Cold Refuge

by Larry Simpson

This book is dedicated to my children Jean, Mike, Mark and Jake. The first three were born in Frobisher Bay/Iqaluit, and the last was born in Africa. All of them have enriched my life.

NOTES TO THE READER

This book is fiction, an imaginative play on what possibly could have happened in Foxe Basin in 1944 under certain circumstances, if all the stars and *inuksuks* had lined up right. The historical underpinnings of my tale are real: the German weather station in Labrador and the U.S. air base in Frobisher Bay, the shuttered trading post at Igloolik, the RCMP patrols, the *Nascopie*, the explorers Hantzsch and Freuchen, and so on.

Any similarity between any character in this book and any Inuit, living or dead, is purely coincidental. The Inuit characters are an imaginative remix of the personalities and traits of hundreds of Inuit I have known during my thirty years in Nunavut. The particular Inuit names assigned to Inuit characters are very much a random selection, as is the way of fiction. I am aware that Inuit names are important and sensitive attributes of Inuit culture and identity, and for that reason I have often used Inuit names more typical of other regions. I have endeavoured to achieve a respectful and balanced portrayal of Inuit at a time when they were facing rapid change in their lifestyle and worldview. My own Inuit-status daughter would insist on that.

Likewise I have had to crawl into the skins of Mounties and *U-bootwaffe,* sub-cultures in their own right, and at a time when I was not yet born. I hope that if I got anything wrong, at least the portrayal is positive on balance, and I stand to be corrected.

Terminology

In this book I use the terms *Inuit* and *Eskimo* depending on the point of view and context, and keeping in mind that the story is set in 1944 when the Eskimo label was widely used by others in reference to the people who have always called themselves *Inuit*, "the people". The proper term is *Inuit*.

I also use both metric and British standards of measure (feet, miles, pounds and meters and kilometers, etc.) again depending on the speaker (Canadian or German) and context.

Cold Refuge

PROLOGUE

Up until May of 1943 Germany was winning the Battle of the Atlantic. Its submarines, organized into U-boat wolf packs, came very close to choking off Britain's lifeline of resupply convoys from North America.

Germany recognized early in the war the importance of forecasting weather in the North Atlantic, where weather moves from west to east. A number of manned and automated weather stations were established at strategic locations in the far north from Svalbard to Greenland to northern Canada. One site was WLF-26, *Kurt*, an automated weather station powered by nickel-cadmium batteries in northern Labrador. The station measured temperature, humidity, wind-speed and direction, and atmospheric pressure. These observations were broadcast by radio in coded 120-second weathergrams at three-hour intervals to German receiving sites in northern Europe. This weather information was then used by U-boats in their convoy search and attack planning. *Kurt* was installed in 1943 by U-537, which was subsequently sunk with all hands in the Pacific. It was left to another U-boat to service the weather station.

* * *

Frobisher Bay, on Baffin Island in Canada's Eastern Arctic region, was the site of remote airstrip construction by the United States commencing in 1942. The purpose of the base, code-named *Crystal II*, was to facilitate the ferrying of light bombers to Britain utilizing the so-called *Crimson Route,* which also made use of airstrips in Greenland and Iceland. This hopscotch approach enabled designated aircraft types with limited range to fly from North America to bases in England. Hence the lethal U-boat attacks on convoys carrying this valuable cargo could be avoided.

* * *

In 1944 the Foxe Basin region was inhabited by only a few hundred Inuit who were living a nomadic and traditional lifestyle. Igloolik, long a site of Inuit seasonal residence, was the only community in Foxe Basin with a Hudson's Bay Company trading post and a church mission. During the years 1943-1945 the Igloolik trading post was shut down due to heavy ice in Foxe Basin together with a shortage of icebreakers, which were in greater demand in strategic waterways including the St. Lawrence River. As government administration and health-care personnel had routinely travelled with the Hudson's Bay Company's ship *Nascopie* in this region, the Canadian government had to look at other bare-bones means of monitoring the welfare of these isolated Inuit who were belatedly recognized as Canada's northernmost citizens. The annual RCMP dog-sled patrols from

Pond Inlet to Igloolik were one means of fulfilling this role while asserting national sovereignty.

Inuit legend in the Foxe Basin area is generally a good fit with the western world's more detached methods of recording and interpreting history. Inuit legend contains accounts of Inuit families in seasonal camps strangely disappearing without a trace, their iglus or *tupiq* tents undisturbed. Various purported agents of Inuit kidnappings have been the Russians, reportedly having left aircraft tire tracks where they landed near the camps, and, in a previous era, Germans using submarines. There has been no definitive verification of these various accounts, which over the years have gradually settled into the misty territory of myth.

Route of U-807

Pond Inlet

Greenland

Arctic Circle

Baffin Island

Netilling Lake

Davis Strait

American Airbase

Frobisher Bay

Resolution Island

Canadian Bomber Attack

Labrador Sea

x1

Igloolik

Foxe Basin

Hudson Strait

Kurt Weather Station

Quebec

Southampton Island

Hudson Bay

PART ONE

I

August 16: Northeast of Nain, Labrador

Oberleutnant Karl Hansen cursed the slow progress of transferring fuel, men and supplies between the two U-boats bobbing out of step in heavy seas. He looked down from the tower of his own U-807 at the sleek lethal lines of a Type IX attack submarine linked by a damned fuel hose *cum* umbilical cord to U-494, a fat and clumsy Type XIV tanker sub. He knew he should be more grateful for the much-needed rendezvous at sea with the 1700-ton mother boat. Soon he could carry on with his mission without having to return for resupply to his base in Lorient on the coast of France. These cargo boats were affectionately known as the *Milchkuh* for their role as "milk cows". They kept the fighting boats out at sea and attacking enemy convoys, convoys maintaining the cursed lifeline of men and war materials to England from North America. But this was taking way too long . . .

Hansen sighed and went to join his Second Watch Officer in sweeping a clear blue sky for possible airborne threats from enemy bases in Greenland and Newfoundland. He looked over at young Franz on his twin 20 mm flak gun, the sad remains of his boat's defensive armaments. The gangly youth appeared to be vigilant and perhaps even hoping for targets. Fool kid! The Commander scanned the heavier defensive armaments of the larger boat, quad 20 mm guns and two 37 mm guns and a couple of machine guns. The men on those had their fingers on the triggers too, which gave him a measure of satisfaction. He turned his gaze on their last two torpedoes being floated over to the *Milchkuh* for better use by other attack boats in the North Atlantic, given that the special mission of U-807 above all stressed avoiding contact with the enemy. He saw cases of tinned meat and fish, powdered milk, bags of potatoes and onions and even apples being manhandled onto his boat, and passed down through the forward crew hatch. And he caught a whiff of some fresh-baked bread too, still warm out of the oven. He noted that the dinghy from U-494 had completed the shuttle of nine of his crew for treatment by the doctor, men who had suddenly come down with a serious case of food poisoning. In return, U-807 received a man from the cargo boat, a tall trooper in infantry fatigues carrying what appeared to be his own personal arsenal of weapons in multiple cases and tubes. Hansen acknowledged him with a nod and assigned a man to help him stow his gear and weapons below. Lots of time to go over the special mission with him once they got off the damned surface.

* * *

Oberfunkmeister Markus Winkler, senior radio petty officer on the boat, was in the tower alongside the Commander. He was not there to contribute his bespectacled eyes to airborne threat-detection, but rather his ears. His ears were just a little larger than usual and did protrude a little more than usual. However, the sense of hearing that blessed Winkler was second to none. On this occasion he was not wearing his big headphones to link him to sounds in the watery environment below. The real threat here, at maximum vulnerability while refueling on the surface, was from above. By mid-1944, now that the enemy had extended their offensive reach and surveillance technology throughout the North Atlantic, there were no more safe gaps for the boat to hide in.

Winkler was also attending to the *Fumb Naxos* radar detector. All active sensors and transmitters including radar were switched off, given the enemy's enhanced capability of homing in on German radar and radio signals with direction-finding equipment. And even with the Naxos device there was concern that the enemy could somehow detect it. Winkler glanced over at Franz on the flak gun. The gunner possessed the keen vision to complement his own keen hearing. Perhaps they could somehow merge their senses by working in close proximity to one another. Wishful thinking, perhaps . . .

Franz was a noted marksman on the 20 mm gun, though he had not yet fired at the enemy. Commander Hansen was recognized as having a special touch when it came to keeping his boat and crew away from danger. So Franz had to make do with occasional target practice on cast-off floating garbage, and that one time off the Ivory Coast with an albatross coming at him out of the sun . . . To the novice gunner from a farm near Stuttgart, the huge bird with the three-meter wingspan looked so much like a diving bomber that he emptied the two ammunition boxes on his twin gun at it. He was just beginning to fathom that the debris was in fact . . . feathers . . . when he finally made out the Commander shouting at him to stop. After that he hesitated when he saw wings coming out of a blinding sun, especially when it was slipping toward a shimmering horizon, like now. Yet he knew there was a thin line between jumping the gun and a costly delayed reaction.

The gunner's 360-degree scan brought him back to the sun, sinking lower with skies behind it already turning a muted crimson. Though just hours ago he had gloried in being on the surface and miraculously under a blue sky with sunshine again, Franz had found himself wishing for overcast conditions. On the other hand, he knew that cloudy conditions can also favour an approaching enemy bomber. He would just do the best he could do under the circumstances. Just then he saw . . . another albatross? Instinctively his finger tightened on the trigger, and the last thing on his mind was that this location between Labrador and Greenland was far from the habitual airspace of an albatross. He had learned that estimating the size and distance of an approaching airborne object is largely a function of what best-bet category the object of interest is mentally slotted into. A diving bomber five kilometers away looks much like a gliding seabird at a fraction of that distance.

Franz deliberately forced his gaze away, then back to the approaching wings. His heart beating like a drum, Franz glanced at Winkler to see if he registered any cognition of an airborne threat, any other sounds beyond the thrum of the boats' diesel engines and the myriad sounds of cargo exchange. Winkler's eyes went huge and he turned to the Naxos radar detector to see if there was any confirmation, knowing in a heartbeat that a bomber descending on its prey would have switched its radar off. Winkler spun his head around to face Franz and shouted "Bomber!" Just then Commander Hansen lowered his binoculars and shouted, "*Alarm,* enemy aircraft!" a split second before their 20 mm gun began spitting out rounds. Now they could hear the plane's radial engines too. The target was still a little far out for the twin 20 mm, but it was best to throw everything you could at an attacking bomber to degrade its bomb aiming capability. The guns on the *Milchkuh* presently opened up. Franz, a keen student of aircraft types and recognition silhouettes, called out "twin-engine aircraft, Canadian Hudson bomber." Commander Hansen turned to see their new infantry trooper calmly pouring automatic fire out of his STG 44 assault rifle[1], the limited-distribution one with the big 7.92 round in 30-shot clips. By now a fierce stream of steel was invading the diving bomber's airspace.

Still the bomber came on, firing the machine guns in its nose. As the defensive fire from the two U-boats closed in on the aircraft, its pilot chose to abandon the bombing run. When the plane banked sharply to starboard, its wingtip just clearing the swells, the gun in the dorsal turret was still able to target the U-boats. Winkler watched in horror as a line of geysers marched in a ragged line across the water like grotesque wild flowers toward the larger U-boat, the one of most strategic interest. Four men on the *Milchkuh* went down, including two on one of the quad 20 mm guns. Then the bomber receded in the distance,

---

1   The German STG 44 assault rifle is considered the forerunner of the Russian AK-47

but the German crews knew it would be just a matter of minutes before it was back.

"*Fluten! Fluten! Fluten!*" Emergency dive! In seconds fuel hoses were uncoupled, diesel engines were stopped and electric motors engaged, hatches secured, tanks flooded and hydroplanes set to drive the bow down from the surface's icy grip. Commander Hansen stood by while the seasoned deck crew executed their controlled free fall through the conning tower hatch to the control room floor below.

* * *

Markus Winkler slumped forward on his perch to reclaim the cramped workspace that he called his own. Nothing but silence on the radio and hydrophones, no immediate threats but no news either . . . The Commander's eyes were haunted when he looked over at the radio operator every few minutes. Did U-494 manage to survive the sudden attack by the Canadian bomber? At first light the next day Hansen had given the order to surface and check for debris or an oil slick from U-494. And possibly survivors if the ponderous *Milchkuh* was holed before it could submerge . . . Nothing! Winkler knew escaping in their own more dive-capable boat was a miracle in itself. The last few days had been a confusion of events that would tax even those with a nervous system more robust than his own.

Winkler's thoughts returned to the new man they had taken on when he saw the trim figure moving through the narrow passageway from the forward torpedo room/crew quarters. This was the one already dubbed "Soldier" by the crew. He was sidestepping like a boxer as he dodged crates and hams and sausages dangling from water pipes and valves before coming through the hatchway with fluid ease. Winkler was a four-year member of the *U-bootwaffe,* and he was surprised at this display of balance and composure in an infantry type so recently planted in the cramped spaces of a U-boat on patrol. Winkler played back in his mind the air attack alarm sounding and the cool composure of the trooper as he fired upon the attacking bomber. Then the way he followed the deck crew unhesitatingly through the conning tower hatch to the control room floor and dropped like a cat, not needing at all the steadying hands of the man posted below . . . The trooper seemed genuinely offended by the crashing sounds of his considerable mass hammering the metal plating of the floor.

Now what would be the purpose of this new addition to their crew? Winkler fought back the unacceptable physical excitement he felt as he gazed upon this specimen. Tall and slim with good muscle definition showing through his t-shirt, short blonde hair, intense blue eyes, handsome chiseled features, the whole package. Yet he knew the added risks of an apparent new mission heralded by the arrival of this passenger did not bode well for his fragile nervous health in the future. This one they were calling Soldier had already become something of an onboard hero to the crew. He had insisted on taking his own weapon above upon learning to his disgust that the 37 mm anti-aircraft gun had been removed from the boat as "mission redundant". And that the 105 mm deck gun, ripped off in an Atlantic gale on the last patrol, had not been replaced. All that remained was the twin 20 mm flak gun manned capably by Franz. The mission was supposedly all about avoiding detection, but here they were, obviously detected and quite suddenly a target.

Winkler's dormant headphones came to life. He called out to the Commander and reported that an encrypted message to U-494, the *Milchkuh*, was coming in from *BdU*, U-boat Command in Germany. Winkler's pencil scurried over his pad as he expertly recorded the dashes and dots, ready for the Enigma machine to generate a message for the Commander. No doubt it was another order to U-494 to report in. Winkler handed over the message and resumed his thoughts. Despite the momentary diversion with the radio he felt the familiar nausea and cold sweat starting to work on him again as he contemplated the fate of the other boat. There were only a couple of these Type XIV tanker boats left out of ten completed to date. Presumably one less now . . . Winkler knew a few of the U-494 crew from training days. That was four years ago and already the youngsters were the old hands. He felt the tears and shakes trying to get the upper hand and he wondered if the Commander would be able, or willing, to talk him down again. Winkler suspected that the fact he still found himself on this boat was a tribute to his valued sonar and hydrophone skills, and what his fitness report called his "sixth sense of spatial awareness and direction when submerged". These skills had already saved U-807 before, in an underwater contest with a British submarine in the North Sea. It was a first for a U-boat to launch an unguided torpedo, a standard G7a driven by a motor running on steam, at a moving underwater adversary and actually hit it. Just a set of earphones linking an array of passive hydrophones on the boat's steel skin to Winkler's nervous grey matter, scanning through fluttering eyelids a myriad of location possibilities in three dimensions of dark fluid space . . . Fortunately for the Tommies the torpedo was a dud and did not explode, but the hit rattled the British sufficiently that they broke off the engagement.

2

August 18: East of Hebron, Labrador

Commander Hansen wiped the sweat from his brow and stubbled cheeks. It seemed strange to be sweating off Labrador, where floating ice was as dangerous as an anti-submarine aircraft based in Newfoundland or Greenland. He observed the young army sergeant approaching for their requested 1800-hour sit-down. Time to get to know each other. Hansen had made the request to *BdU* for a "special forces type" to assist with special operations involving landings in enemy territory.

In the past two years U-807 had taken on more than its share of special missions, more often than not in northern seas: infiltrating and extracting agents, surveillance, the occasional attack on strategic targets in enemy ports, and the welcome softer missions such as servicing unmanned weather stations such as the one coming up near Cape Chidley in northern Labrador. These special missions often needed specialized talent and aggressiveness apart from the naval variety. It appeared that Hansen had received his man all right. It took a bit of sting out of the fact that he was still waiting for upgrades to his older Type IX boat to enhance the crew's survival prospects. Better radar detectors for a start, and a *schnorchel* to let him make way and charge his batteries while under water like a true submarine as opposed to a steel-coffin submersible. But, by this stage of the war, U-boat skippers who were still breathing had learned not to expect too much. The Happy Days of 1942 were over and U-boat losses at best were now on a par with enemy ships dispatched to the bottom. Even "the Lion" Karl Donitz, *Kriegsmarine* Grand Admiral and devoted mentor of the *U-bootwaffe*, had gone relatively silent, other than to babble intermittently about emerging technology that would soon turn the war in Germany's favour. For example, the advanced Type XXI electric boat that could stay submerged for days and still outrun convoy escorts on battery power alone. And reliable homing torpedoes to replace the earlier generations still in use and still plagued by an alarmingly high failure rate. Empty words, Hansen concluded.

"Sergeant Wolff reporting as ordered, sir." The Commander turned to acknowledge the trooper, pointing out a crate for a seat.

Helmut Wolff could see that there might be some truth in what he'd heard about the Commander not being big on formalities such as uniform dress and saluting on board. He was happy with that, and tired of incompetent officers putting his life on the line. He preferred smaller, more loosely structured operations offering more scope for personal initiative and cunning. And good no-frills teamwork when he couldn't go solo . . . Maybe the Old Man would be the same way. U-boat types were considered elite and were selected for fitness including intelligence and an ability to tolerate stress. Sergeant Wolff could relate to that. He had survived two pulverizing months with a recon unit attached to *Panzers* on the Russian front and now every new day was a gift from God, if only he could believe in God after what he'd seen and done there.

Hansen looked through the binder in his hands. "Selected for special forces and winter warfare training, assigned to a *Bandenburg* commando unit. Fighting underground saboteurs on skis in Norway, let's see . . . skirmishing with the Greenland Home Guard and American commandos while covering a withdrawal from one of our manned weather stations . . . "

"*Jawohl! Herr Kaleun.* It seems my time spent in Greenland with my scientist father and learning some land and language skills from the natives caught somebody's attention."

"Called back to Germany and assigned to a commando unit on the Russian front . . . "

"Yes, to a reconnaissance unit. Wounded at Stalingrad and evacuated."

"Had your heel shot off? You didn't show it up above and coming down the passageway just now."

"Thanks to the best surgeons in Berlin and to special boots. I can't run as well as I could before, but I can still walk a long distance at a good pace."

"Hmmm, I see here that before the eastern front you were attached to a U-boat for special duties. A tropical adventure in Cuba, of all places?"

"I was with a boat carrying out reconnaissance in the Mississippi Delta area and the Caribbean, and I was still aboard when the boat was depth-charged and damaged off Cuba. The Commander sent me on an errand to get some machine parts from a plantation owned by a sympathetic German. I had to do a two-kilometer night swim to the beach and up a river near

Matanzas for that one. But since then I've been freezing my ass on northern missions."

"And so have we. It looks like our paths have finally crossed."

Commander Hansen hesitated before continuing. "Will we win this war?"

The trooper paused in turn. "Well, I experienced some of our military defeats on the eastern front, it's over in Africa and Italy for us, German air superiority is a joke, and you know all about the Battle of the Atlantic. It's not a walk in the park for us any more, as the Yanks would say."

The young man demonstrated either courage or foolishness to speak out like this to a commanding officer, Hansen thought. "You have spent time in America?"

"Yes, a couple of trips as a youth with my father to scientific conventions. New York, and also to Montreal in Canada."

"No mixed loyalties . . . or sympathies?"

"I am German, just a well-travelled one. Doing a job and trying to do it well when circumstances allow. My father believed in the cause, or should I say in seeing things through, though he was no Nazi . . . " He hesitated. "And so it is with me."

Commander Hansen was relieved that Sergeant Wolff was *Heer,* army through and through. He was not from the *Waffen SS*, an elite fighting force to be sure, but with too much baggage given their Nazi party associations.

"And your father passed away when you were on the eastern front, I see."

Soldier nodded.

"Well, welcome aboard, Sergeant Wolff. Cookie has announced dinner so let's get some food in our bellies."

* * *

Soldier sat at the small table with six others on dinner shift, while Cookie scurried around ladling out potato soup, sausages and cabbage, and passing a plate of still-warm biscuits. Not bad fare, he thought, given the war was in its fifth year and the boat had not been back to its base in Lorient, France for over two months. The crew, looking fit but understandably pale, were friendly to him though obviously curious. It seemed to be almost a skeleton crew now, after a goodly number of them were suddenly taken ill and transferred to the tanker boat that he had just de-shipped from before the aircraft attack. He gathered that some of the crew were working longer shifts now, while some functions had gone by the wayside. Now that the boat's mission profile stressed avoidance of the enemy and not the routine convoy interception and attack . . . A dearth of guns and torpedoes on the boat was an ominous shortcoming to him though. Being well armed, in his experience, was always a correct step toward survival in a hostile environment, and that was just about right with the bomber attack. He patted himself on the back for bringing his assault rifle to complement the assortment of arms he had with him for close-in work. The Commander had explained to him that for a short period *Kriegsmarine* doctrine called for U-boats caught on the surface to shoot it out with attacking aircraft. That was considered a safer bet than offering up their backsides in the passive emergency dives that put them at maximum vulnerability. A few enemy bombers were shot down initially but soon the enemy adapted their tactics and odds went against the boats again. And so doctrine shifted back to emergency dives and hoping for the best.

Soldier knew that he was but a passenger on this voyage for now. With fewer crew on board and no torpedoes in the bow quarters to share space with, there was less crowding and more opportunity to lounge at the dining table with elbows up. Still only two smelly shitters for the whole crew to relieve themselves in though . . . He looked at the banks of instruments and pipes and valves and machinery. What a fucking maze! And in the heart of the boat the engines and motors and batteries ate up two-thirds of the space in the pressure hull. At least he had the run of the boat, though a very slow jog might be more like it.

* * *

U-807 was on the surface, slicing through easy swells, the two MAN 2,200-horsepower supercharged diesels driving its streamlined 80-meter hull at a respectable but fuel-conserving ten knots. There were no signs of ice or bergs, though the growlers could sneak right up on you. On this day in August and at this point off Labrador the days were still long and the nights shorter, but soon this would start tipping the other way. There was a full moon that made the boat and its wake all too visible from the air. Still, the batteries needed to be charged daily on the surface to be effective. Even in the darkest night they weren't safe. The enemy patrol aircraft had superior radar as well as huge searchlights, the cursed Leigh Lights that they could turn on at the last minute just before bombs away.

Commander Hansen and Soldier were in the *Wintergarten*, the elevated rear of the conning tower. They smoked cigarettes and commented on the moon's play with the shimmering wake as they made good time up the rugged Labrador coast toward Cape Chidley. Felt, as much as seen in the moonlight, was the haunting specter of the mighty Torngat Mountains towering over them at 1,500 meters. More intimidating, however, was the uncertainty of water depths and shoals off this coast. Their charts for these waters were few and unreliable. On top of that, huge mountains of ice calved off of Greenland glaciers paraded down iceberg alley dragging their backsides hundreds of meters deep, while growlers menaced at surface level. Petty Officer Winkler had just reported there was nothing out there making noise of the enemy-threat variety so soon he would be relieved by the Second Watch Officer and go below for some hot coffee.

* * *

Chief Berg-Nielsen, a career *Kriegsmarine* man, was thinking about their upcoming stop in northern Labrador. The last time U-807 had made a maintenance call at an automated weather station they had managed it quite well on their own, without the bloody infantry along. It was a bitch though, unloading the heavy replacement canisters of nickel-cadmium batteries and manhandling them to their final destination. And yes, this time around they would be more vulnerable exposing themselves with less armament above. So maybe having the trooper along wasn't such a bad idea after all. It seemed to Chief that there were some other bigger plans in store for their boat, and the Commander was being bloody secretive about it. What he knew all too well from his own supervisory role on their last trip to base was that the streamlined shutters in the external fairing over the four forward torpedo tubes were sealed and strengthened. Then additional steel sheathing was welded onto the foremost faces of the bow. After that the boat was stripped of its 37 mm flak gun. The posts and railings and antennas on the conning tower that were still fixed and rigid were replaced with bending and collapsing ones, and the lower external casing around the tower was strengthened with more steel. Chief naturally knew what that was all about . . . Ice! Moving through ice and possibly even surfacing in ice! Chief was the single most informed person about the boats' operating status including mechanical, electrical, and hydraulic systems. He knew enough about his boat and about ice from his operations in the Barents Sea and Greenland Sea to be concerned. Even with the minimal ice strengthening possible on the inherently fragile superstructure of a Type IX U-boat it probably wouldn't survive a surfacing through much more than a meter of ice. And that was new ice, definitely not the old multi-year pack ice that could peel back their hull like a tin can. The Commander, when queried about their current mission, had just repeated that that their boat had more or less by default become the "northern missions" boat. Ice boat! Chief winced. He would get the story on this mission soon, because the Commander valued his expertise too much to keep him in the dark.

* * *

Soldier stretched out on his bunk. It was a luxury to not have to hot-bunk, to share his bed on alternating shifts with another man. The Commander had commented that, despite the unfortunate crew loss, they still had enough manpower and skills for the kind of work they had to do, 30 good men besides himself on board out of a normal crew complement of 46. The Commander was a different breed, Soldier reflected. Competent, yes, but definitely outside the norm for German officers who, even on U-boats, tended to be competitive on the one hand and obsessed with duty and chain of command on the other. He was a thinker beyond a doubt. The attributes and attitudes that might have raised eyebrows at *BdU*, U-Boat command in Germany, were no doubt precisely those that enabled him to succeed in unorthodox missions. Soldier had observed that the Commander routinely ignored radio messages from home base calling on him for status reports. When queried, he had explained that making these reports was virtual suicide now. Now that the enemy had good radio direction finders and effective radar to catch them on the surface charging batteries or exchanging radio signals, or refueling. The Commander had added that, by all appearances, the enemy had cracked their Enigma codes and seemed to have a pretty good picture of German U-boat operations in the Atlantic on a day-to-day basis. The surviving boats were those with commanders who could bend rules and think outside the box, while still getting some tonnage figures of enemy ships sunk to call in when deemed safe to do so. Hansen had casually dropped an interesting fact on him. The U-boats that engaged in the boldest actions generally did so on the Commander's daring and initiative, not on the orders of *BdU* in Germany. Soldier smiled, thinking that *Oberleutnant* Karl Hansen certainly looked like a character, longish hair to go with his scruffy red beard, and occasionally wearing an African tunic he had snatched from a coastal freighter boarded off Senegal. In spite of his renegade persona it appeared that his crew adored him. Soldier suspected that the Commander cared more about the welfare of his crew than he did about enemy tonnage figures, and this might explain why he was still *Oberleutnant sur zee* and not *Kapitanleutnant*, which was a more common rank for officers commanding this type of boat after more than two years at war.

3

August 19: Southeast of Cape Chidley, Labrador

Commander Hansen scoped out the approach to the weather station with his binoculars and found nothing to alarm him. He had actually made out the antennas and drum canisters on top of the hill when they were still three nautical miles out. He wondered if other sea traffic along the Labrador coast had observed the weather station, which for some reason had stopped transmitting weather data some four months earlier. He himself had benefited from the station's automated broadcasts of weather data in carrying out their missions. Sabotage could be the cause of the interruption in weather data transmissions, but Hansen guessed it was more likely a technical problem or just prematurely depleted battery power. He looked forward to hearing Soldier's full report. Sergeant Wolff had been first to exit the surfaced boat with his surveillance kit in a small dinghy. Thus far he had messaged by light that everything looked good, to bring the boat in and commence offloading. The Commander was relieved to see they were blessed with calm seas as they closed on the beach below the weather station. U-807 was soon positioned behind a grounded iceberg and the crew commenced to offload the canisters from the deck onto six-meter flotation rafts. Hansen looked appraisingly at the iceberg, which served to shield them from view to a moderate extent. And the berg was a fairly safe 100 meters from the stern and rooted on the bottom outside the boat's piece of beach. The winds were favourable and exiting this location and making headway out to deeper seas should not be a problem. Hansen gave the order to blow all ballast tanks and raise the boat as high as it would float in the water. The Chief shouted orders and a dozen men went to work scouring the upper hull and conning tower. Other men followed with brushes and pails of primer paint. They would be here a good 12 hours doing the weather station maintenance. Meantime, the boat would get some of its own maintenance as well as some cosmetic attention.

* * *

Soldier watched as the boat crew managed to muscle the 100-kilogram Ni-Cad battery canisters out of the rafts and onto the beach. After a breather they started to roll the canisters up and over the uneven ground, 100 meters inland and another 60 meters uphill. They laid down mats and lengths of pipe here and there to facilitate movement of the canisters while reducing wear and tear. Soldier thought about going down to lend them a hand with the grunt work but decided his place was up here on the high ground scanning the surrounding terrain through his rifle scope. He had found signs of earlier site visitation by persons unknown, most likely Eskimo[2] hunters. Presumably the hunters would think this installation is the property of the Canadian or American government. He did find some .303 shell casings, a caliber sometimes used in the north since surplus British Lee Enfield rifles became readily available and inexpensive following World War One. There were no bullet holes in the weather station equipment so it was not readily clear what the shooters were aiming at. He knew for a fact though that the Eskimos do not waste their precious ammunition. He raised his rifle and scanned the rocky terrain to the west again.

When the first of the canisters made it up the hill Soldier sent a sailor back to the boat for stencils, black paint, and a few other items. Before long the newly erect canisters were marked "Canadian Weather Service". Soldier was aware that Labrador and Newfoundland were not Canadian territory, but they were nevertheless allies in the war effort and so the label would be credible. The .303 shell casings and some American cigarette and chewing gum packaging were scattered around the site. The final touch, thanks to the Chief's largesse, was a green 7 Up pop bottle with a bathing beauty and bubbles on the label, a clever way of repatriating some war booty to enemy territory. The German sailors chuckled but were obviously impressed with the subterfuge. Soldier then requested two of the men to stay with him as the others trudged down the hill toward the boat. He raised his STG-44 to his shoulder and pressed his eye against the optics. Before the other men knew what he was up to he squeezed off a shot, shifted his aim to the right and squeezed off another

---

2   While the *Eskimo* label was still widely used by others in 1944 the proper
     term is I*nuit*

one. The sailors were startled, fearing the enemy had found them out, but were unable to make out any targets in the hilly boulder-strewn terrain.

"Relax, it's just some fresh meat," Soldier announced as he stooped to pick up the empty shell casings. Thirty minutes later the men were humping caribou meat down the hill to the boat. On the way down they passed Petty Officer Winkler and the boat's electrician on their way up, respectively carrying a binder and a bag of tools. They would need an hour to do the new connections and testing to bring the weather station back up to operational status.

When Soldier and Winkler returned to the boat with the remainder of the meat it was obvious that Commander Hansen was not pleased about the unauthorized shooting. Still, he could not hold back the smile that came to his face. Food was always an issue for a U-boat on patrol, and any fresh food was a delicacy. Then it was Soldier's turn to smile as he took a close-up look at the upper surfaces of the boat, which were now a mottled white colour instead of navy grey.

* * *

The Commander filled his coffee cup again, closed the curtain, and sat down at the little desk in his small personal space. He studied his orders along with the maps and charts again and then called for Chief. Berg-Nielsen had served as Chief with him for two years, a long time in the U-boat war, and the Commander trusted him completely. In fact the older grey-haired seaman was almost like a father to him, his own father having been lost in the trench warfare of the Somme. Hansen's blue eyes twinkled. "Well, Chief, how goes it?"

"Busier without the second engineer after he went over to the *Milchkuh,* and the *Bootsmann* navigator too. But that couldn't be helped, I suppose."

Hansen thought he saw a searching look in the Chief's eyes but he let it go by.

Chief relaxed into his chair and let his thoughts drift. A puzzle caught in his mind and he looked up. "I must say I am curious about this particular location for the *Kurt* weather station. This is by all indications a fine location, but the navigation in here is not easy. How was this particular site selected by U-537 last year? It would seem to require some foreknowledge of the bottom and the terrain in this rugged country."

"Ah, my friend, if I tell you the details I would have to shoot you. But let it be said that the Moravian Church has been well established along this rugged Labrador coast for more than a century. In fact, there is a Moravian mission on *Killinek,* an island just to the north of us."

Chief showed some surprise at this, but waited for more.

"Most of the Moravian missionaries have been German, though there has been a trend in the last decade or two to bring in replacements as required from England. This has caused some resentment in some circles, as you can imagine. Enough said?"

Chief winked and nodded. "Yes, but if there are indeed Eskimos in some church community just to the north of us, then we must be very vulnerable to detection by them!"

The commander smiled and nodded. "Yes, but this risk is much reduced at this time of year as the Eskimos over there are presently engaged in their annual harp seal hunt, on the other side of Killinek Island. We will be sure to be submerged when we go by!"

"Well," Chief said, making an exaggerated bow, "I am impressed by your vast store of knowledge in these matters."

"Don't be overly impressed, Chief. I fear I know only enough to get us into more trouble. We shall see."

Commander Hansen shared a comfortable interlude of quiet with his comrade and then pointed at his map. "And now we are heading up here, Chief. What do you think?"

Chief stared at the spot where the skipper's finger rested on the map, more than 200 nautical miles north of their position off northern Labrador. He took a deep breath. "Really? Baffin Island is not even on the Lion's grid." The nearest squares on Admiral Donitz's Atlantic operations map were to the south and east below Greenland. The Chief saw that the southern part of Baffin Island was called *Meta Incognita* and he thought that was probably appropriate. Unknown Land . . .

"The thing is," the Commander went on, "Sergeant Wolff, now more commonly known on the boat as Soldier, already knows about these orders. This project of his has apparently been discussed at the highest levels."

Chief knew what that meant, Donitz and probably even higher. He drew his fingertips in a vertical line between his nose and his upper lip.

Hansen chuckled at Chief's indiscretion. "That reminds me. As you know, I took the opportunity before departing Lorient to press again for a *schnorchel* so we can hide underwater for longer periods, in keeping with our growing reputation as the 'invisible boat'. U-494, rest in peace, carried a message to us from Admiral Donitz saying only that we are next for the *snort*."

Chief nodded, knowing most Type IX boats had been fitted with a *snort* at their home base in coastal France. Thus the boats would be less vulnerable to air and sea attack while running their diesels underwater. He also knew full well how much good it did to protest at this late point in the war. He could have offered as a consolation the fact that a *snort* would be just one more problem while operating in an area of uncertain ice cover and with enemy radar apparently able to pick up even periscopes, but he opted to remain silent on that well-covered topic.

"Well, Karl, I know we don't have equipment to install another automated weather station on Baffin Island so why in the hell would we be going into Frobisher Bay? I gather the starring role in this drama will be played out by our new *Heer* talent on board."

The Commander smiled. "Indeed, my friend, you win the prize. We are landing Soldier close to a fledgling American port and air base at the end of Frobisher Bay, so he can carry out a reconnaissance. Presumably to make a plan for a future raid . . . Apparently he has done similar things in Norway and Greenland, not to mention Russia."

"Port, you say? There is one hell of a tide in there, one of the world's highest at over 15 meters," the Chief remarked, recalling how the extreme Bay of Fundy tides had spelled doom for at least one U-boat seeking targets near Saint John, New Brunswick. "The Yanks must be beaching their cargo ships and unloading at low tide, unless they have constructed some kind of a breakwater and landing platform, which would take a lot of rock and no shortage of bulldozers and other heavy equipment. What's the strategic interest up there?"

The Commander glanced at the intelligence part of his orders and allowed that the Chief was pretty close in his speculations. "Apparently, one of the surviving aircrew from an American fighter-bomber that was shot down in Germany divulged, under duress of course, that he had ferried the plane to England from America by way of this airstrip in Frobisher Bay, and others in Greenland and Iceland. For the past two years American freighters have been transporting materials, equipment and fuel to the end of this Frobisher Bay. They've been working around the clock in the short summers to build runways and buildings to refuel and service light bombers on the way through. I gather a lot of their aircraft en route to England in the convoys were being re-routed to the bottom of the ocean, thanks to our U-boats." He paused. "But at the rate our U-boats are being sunk now there won't be much of a gauntlet for the convoys to run, certainly by the time a raid on this Frobisher base can be organized."

Chief chewed this over for a moment and then replied, "At least there is little shipping up this way and only a few scattered Eskimo outposts, so the Americans and Canadians are probably not too worried about U-boat threats."

"That's correct, Chief, and assuming this *Kurt* weather station has not been discovered, there is no known German presence in this area, and therefore probably not much in the way of air patrols either. The flyboys tend to fly where they've had results in the past. But it would be a bitch having one of those ferried bombers fly over us, even if they are not armed. We know their approximate route, so we shall be vigilant. On their way from the American Midwest they would fly over the western part of Hudson Strait, well off our track." His finger touched the map. "In any case we will have to go submerged most of the time by day and we'll need to keep our wits about us at night when we are running surfaced with those monster icebergs along our path, not to mention the potential for enemy aircraft."

Chief nodded. "Having someone sight us would surely give the game away. We'll get some fog as well as darkness to blanket us but that may be as much of a curse as a blessing with our poor maps and charts for this area. And the icebergs . . . "

Commander Hansen stuck his head outside his cubicle and called for Soldier, who was waiting at the dining table to be summoned.

"So," Hansen directed his gaze at the young man in fatigues, "we know less than you about the specifics of your landing and I am just the taxi driver on this one. So can you be so good as to fill us in?" He passed around some small glasses of *schnapps* from his private stock.

Soldier met their gaze confidently. "*Jawohl! Herr Kaleun.* As you know, this is a reconnaissance. If it looks worthwhile we can come back in greater numbers and shut down the Frobisher Bay base."

The Commander and the Chief looked at each other. "Greater numbers? No doubt brought in by U-boat? How many are these greater numbers to do such a job?"

"Well, we shall see. Our men would lie low until the opportune moment, but I think ten commandos could do it, once we are suitably dressed in American uniforms and with the element of surprise. The base is a crude one with the sole purpose of keeping those enemy aircraft on the way to the front, though it could also be a secondary base for patrol aircraft flying out of Greenland and Newfoundland. A guess is that there are probably fewer than 100 men left there now, mostly heavy equipment operators and such, with a small communications and radar unit. I will be surprised if there are ten men on the ground with loaded guns. They will feel isolated and a long ways from the war."

"Famous last words," said the Chief.

Soldier continued. "Our objective would be to blow the fuel storage tanks, or more likely thousands of 45-gallon drums concentrated in storage dumps at this stage. Then the bombers can't refuel. Then we destroy the radio and radar equipment, disable any heavy construction in the middle of the runways . . . Destroy any aircraft on the ground, and hole any freighters or small pursuit craft on the beach. That's it in a nutshell, then withdraw and rendezvous with our U-boat down the Bay."

The Commander raised his eyebrows and chuckled. "Unless something goes wrong in all that."

"Exactly," said Soldier, wearing the smallest of smiles.

"Well, I suspect any future raid based on your observations will be too late for this year in any case. In less than two months the weather will pretty much shut down this base for the year. And anyway, who knows how much longer this war will last?"

Soldier nodded, deadpan.

4

August 21: Northeast of Cape Chidley, Labrador

Commander Hansen was at the tower bridge having a cigarette with Soldier. Wolff was proving to be a keen student of U-boats, having plenty of time and no defined duties onboard. Oh yes, he was now coordinating chess tournaments and such. Soldier turned to take the coffee flasks handed up through the hatch. The Second Watch Officer swept the overcast skies for enemy aircraft. It was early evening and the day was fading more quickly with the overcast conditions. The water was dark and choppy, looking ominously cold and inhospitable. They had spotted some white beluga whales in eastern Hudson Strait, and even a polar bear swimming more than 20 miles from land. And seals . . . harp seals in herds and solitary ring seals. Ducks and geese as well, and Hansen had been tempted to give in to the men's request to pot a few for dinner using a shotgun they had seized from a fishing boat off Newfoundland.

As they approached Resolution Island outside the opening of Frobisher Bay, there was some obvious underwater turbulence from tidal currents. They were running the diesels at standard cruising speed yet they were only making seven knots instead of the usual ten. Occasionally the boat would have to turn to avoid icebergs floating south with the current, though once out of the current's icy grip the boat was steered alongside a majestic mountain of ice that looked relatively stable. The crew chipped off hunks of thousand-year-old ice for special tea and other drinks. Soldier seized the opportunity to scale the iceberg using some mountaineering equipment in his kit. Soon he was enjoying a superb view with his binoculars from 30 meters up, and he returned with a report that no pack ice was immediately in their path but that some was moving their way through Hudson Strait to the west. They were approaching the peak of summer in this Arctic region, in the short interval between melt and break-up of last year's ice and the onset of new ice delivered by an incoming winter.

No aircraft or ships had been spotted heading to or from Frobisher Bay. Hansen reasoned that quite possibly a freighter or two could nevertheless be headed toward the base. They wouldn't do so without an escort and maybe even an icebreaker as well. Ice and weather were the known enemy here, but current American naval doctrine had ruled somewhat belatedly that even their small convoys must have military escorts. The Yanks had learned their lesson the hard way during the U-boats' first Happy Days of hunting off the North American coast in 1940, when their unescorted convoys took such a beating and suffered unsustainable losses.

* * *

Winkler was monitoring radio broadcasts from the Frobisher Bay base and from what sounded like American weather stations at Lake Harbour on south Baffin Island and further up the Baffin coast at Clyde River, north of the Arctic Circle. There was also radio traffic between isolated Hudson's Bay Company trading posts and between religious missions scattered here and there across the region. The Commander had joked that HBC was not only an abbreviation for the oldest incorporated company, the Hudson's Bay Company, but also stood for *Here Before Christ*, meaning the traders came to get the white fox and other fur from the Eskimos before the churches—primarily Catholic and Anglican—arrived to capture their souls. Winkler monitored other, more somber, radio transmissions from U-boats losing their battles with the convoys. Small escort aircraft carriers were taking their toll on the remaining boats. It was the same for the long-range B-24 Liberator aircraft, and for the increasingly effective corvettes and destroyers on regular convoy escort duty. Furthermore, there was better inter-service coordination now against the harried U-boats, with navy ships talking to patrolling aircraft. There was no safe part of the ocean anymore. The so-called black gap in the North Atlantic south of Greenland had closed with the extended reach of the enemy aircraft and their detection technology. Almost every day Winkler's heart raced as he heard another U-boat sending out a final message to home base: "Bombed by enemy aircraft while recharging batteries on surface, taking water."

Winkler felt safe in the here and now, all but removed from the war. Still, the Commander had not yet informed the crew what their current mission was, and how Soldier would fit into it. The radar on the boat was primitive, though returns from icebergs had given him a scare until visually confirmed. Radar was rarely used in any case, given its telltale signature. But the hydrophones, the latest technology available in the *Balkon-Geraet* array, were an amazing extension of his own sensory apparatus. Around Resolution Island he thought he could hear the action of the water currents and tides working against bottom and shore contours. He could hear a buzz of marine life around the larger icebergs. And he could hear marine mammals, especially whales! Whales opened up an exciting new world to him. He found their sounds fascinating. Winkler knew that he was blessed with acute hearing and a special ability to analyze sounds as to source and character. A kind of second vision . . . He tuned in even when off-duty and half-awake. At some point the glorious sounds beyond coalesced to bring forth special meaning to him, personal communications made of bits and pieces he was beginning to understand in some holistic way. And somehow he could visualize the mammals that made the sounds. He fancied that the whale songs were like a symphony orchestra, his ears the privileged audience.

*   *   *

The Commander was with Chief in the control room as U-807 eased quietly through the fog on electric power in the midst of scores of small islands just 30 kilometers out from the end of Frobisher Bay. With virtually no charts, he was depending too much on the fathometer to keep the boat from running aground. The shallower the water, the trickier the tide became. It was dangerous to submerge in such conditions so they were hoping the fog would hold a bit longer despite the hazards it brought with it. The Commander had identified a likely spot on the map, courtesy of the Canadian Geographic Society. Here they could submerge the boat behind some small islands, assuming sufficient depth, where the known currents and prevailing winds should keep drift ice and icebergs away, and where they would likely be out of the way of any larger vessels heading toward the base.

The Commander nodded at Soldier. "Not quite dark yet but time for you to load up. This fog should help to conceal you until the dark settles in."

5

August 23: Frobisher Bay

Soldier loaded his pack containing surveillance gear and weapons into the dinghy. He pulled at the Evinrude outboard motor, reportedly taken from a seaside home in Maine two years earlier, and it sputtered into life. He could see perhaps 100 meters into the fog but it looked as though he could manage if he kept just off the western shore.

Most floating ice should be on the other side of the small islands. He made good time even at half throttle to keep the engine noise down, so as not to attract a curious Eskimo hunter with notions of a social visit. Up ahead he spotted a smaller castoff from some distant glacier now jammed up against a point on the western shoreline, but for the most part it was smooth passage. At one point he was startled when he thought he saw a rock immediately in front of him through a patch of fog as he moved through calm water. It turned out that the rock was a walrus, and it splashed off to the west. The fog was lifting now and there was a breeze blowing onshore from Davis Strait. Soldier shut down the outboard and with the light of a half moon peeking through overcast skies he raised a sail rigged from his reserve parachute and ran silent the rest of the way in. He thanked his lucky stars twinkling above that he was able to trade off his cloak of fog for this cover of darkness. Now he would sail the dinghy quiet as a dream right into Koojesse Inlet, just to the west of the Sylvia Grinnell River mouth. The base would be a three-kilometer hike to the east.

* * *

Sometimes it was better not to ask. Chief and the Commander trusted one another and that was enough. They had served together for two years and still liked each other, which meant something in the stressed environment of a U-boat on constant combat patrols. Chief was 20 years the senior of the Commander, who at 39 was considerably older than the average U-boat commander since the unsustainable crew losses beginning in the first few months of 1943. Chief hoped to retire when this was all over, with his wife to a small cottage on the sea somewhere, a more temperate sea perhaps. Perhaps the damned arthritis that plagued him so much in the North Atlantic would ease up. If he ever saw another dripping pipe or valve again it would be too soon. He and his wife would tend the garden and fish for cod, by God, yes, he would have fresh food every day! And they would entertain their grandchildren when they visited. Chief pulled his mind back to the present. The new mission was understandable, though perhaps extreme, given the dwindling resources of the German military machine. But he sensed that there was something else happening here under the surface.

Nine men had fallen sick just before their scheduled rendezvous with the doomed *Milchkuh*, and they were now in their steel coffin at the bottom of the ocean. A few of them had been casual friends, but most had not been. In fact, if he had to draw up a list of those on board most likely to be unproductive or even troublesome given their current mission, the nine names on the list would have been right up there. Like the First Watch Officer, a fucking Nazi youth the likes of whom the U-boat fleet prided themselves at keeping off their boats for want of common sense, let alone for lacking technical proficiencies. The skeleton crew remaining in the boat now were a good working team with the required skills and temperament.

* * *

Soldier stashed his boat and gear behind some big rocks above the high tide mark on the shore. He could see in the low light that he was near the circular rock foundation of an old Eskimo house, probably a thousand years old. Pieces of whalebone and caribou antler were strewn around, which suggested that this had long been a good hunting area. He hoped there would be good hunting for him as well. He looked at his watch and decided to rest for a few hours. Then he would hike over the height of land and somehow get across the river separating him from the base area. With just a touch of ghostly radiance sifting through thinner shades in the overcast sky he did a 360-degree sweep along the horizon with his Zeiss binoculars. Not seeing any sign of life, he dropped his weary body to recline against his pack for a few hours of needed rest.

* * *

U-807 had less than three meters of water over its tower now, as it rested on a sandy bottom between a small island and the Baffin shore to the west. They had pulled the plug in the boat just before midnight, their flooding sounds masked by the incoming tide. It had been darker than usual thanks to an overcast sky. No lights from other boats or camps had been visible, nor had there been any exterior illumination from their own boat. The crew wore sweaters and long johns against the clammy temperatures, which so far was no worse than what they had found in the Barents Sea the year before. It was quiet time and the crew took advantage of it by reading or resting in their bunks. The Commander and the Chief conversed in low voices and pointed out various features in the maps and charts under a red light. They would surface the boat in the narrow channel in just over 18 hours to take Soldier back on board. They hoped the moon would slip behind some clouds, and a little more fog would be nice too.

Petty Officer Winkler was wearing his headphones as usual and looking very far away. He felt his ears and his brain were learning to distinguish between different whales at this point, though he conceded to himself that it might have been just his imagination at work. Earlier he had heard with his hydrophones the sounds of a small motorized craft in the water, off on the eastern side of Frobisher Bay. It seemed to be coming from the same area as one group of whales. He listened, fascinated, but his sense of euphoria was soon replaced by a terrible dread when it occurred to him that some Eskimos might be hunting the whales, whales that were perhaps trapped in a bay or inlet. And they were probably hunting with rifles using the same bullets as the shell casings Soldier had found at *Kurt* weather station. Winkler swore under his breath and ripped the headphones off. He had already been sufficiently depressed thinking about the painful loss of his special friend Albert, who had served as steward on the boat. The young man with the shock of black hair and the devilish smile had been one of the stricken crew transferred to the sick bay on the *Milchkuh*. Winkler's slight frame trembled as the tears came again.

* * *

Soldier looked at his watch in the beginning light of the new day, and it was not yet 5 a.m. He did some quick push-ups and deep-knee bends to limber up, then smoothed down the green army fatigues that were a clever copy of the American army dress. A quick wipe-down of his Thompson submachine gun with folding wire stock reassured him that he had some good close-up firepower should he be surprised. He tucked it back into his backpack and then did a check on his Colt .45 pistol, an American Mk 2 hand grenade, his binoculars, a small camera, canteen, and some snacks. He started walking across the tundra and up the hill, from which he should be able to identify a crossing of the Sylvia Grinnell River to the base beyond. The river was a little higher and wider than he had expected, but he could see a wider section with rocks spanning the width where he might be able to wade across. As Soldier got closer he could see that the current was too strong for wading in the shallow sections. He could swim across the narrower and deeper part closer to the river mouth but then he would be seriously wet and cold, possibly even become hypothermic in the icy water. That could jeopardize his mission. As he scoped the river toward the mouth he could see an Eskimo camp on his side, red fish fillets and sliced caribou hanging from a line to dry. And there was a seal-skin kayak pulled up on the rocks . . . Eskimos, in his experience, were early risers. When they came outside to greet the new day they would find him waiting.

* * *

Silasie drank the tea handed to him by his wife who was already up with the little one. He chewed on a piece of bannock taken from the pan over the primus stove and smeared strawberry jam on it with his hunting knife. The Americans were running a small canteen for their men and their local workers. They had quickly learned what they should stock to keep the natives happy. Jam, lard, baking powder and flour for bannock, tea and sugar, ammunition, rope, but not much else. There was no HBC trading post here yet, though there was one down the north shore of the bay at Ward Inlet. Soon Silasie would go to the officers' Quonset hut again and inquire if they had any work for him yet. They had told him already that he was a quick learner on the D-2 Caterpillar and other equipment, and that he should return when their next ships came in with more cargo. That was expected any day now, they had told him. Silasie held his hot tea aside as his naked two-year-old son crawled onto his lap. This is a good place to camp. His wife could snag *iqaluk* arctic char and maybe even shoot a *tuktu* caribou walking along the banks of the river.

Silasie's hearing picked up the sounds of stones turning and he lifted up the tent flap to peer out. A tall *qallunaaq* was down by the river looking over his kayak. He wore the clothing of an American soldier and carried an army rucksack. Silasie put another piece of bannock into his son's mouth, rubbed his nose against the little one's nose and went out of the tent to greet his visitor. "*Qanuippit?*" he called out in greeting. Maybe this *qallunaaq* would know when the ships were coming in and if there would be more work for him soon. He looked young, so he might not be a boss yet. Silasie wondered what the man was doing on this side of the river and what he was doing near his camp. The visitor had his camera out and was snapping pictures of his tent and kayak, much as some other soldiers had done when they came down to fish for arctic char in the river. Silasie was more than a little surprised when his visitor answered "*qanuinngittunga*" to his greeting. He is fine.

* * *

Hansen took advantage of his bottom time to read a St. John's newspaper that had been trading hands on the boat for just about forever. Two years ago, a lifetime ago, he marvelled, U-807 had taken its crew up the St. Lawrence River to within a few hundred kilometers of Quebec City, as well as close enough to St. John's and Halifax to imagine that they could go pub-crawling. The crew had been amazed that the Canadians and Americans were so slow in getting the idea that they were at war, and that the enemy was indeed at their doorstep. Freighters were often unescorted, some aircraft patrols did not seem to be armed, and their navy and air force did not seem to work well together. Furthermore, there was no blackout policy in coastal cities nor were there safeguards against the Germans using Canadian navigation aids and weather reports. U-807 had scored a freighter in the Gulf of St. Lawrence, another in the Strait of Belle Isle west of Newfoundland, and even one coming out of St John's harbour.

Now things had changed. U-807 returned to the same areas of operation earlier this year, this time narrowly escaping bombing and depth charging from a more prepared foe. And little on their tonnage score to show for it . . . This was after getting battered by winter storms so fierce that the waves ripped their 105 mm deck gun off its mounts. The year was getting off to a bad start until they were finally ordered back to their home base at Lorient for provisioning and re-fitting. There they learned that their role in special operations was being ratcheted up a couple of notches. Their enthusiasm was dampened somewhat at the news that the boat that had originally installed the *Kurt* weather station, U-537, had gone to the bottom in the Pacific with its crew. And that U-867, just departed from its base in Lorient and en route to Labrador to install a second automated weather station there, was sunk by an RAF bomber, all hands lost. Then there were the unsettling rumours that U-807 could receive orders to transport German scientists and secret superweapons and materials to Japan, possibly through a less-guarded Arctic route. It appeared that news of the recent successful traverse of the Northwest Passage, by the RCMP's tiny wooden vessel the *St. Roch*, had travelled quickly and widely indeed.

U-807 had been forced to depart its base submerged with a reduced speed of seven knots through the Bay of Biscay and most of the way around the Shetlands, daring to surface only at night to charge batteries. It was now a deadly game of cat and mouse for a U-boat just to survive. Back in *Schwartzer Mai*, Black May of 1943, 20 U-boats were sunk by allied aircraft and warships, including the one Donitz's own son was serving on. By early 1944 more than a third of U-boats heading back out to sea from their fortified bases in coastal France were destroyed. It was speculated that U-boat provisioning and repairs would soon be moved to Norway, and the word was that Admiral Donitz had moved his headquarters from Lorient to Paris.

Ah, it was soothing to think about earlier times. Hansen smiled in recollection of their boarding a wooden 15-meter fishing boat off the coast of Newfoundland to see what they could scavenge from its food lockers and fuel and lubricants stores. U-807 had missed a rendezvous with a *Milchkuh* tanker boat and was running low on torpedoes and ammunition. And food! As they observed the gillnetter through the periscope he had shared with the crew the news that the fishing boat had no radio antenna, and the opinion that a fishing boat so unequipped should more properly be considered a looting opportunity than a target. The Newfoundlanders were initially shocked as a U-boat surfaced beside them, while being quite composed and even polite as they surrendered their scant booty including several tubs of fresh cod. Having loosened up somewhat as German gun muzzles were lowered and they were offered French cigarettes and chocolate, the Newfoundlanders responded with a jug of screech. This elixir turned out to be a potent rum traded from Jamaica for salt cod. At this offering, the Commander had smiled and poured the golden liquid into tin cups quickly produced by the fishing crew, finally yelling "down the hatch". As the boarding crew prepared to push off, he had relented and handed back half the crates they had just seized as war booty. But they kept the cod and bologna, the apples and fresh milk, and the 12 gauge shot gun with two boxes of ammunition found in the cabin. The Newfoundlanders had reciprocated by offering up half the remaining screech from their stash. Hansen and the Chief, who both spoke passable English, had joked about the Newfoundlanders' peculiar English dialect and went so far as to wonder if it could perhaps be used for coding messages to naval headquarters, replacing the possibly compromised Enigma machines and codebooks.

More glorious memories from the Happy Days . . . Cruising on a glassy surface along the Labrador coast, the crew sunning in shorts on the deck with little fear of attack. They passed small fishing communities with clothes hanging on the line and smoke curling up from cook-stoves and fish smokers, all in all a hauntingly beautiful and peaceful scene for the war-weary crew. And then there were the more security-conscious patrols up the St. Lawrence River with the crew taking turns at the periscope to view the tranquil pastoral scenes, a church with a steeple in every small village, with cows and sheep and with children playing. Someone suggested that perhaps nobody would notice if they just moved into the village and set up house. What a life! The crew joked but there was longing in their eyes too, thinking about what might have been, either at home or over here. At night they would sometimes sing along to the improvised Lili Marlene tune "The Schnorchel", their favourite verse:

> *Now the Convoy Commodore's*
> *Growling in his beard:*
> *The local strategic thinkers*

Are really rather weird!
But when we're sent on ops once more
We'll want nothing better than a St. Lawrence shore
With you, Lili Marlene!

And occasionally a boisterous Teutonic-accented rendition of a Newfoundland folk ballad heard over the radio when patrolling the Strait of Belle Isle and outside St. John's Harbour, just one verse sung over and over with hands slapping the knees:

I's the bye that builds the boat
And I's the bye that sails her
And I's the bye that catches the fish
And brings them home to Liza

Well, Hansen reflected, Liza didn't get the fish that one time we snatched it from those byes . . .

* * *

Soldier thanked the friendly Eskimo who was somewhat surprised that this *qallunaaq* could speak some of his language, a different dialect certainly but yet understandable for the most part. He had told Silasie that he had been based with the US military in Greenland for some time, and that there were some Eskimo workers living near the base. But now he was in a hurry to get back to the base for his morning shift. After some small talk, Soldier asked for the use of Silasie's kayak, handing him some chocolate for the little one. He felt three pairs of eyes upon him as he expertly paddled himself with his pack across the narrows. Once on the other side, he wound twine around a rock and threw it back so the kayak could be retrieved. Soldier waved at the smiling Eskimo and called out, "*Tagvauvutit*".

Just a kilometer up and over the slope was a panoramic view of the whole flat base area extending from the landing beach at the northern end of the bay to a long gravel airstrip running approximately north to south. The terrain was rocky and rugged but it was softened by meadows of tundra grass. Where the landscape offered shelter and where there was generous exposure to the sun, random late-season patches of bright yellow arctic poppies and purple saxifrage persisted.

Soldier's analytical mind kicked in. He noted that there was a huge supply of natural gravel here. There was a good unobstructed approach to the main airstrip. There were surrounding hills offering good potential sites for anti-aircraft guns. But Soldier knew that a German air attack at this remote location would be out of the question. Germany had no long-range bombers to compare with the heavy American and British bombers, just a few surviving four-engine Condors that were used sparingly for reconnaissance. Soldier lay prone between two rocks and continued to sweep the area with his binoculars. He could see that the main north-south runway of approximately 1,500 meters was being extended to the north and a shorter east-west runway was in the final phase of construction. It appeared that most of the heavy equipment operators remaining were black soldiers, presumably attached to a military engineering battalion. There was only one aircraft, a twin-engine C-47 Dakota transport plane parked beside the main runway, likely for logistical support.

No light bombers were on the ground, though they could come through at any time. Two rows of Quonset huts were probably for housing construction personnel while the two larger buildings could be a mess hall and administration offices. He could see a generator building to supply the power, and in three locations bordering the main airstrip he could see large concentrations of fuel drums. An aircraft hangar was under construction, probably so an aircraft engine could be quickly repaired or replaced out of the weather to keep those enemy warplanes flying to the war. There was a radio and radar communications structure on a hill on the northeast corner of the base area, with a winding road linking it to the base. He could see two security huts, one near the beach area and one off to the side of the main runway. Probably the biggest challenge up here, Soldier mused, would be keeping caribou off the damn runway when the ferried warplanes were on final approach. Soldier did not move a muscle as the sun arched through a partly cloudy sky, in spite of the tormenting mosquitos. He was confident that nobody had observed him, other than the Eskimos earlier on.

Soldier completed an inventory of construction equipment, small trucks and jeeps, buildings, possible infiltration and egress routes. He made a count of armed soldiers and military police, concluding that there were only a handful of routinely armed men on base and no armour or heavy guns, just a jeep and a half-track with what appeared to be Browning .50 caliber machine guns mounted on them. These were usually parked at the security huts or alternately doing patrols of the base and runway perimeter. There were no trenches or bunkers or fortifications of any kind. Yes, he calculated, ten German commandos in

American uniforms with the element of surprise could do it, once they commandeered the American jeep and half-track. Ideally they could hit the base when there was a flight of bombers on the ground as well, to up their score.

Another look south down the Bay from his elevated position revealed no sign of the approaching ships that the Eskimo had mentioned this morning. A dozen quick pictures and it was time to get back to his dinghy and lie low till evening and the light faded. To get across the river again he would have to find a place where he could wade and swim across, clothes bundled above him, and not drown in the process. He knew he could not risk encountering the curious Silasie again, and he had no desire to ensure his silence by killing him. Silasie's wife had peeked out at him too, holding the baby through the tent-flaps with some urgency while he let loose with a stream of urine. He knew that news could travel fast about the strange American who had arrived at their camp from the west and who could speak their language, but he hoped the news would fall only on Eskimo ears for the time being.

6

August 24: Frobisher Bay

Petty Officer Winkler clutched his headphones and called for the Commander. "Propeller sounds, three or more ships, coming up Frobisher Bay."

"How far?"

"Estimate 20 miles."

"*Scheisse!*" cursed Commander Hansen. He looked at his watch, still an hour before their surfacing and rendezvous with Soldier.

* * *

Soldier steered his dinghy along the shore to the agreed pick-up point. Still shivering from his icy swim across the river, he cut the motor and dropped a small anchor. Bobbing up and down in the heaving sea just a stone-throw from the Baffin shore he could feel the tidal currents pulsing through the thin material of the inflatable boat. At two minutes past midnight he could just discern a small hooded light pointed toward shore. He headed for that and was soon able to draw out the whitened mass of the conning tower against the black undulating ocean and dark sky. There was a purplish twilight and he could see the U-boat from 200 meters out, which left him wondering how effective their new camouflage paint really was. At least when there was little ice on the ocean and no snow as yet on the land . . . Soon he could hear the waves washing against the hull, and moments later the skin of the dinghy rubbed against the mother ship. He sensed the urgency of the waiting crew when he was quickly pulled up and spirited below. After having heard Silasie's news that more ships were coming "soon" Soldier was not surprised to hear of the small convoy approaching the base. The Commander was making ready to slip behind the larger island off their port bow until the small convoy passed, gambling that the island's elevation would be enough to hide the outline of the conning tower, from eyes and from radar. They did not want to make flooding sounds in a dive, and in any case the bottom here was too shallow and irregular for safe navigation while submerged.

The Commander's face showed tension as more than two hours passed while the small enemy convoy proceeded in a column up Frobisher Bay to the base. The convoy was made up of an icebreaker in the lead, a freighter, and a destroyer escort at the rear. Winkler monitored the radio communications between the vessels and the communications hut at the base and he communicated this in low tones to the Commander. The whales had gone quiet.

Finally, Hansen looked up at the pre-dawn sky. "We can see well enough now. Let's sneak away on the surface. Both electric motors half-ahead for an hour. We still have some outgoing tide in our favour and should make ten knots. Once clear of these islands we can start the diesels to charge batteries and fire up the air compressors too. By the time that's done we will be in deeper water and can go to periscope depth."

The Commander looked at each of the other men clustered in the control room—Chief, Soldier, and Winkler. "There's no fog cover and the American weather station is promising blue sky and sunshine for our return cruise down the Bay. I would say we stand a fair chance of getting back out into the open sea without running into any more ships or being spotted by an aircraft on this heading."

"A piece of cake compared to the Bay of Biscay these days," added Chief. "We should come here more often."

* * *

Captain Eggars peered out from the bridge of his freighter loaded with heavy construction equipment, drums of aviation gas, and steel beams to drop onto the beach at Crystal II. He had main engine problems and was too damned slow for the rest of the convoy, which had left him behind once past Resolution and into Frobisher Bay. The pack ice was negligible and the icebergs were out in Davis Strait where they belonged, and indications were that the winds would not be herding them his way any time soon. Eggars had made this same run last year and at that time he and his crew had worried more about storms and ice than anything else, once they got past Newfoundland anyway. But that all changed when *Chatham*, a freighter with 4000 tons of construction equipment and fuel, was sunk by a U-boat off southern Labrador. With that in mind, Captain Eggars just wanted to unload and get the hell out. He looked over and saw the Canadian corvette escort coming up on his port side again, constantly ranging around him in circles and doing soundings with its sonar. Going by the book, Eggars smiled, even here. Part of that was probably just going crazy babysitting this tub and wishing it was all over with. "Just like watching paint dry," the skipper of the corvette had commented. He had also professed disbelief that two small freighters had an icebreaker and two warship escorts assigned to it. It certainly smacked of overkill! But Eggars knew the superfluous contribution of the Canadian icebreaker and the corvette escort was all about sovereignty. Ottawa politicians, not to mention the military brass, were still pissed that the Americans had launched into airstrip construction on Baffin Island, Canadian territory, without official permission from Ottawa. So it was about flying the flag as much as anything.

* * *

Winkler was more focused than usual on his headphones. The skipper had maintained full speed with the electric motors at periscope depth, which slightly downgraded the effectiveness of his *Balkon-Geraet* hydrophone array. Still, his hands came up to clutch his headphones. "Commander! Propeller sounds! Two more ships coming our way up Frobisher Bay, one probably a freighter and the other possibly an escort."

"Range?"

"Maybe 15 nautical miles at the most." Establishing range and direction was an art as much as a science when hugging the surface at this speed with periscope up.

Hansen looked at the instruments, particularly the fathometer. Batteries not fully charged but time to get under. "*Auf Sehrohrtiefe!*" The men operating the hydroplanes hustled to take the boat to the new ordered depth of 100 meters. "Change course ten degrees to starboard!" He looked over at Winkler holding his headphones in concentration, raising his eyebrows.

"Heading our way!"

"*Scheisse*! Report any changes."

Five tense minutes later Winkler grimaced. "He's increasing speed and coming right at us!"

"He's left the freighter to do some hunting," growled the Commander. "Fathometer is indicating 300 meters here. *Tiefer, schnell, tiefer!* Dive to 200 meters. Silent running."

The pinging from the enemy warship's sonar was nerve-wracking. Water conditions were in the U-boat's favour, changes in salinity with some thermal layering caused by relatively warmer Atlantic water mixing with colder Arctic waters. This would mercifully play havoc with the enemy's sonar. A first salvo of depth charges was off-target, and their destructive force was muted by water pressure at their depth. Commander Hansen glanced at his watch. "We'll hold out till dark and then try to continue south. Let's hope they're worried about another German U-boat in this area and head back to look after their freighter."

Chief added, "And let's hope the destroyer that passed us earlier with her little flock does not come back out to lend this one a hand." The Chief made a face as he considered their battle prospects with no deck gun and only the two stern torpedo tubes remaining functional and with only two torpedoes. Given their past experience, one of the G7a's stood a good chance of being a dud. Not much to fight it out with a warship if it came down to that.

Hansen stared at their poor excuse for a chart. "If we can make it into this channel here we can turn the corner and go west into Hudson Strait and try to hide under the drift ice we observed moving east. That would stop or slow down the surface ships and we can worry about finding our way out again later."

Chief spoke up. "That's still 40 nautical miles from here, six hours on electric motors."

The Commander sighed. "And probably the only chart work done outside of Frobisher Bay's main navigation route was courtesy of the American explorer Francis Hall in the last century." He paused, then added, "Gentlemen, on our right we have *Meta Incognita*, and below us we have *Meta Incognita*."

The escort, sounding like one of those cursed Canadian corvettes, was on to them again, running a box pattern at high speed, slowing and stopping at intervals to try to fix the U-boat's position. U-807 was northwest of Resolution Island by the time they could hear the propellers of the destroyer coming in fast to join the hunt. From the charts and tide information they had it was likely the water at the surface would be churning. This could make matters a little more difficult for the hunters, particularly with some ice moving in the current. As for the prey, they would have to just hope they did not drive their U-boat into some shoals. The Commander gave the order to bring the boat up 50 meters. They held course for the next hour and found new hope when Winkler reported that the warships were moving away. But they could be trying to move through drifting ice to get in front of them. The Commander gave the order to drop the boat onto the bottom and listen.

Commander Hansen felt a strange sense of relief knowing that the enemy warships had given him a timely cover and apt send-off for an adventure he had thus far only dreamed about. He was clearly thinking outside the box as required by a U-boat commander to optimize prospects for survival. Even so, his next move could conceivably doom his *Kriegsmarine* career while endangering his own life along with those of the crew. He thought about this, the notion of relative risks. What he envisioned seemed no riskier than heading home across the Atlantic in their tired boat with insufficient diesel fuel to make it to their bases, bases that were being overrun in the enemy's massive invasion at Normandy. He had to talk to the crew very soon about their alternatives. Commander Hansen pulled out a file case and unlocked it to peruse his personal library of the exploration of Foxe Basin . . . reports, charts, crude maps and sketches. He closed the curtain of his small berth, thinking with mixed satisfaction and dread that this undertaking could well go leaps and bounds beyond a stealthy cruise up the St. Lawrence River.

7

August 26: Eastern Hudson Strait

The Commander nodded to Chief, looking at the water temperature reading. "There may well be ice up there. No indications of surface light from the periscope. We have to surface before we run out of battery power and air. Hold the boat at 50 meters and we can trim the boat for a slow rise to the surface with bow up at a 20-degree approach angle." He knew this would be easier said than done, compensating for the unequal volumes and weights of water displaced respectively by the higher bow and the lower stern at different depths and corresponding water pressures, in accordance with the physics outlined in Archimedes' Principle. This would require a delicate process of pumping water from the bow trim tanks to the aft trim tank to balance the boat on its longitudinal axis to the desired attitude. On the other hand, the Chief was superbly competent, and this is what he was paid for.

Chief, engaging his engineer brain, sighed and nodded in return. He understood the other driving problem as well. There was no way of knowing for sure, with their crude instruments and darkness above, if they were under open sea now or some concentration of ice cover. An upward-beamed echo sounder could be useful here, though it still wouldn't give accurate values on ice thickness. The periscopes would be of limited use submerged without effective lighting and in any case they could not risk ice-damage to the scopes as other U-boats had experienced in escape and avoidance measures in the Barents Sea. Hansen had reviewed the tactics of another U-boat commander who was forced into a risky escape under ice pack. The boat rather crudely identified areas of thin or spotty ice by pioneering a low-buoyancy "bow-knocking" approach with a controlled rise of one meter per minute, presumably to protect the electronic equipment in the conning tower and the guns, and to avoid surfacing with hatches blocked by slabs of ice. Similarly, U-807 would attempt some of these bow-up probes. The hope was that if they hit thin or broken ice they could break through with no appreciable damage to the boat. Or else be handed a glancing blow from heavier ice and be driven back under, again with no appreciable damage . . . Chief gave his belated thanks that U-807's bow and front tower casing had been strengthened with additional steel plating for just such contingencies of operating in regions of known ice prevalence. One of the new Type XXI boats would have been so much better for this area of operation, though.

U-807 surfaced easily in ice-free water and the release of tension was palpable. From the bridge, Commander Hansen could see that there was significant pack ice to the west in Hudson Strait. Not knowing where the warships were, the Commander gave the order to proceed with both diesels half ahead on a northwest heading. They had to top up their batteries and compressed air as their first priority. And it would not hurt to put a little more distance between the boat and where the enemy warships were most likely to be . . . Presently they were easing through broken ice with pieces up to 30 centimeters thick cascading off the bow. The impact and scraping sounds were worrisome but what most concerned them were the fewer but larger chunks of multi-year ice, old ice that displayed their history of melt and freeze akin to the growth patterns of an oak tree.

The Commander gave the order for the helmsman to turn the boat six times in the first two hours to avoid threatening patches of heavier ice. Two men in waterproof gear were positioned on the bow wielding poles to fend off this heavier ice, though the poles were having little effect. A speed of about eight knots seemed optimal in terms of generating a good bow wave to lift and deflect ice pans ice while proceeding with a measure of speed. At this pace they could still effectively maneuver around the heavier ice, which was presumably drifting down from Foxe Basin. Hansen saw that the ice they were encountering now was darker than that of Davis Strait and Labrador, probably due to sediments kicked up by currents and tidal action.

Hansen was scoping 360 degrees with his glasses. There were patches of fog ahead, but presumably the enemy warships were further east of their position. Yet it could be only a matter of time before there would be patrol aircraft with bombs and depth charges hunting them, perhaps even using the Frobisher Bay base. A U-boat had shown up in their own backyard and would be considered a security threat of the highest order.

"*Alarm*! Ship 40 degrees off the port bow," barked the Second Watch Officer. "No, two ships." Their bow waves indicated high speed, and the ice cover immediately between the hunters and their prey was negligible.

"Fluten! Fluten! Fluten!" ordered the Commander. Dive the boat! Thirty meters down, the order was given to the helmsman to turn 45 degrees to starboard.

The boat's batteries were only half-charged, which was of obvious concern. But there was some water depth here and perhaps still some thermal layering of Atlantic and Arctic waters, perhaps even shifting salinity as the less saline Hudson Bay water with its huge influx of river water mixed with the more saline ocean water.

As the first depth charges exploded around them the Commander gave the order to drop the boat onto the bottom again. The boat shuddered and scraped as it settled at a depth of 220 meters, shifting slightly to port on its vertical axis. Pinging from the ASDIC's on the Canadian corvette and American destroyer was continuous and terrifying, but the crew prayed that the Commander was correct in claiming the enemy's sonar returns here would not reveal their true position. The exploding depth charges were still a reassuringly safe distance off their port bow. Hansen and the others clustered in the control room held their breath and waited. You could have heard a pin drop. "Damn their radar! And they were just sitting there dead in the water in a handy fog bank waiting for us." Soldier watched the Commander, keeping quiet. He was feeling at a loss to contribute anything useful here while struggling to keep his own stirred-up Stalingrad demons at bay.

Winkler listened through his hydrophones. "They're circling over us," he whispered.

A long and tense two hours later there were no sounds of ships' propellers at the surface. Hansen gave the order to take the boat up to periscope depth. No threats of the warship kind or from heavy ice cover either so the order to surface was issued. The boat's bow banged benignly into some pans of ice, though the noise through the hull was unnerving. Commander Hansen was on the bridge with binoculars within minutes. A large slab of ice measuring approximately three meters by four meters by 30 centimeters thick lay on the foredeck.

Soldier, at the Commander's side, looked down and commented, "Ah, a little more camouflage."

U-807 was making 11 knots on a westerly bearing in Hudson Strait along the rugged Baffin coastline. Daylight was fading fast when Commander Hansen gave the order to steer for a sheltered bay on the northeast corner of Big Island that was situated off the inlet leading into Lake Harbour, site of a Hudson Bay Company post and Royal Canadian Mounted Police detachment. And according to Winkler, there were all the signs of a manned American weather station there.

The little harbour they found themselves in was a beauty. It was protected on three sides with a sandy beach on the shore and a sizeable stream for fresh water, and water deep enough for them to submerge quickly if they had to. For now they were surfaced but sitting low in the water with decks awash, the white tower looking like a cousin to a small berg. Full darkness had descended upon them to accompany the drizzle from overcast skies obscuring the moon. The hydrophones would give warning if the warships ventured back this way, but Hansen had little reason to believe that would happen without some daylight. It was time to have a sit-down with Chief and bounce a few things off him. Once he was onside, they would talk with Soldier and see if they could achieve a meeting of minds. But now it was mealtime and Cookie was preparing the last of the Labrador caribou in a hearty stew served with thick slices of bread coated with canned butter. The crew were only too aware that the bread was the last of what they had received fresh-baked from the *Milchkuh*.

* * *

Commander Hansen was getting impatient and even a little disappointed in Chief and Soldier as they had their smoke and coffee up top. He looked around at the three protective sides of what they had already dubbed "Safe Harbour" and wished things could be more convivial.

"Yes, Chief, I know you want to go home. But think about it! To head back now into the Labrador Sea and the Atlantic will ensure you never get home. We will run a gauntlet of destroyers and bombers unlike any you have ever seen. We were already low on fuel when that bomber cut short our refueling. And there won't be another *Milchkuh* to give us more fuel and supplies. We are really on our own until we get back to base, which is almost certainly overrun by the enemy by now. The only reason we are still alive at this point is this ice. The ice has become our friend!" Hansen paused and continued. "And then there are the latest developments in Germany, which I gleaned from the skipper of U-494, before the blessing of the bombs."

Chief winced at this gallows humour that went with a U-boat crew like a hand in a glove. "And what would those latest developments be?"

Commander Hansen raised his hand and said, "All in good time. I'm still digesting them myself."

Soldier was pissed, his natural instinct to hit back. "And I say we should go back to the base and attack now while that is the last thing they would expect from us. Just let me pick ten of your men and use whatever small arms you have on board. Otherwise, as you say with winter coming on, an organized raid could probably not be mounted before next year. That could be too late."

Hansen stared incredulously at Soldier. "Too late for what? A glorious fight to the end?"

When Soldier did not answer, the Commander continued, "We would not survive the raid, one more U-boat sunk, and this war we're fighting can't go on much longer. And the biggest thing . . . probably no more American bombers coming through this base after this year anyway. The enemy will know full well they can transport light aircraft much more safely by freighters in convoy, with most of our U-boats sunk." Hansen sighed and spoke tiredly but emphatically. "Gentlemen, this war is all about attrition. Our enemies are building ships and airplanes and tanks, and shipping fuel and men, faster than we can sink them now. I hear that two Liberty Ships a day are coming out of American shipyards, and their auto makers have turned out literally thousands of B-24 bombers on their assembly lines."

"Fuck Henry Ford!" Chief muttered.

Hansen could see that Soldier wanted to fight to the very end like a good German warrior. What to do? He knew that this man had not served under him for more than two years as the others had, and he was not accustomed to blind obedience and subordination of all thought to his command on a U-boat at war. But there was no doubt he was accustomed to total obedience to his officers in the commando units of the *Heer*, who would unhesitatingly fight to the last man. Yet he showed all the signs of being a free thinker. Hansen knew that there was little room for democracy on the Russian front or in a U-boat at war for that matter. Yet he perceived that he and his crew were stuck in a space between war and peace, and in another light they were already as good as dead anyway if they played out their act to the end.

"Gentlemen." Hansen spoke up after a long brooding silence. "We are at an impasse, and it is larger than this question of attacking or not attacking the Frobisher Bay base. I think unorthodox methods are now required for making some major decisions concerning operations of this boat and crew. Therefore, I propose we meet with representatives of all departments and ranks at 2100 hours in the bow torpedo room."

8

August 27: Hudson Strait

With no torpedoes and the battery canisters removed at *Kurt*, the forward torpedo room that doubled as forward crew quarters provided plenty of room for the gathering men. The word of a 2100 hours meeting had spread rapidly through the ranks and there was a buzz of excitement. Most of the men were awed, never in their short, blinkered lives having been called to a meeting such as this one with all ranks represented. Something big was up. Some men were even of the opinion that the war was over.

The Commander entered the torpedo room, nodding at the officers, petty officers and sailors gathered together waiting for his arrival. Most of them were sitting on crates. There were eight men in the room, and they appeared to be good representatives of the crew as a whole. Soldier was there too, by special invitation.

Commander Hansen smiled. "Well, you are no doubt curious as hell about what is going on? Have we turned this boat into Plato's Republic? A cooperative at sea? Well, not quite. But we have decisions that can best be made together. I will bring you up to speed on what is happening back home, and suggest different possible scenarios for us." He paused. "I am your Commander, and you are sworn by death to follow my orders in defending the Fatherland from its enemies." He neglected to say anything about the crew also being accountable to *der Fuehrer*.

Chief watched and listened to the Commander as he went deftly through his listing of facts and figures to inform the men of their present situation. The advances in the anti-submarine capability of their enemy, the apparent ability of the enemy to monitor the *U-bootwaffe*'s coded communications, the terrible toll on the U-boat fleet and an update on boats known to have been lost in the past three months alone. Then the allied invasion at Normandy, loss of the U-boat bases in coastal France, defeats of the German military machine in North Africa and the Russian front, the failure of the Luftwaffe to gain air superiority over Europe, the bombing of German cities and terrible destruction and civilian loss of life from firestorms. The dissipation of resources needed to fight a war as Germany began to eat itself in the way of a dragon feeding on its own tail, sending youth and grandfathers out to fight to the end . . . As anticipated, news of the assassination attempt on Hitler was absolutely shocking to the men gathered in the stuffy, sweat-smelling room. Men stared and sighed and shuffled their feet, looking back to the Commander for more. Perhaps most devastating to the men was news of the order from their leader Admiral Donitz that surviving U-boats are to ram enemy ships, particularly warships. Hansen chose not to add that this *Rammbefehl* was somewhat open to interpretation.

Hansen paused to look at each of the men, most of whom looked him in the eye. "Now, with regard to our own circumstances against all this background context . . . we are dangerously short of diesel fuel. Thanks to the Canadian bomber attack we did not get our tanks more than one-third filled and we have since burned up a good measure of that. There are no more *Milchkuh* available to help us now. There may be six or eight U-boats in the North Atlantic still out hunting convoys. But they can rarely surface at night to charge their batteries without being attacked by bombers or convoy escorts. I need not inform you about the risks of refueling at sea, in the unlikely event that one of these U-boats on patrol would have any fuel to spare for us. So we are, as the Yanks would say, up the creek without a paddle, gentlemen. Even if we had full fuel tanks we would run a gauntlet going home like we have never seen before. And where would we go? Forget your whoring and drinking in Lorient. Our new U-boat bases in Norway are no less a deathtrap and our boats are being sunk daily trying to get in and out. Three out of every five, the story goes. In short, the war is all but over for us but of course we are still under orders to fight and even to win the war against impossible odds." He paused. "We are pretty much dead already but not quite sure what our particular path to the bottom will be. What we decide here will determine our fates, how and where we die. Or, just maybe, if there is any way we can survive."

"Questions?" Silence in the torpedo room . . .

Commander Hansen prompted. "We can do our duty and point our bow toward Germany and pray we can scavenge fuel from surviving attack boats on the way home. Attack any convoy ships we encounter with the two torpedoes in our stern torpedo tubes. We can be blown up and if we are lucky some of us can be captured. Either way the war is over for us."

Hansen looked at Soldier, who was staring hard at him, then continued. "We can attack the Frobisher Bay base and go out fighting, make heroes of ourselves. The best-case scenario is we would survive and possibly even capture enough diesel fuel from the stocks there to get us home without having to refuel in midstream. But frankly I doubt that we would escape from kicking a hornet's nest like that." The Commander took a breath and continued. "I am ready to surrender my command to any officer on this ship who wishes to assume authority, if there is more confidence in his leadership than my own." He paused to look each man in the eye, but the silence continued.

Soldier spoke up. "It appears that the crew who were stricken ill and shuttled over to the *Milchkuh* are the ones who would have been speaking up here today." More silence. Some men shuffled their feet. Soldier continued, "For the record I suggest we sneak back to the base and attack it. Both to put the base out of action and to secure enough diesel fuel to get home . . . Security will be tighter now but they will still have the same limited defensive assets, and they definitely won't be expecting us to attack. And it's getting darker all the time. The convoy will be on its way back south shortly and the escorts with it. It will take time to get other enemy warships on our tail."

Hansen looked from Soldier to the crew. The young trooper had made some sense and he spoke to their patriotism and will to fight. Yet, he was *Heer*, not *U-bootwaffe*. Uncertainty marked the faces of the men. Some of them coughed, avoiding eye contact with Soldier.

"Any other options?" Chief asked the Commander.

"Well, we could always surrender to the Americans at the base in Frobisher Bay. Spend the short time remaining in this war in a prisoner of war camp."

The Commander was only a little surprised at the degree of outright hostility to the idea of surrender. It was pretty much a non-starter. The only *U-bootwaffe* crewmembers who had ever opted for surrender were some of those splashing about at the oil-slicked surface with their boat sinking under them.

Hansen stood up. "Right, let's go up top for a smoke. Report your final thoughts to me in the morning and I will make my final decision, taking your views into consideration." He immediately regretted using the word "final".

* * *

Captain Black was at the controls of his B-24 Liberator, a four-engine bomber patrolling south from the US airbase in Greenland. His course was a sweep to the northern tip of Labrador and then west across the top of Ungava Bay to Diana Bay, then north over *Meta Incognita* to overfly the Crystal II base, then straight down Frobisher Bay with a turn west into Hudson Strait and finally a hard bank to the right to head back to home base. Once over Frobisher Bay he dropped down to 1,000 feet hoping to see a little of the reported naval action. Nothing! Lieutenant Black followed up with a slow turn to overfly Resolution Island and fly a stretch northwest along the south Baffin coast. The surface was glassy calm and the new day's rising sun was obliquely penetrating the epidermis of the dark ocean. The bomber with *Delta Dawn* script and a bosomy belle enlivening its nose, was over a large island off the Lake Harbour channel when the tail gunner drawled into the intercom. "Ah believe we just overflew a submarine in a little bay down yonder. Ceegar-shaped and a tad submerged. Suggest y'all do a turnaround."

Captain Black produced his best rebel yell and slapped his knee. He threw the large unwieldy aircraft into a sharp left bank, deftly coaxing the controls to reduce airspeed and altitude. "All right! Prepare to drop two 500 pounders from 800 feet on our first run. We'll be right on top of it but with those hills circling the back of the harbour we won't see the sub until seconds before bomb release. So make it count."

* * *

"*Alarm! Fluten! Fluten! Fluten!*" Commander Hansen was thankful he had ordered that the boat be held low in the water, forward ballast tank pre-flooded and decks awash, as a precaution in the event of enemy attack. The Commander called out to the hydroplane operators to steer for a down angle of 20 degrees with full power from both electric motors. Slowly the boat clawed its way down to darker and safer depths, its pressure hull filled with the pungent smell of fear to mask the myriad other odours.

The Liberator barely cleared the hills to the rear of U-807's safe harbour, and sent two 500 pounders hurtling toward a faint chimera of their target. The two bombs exploded 100 feet beyond the bow of the boat, not close enough to do serious damage but close enough to generate more Stalingrad flashbacks for Soldier. By the time the lumbering Liberator circled back over the ocean and returned for its second bombing run U-807 was gone. Two more 500 pound bombs with delayed fuses were dropped ahead of the boat's surface turbulence.

Petty Officer Winkler had his headphones off and hands over his ears, sweating in spite of the cold dampness on the boat and trembling but not from the cold. He had prayed that the hard turn to starboard ordered by the Commander would save them. It did. Two more explosions and no damage other than to the crew's nervous systems . . . Then there were ten long minutes with no more bombs as they descended to 100 meters. The commander gave the order to continue west along the south Baffin coast, and for a full two hours their way was uneventful.

"Propellers!" Winkler moaned. "Screws from two ships, getting louder fast. Their ASDIC has us." The rampant pinging on the boat was a waking nightmare. He wanted to scream but he had to keep it together for the Commander.

Hansen growled. "Amazing how slick they've coordinated with the navy boys to get their hardware after us. The ships must be the same destroyer and corvette, with the convoy left behind in Frobisher Bay base with the icebreaker until this is sorted out. Priority targets and all that . . . "

The Chief and the steering men on the rudder and hydroplanes watched the Commander, waiting for an order.

"We need more ice," was all he muttered.

U-807 was making five knots due west, 120 meters down. Winkler clutched his headphones, eyes wide open and focused far away. "Warships approaching again! High speed."

"Drop another 30 meters, 20 degrees to port, both motors back to one-third."

They were right overhead now! Even Winkler would not hear the depth charges begin their murderous descent until the hammer hit the cap. If the explosive charge fell within 20 meters they were done. Explosions rocked the boat. Pipes burst and water sprayed on men feeling doom was upon them. Other men with ice in their veins moved quickly and efficiently around the boat turning valves and flicking switches to contain the damage. Emergency lighting came on.

"At this depth we're running blind," warned the Chief. "We could smack into the bottom. These old charts show some shoals, though closer to the Baffin coast."

"Agreed. But we need to hold course and speed for another hour. After that we need to go up to top up our batteries and air. Who knows what we will find on the surface?" The look of gallows humour appeared on his face again. "Could be bad things."

"Enemy warships or heavy ice?" queried Chief.

"There be dragons!"

At 1200 hours the Commander ordered a bow-up attitude of 20 degrees for another surface probe. Thirty men held their breath as the bow broke the surface, no heavy impact but definitely the sounds and vibrations of steel meeting ice on the surface. Seconds later the Commander was up through the conning tower hatch scanning for threats. Ice to the west looking heavier . . . "*Fluten! Fluten! Fluten!*" The two enemy warships were coming right at them from two miles away. The first shells exploded on the boat's starboard side. Down, down! Two more explosions bracketed the boat as it fought to escape the surface's grip. The sound of ice banging off the bow and that of some larger ice pans sliding up on the deck to be deflected from the base of the conning tower were terrifying distractions.

* * *

Matt Chisholm, Gunner's Mate on the *Minas Basin*, was happy to be busy. Normally he was cursing his ship for its tendency to roll and pitch when he was trying to aim his 4-inch gun or launch his Hedgehog mortars. It was said that these damn corvettes, built from a modified design of a whaling ship, would roll in wet grass. He was glad though when the skipper took the ship out of the destroyer's wake to find its own path through the swaths of drifting ice. The corvette had less steel in the bow but could out-maneuver a frigging Yank destroyer any day. He got two shots off at the U-boat to match the destroyer's two before the sub could submerge again, but no hits. Maybe he could do better with his Hedgehogs, 24 mortar bombs fired in salvos ahead of the ship where the U-boat was reckoned to be. Matt knew that a U-boat could dive in less than a minute but that its turbulence could be seen for up to five minutes. But here there was current and floating ice so there would be a little more guesswork. On the other hand the ice should help calm the seas to help him get a better aim. He would launch the Hedgehogs to a spot 200 yards off the ship's bow and they would drop in a circle a hundred yards wide, hopefully without hitting any ice pans on the way down. Any one of these mortar bombs with its 30-pound explosive charge would almost certainly do in the U-boat if it could kiss it on its way down. A gang-bang of two or more hits would bring on a healthy climax for sure. Unlike depth charges, which exploded at pre-determined depths, the higher kill-ratio Hedgehogs only went off if they made actual contact with the submerged steel hull. Then Boom! All over for those Nazi fuckers who killed his brother when they torpedoed his freighter south of Iceland . . . And each one of these 24 Hedgehogs had his brother's name scrawled on it. Captain Murphy, hailing from Five Islands just a few miles down the road from his own hometown of Kenomee, Nova Scotia, was definitely okay with that.

* * *

Hansen took solace in knowing the enemy warships could not approach at full speed with so much drift ice on the surface, some pans almost a meter thick. No doubt the ships were firing while maneuvering at high speed through channels in the ice cover. Hitting old ice this thick with a hull not ice-strengthened could remove a warship as a threat, all things being right. But the destroyer and corvette were relentless as terriers after a rabbit. They were over the U-boat before it could reach a depth of 100 meters. They dropped depth charges and fired Hedgehog mortars, some of the latter apparently hitting floating ice on the surface. The enemy was motivated, hungry and closing for the kill. Soldier was slammed into a bulkhead as another depth charge shook the boat. Two more knocked the boat sideways, first to port, then to starboard. The next explosions were 200 meters off to port. Winkler reported that the second ship, the corvette, had broken away from the destroyer and was now on their starboard side and moving parallel to the U-boat. The pinging was terrifying and there was no indication of more thermal layers here to help them hide. Hansen took the risk of dropping U-807 to a depth of 150 meters, then ordered 50 more. They would have to risk the shoals.

Commander Hansen knew it was time to play his wild card. "Pump waste oil from the holding tank, eject garbage from the aft torpedo tubes. Kicking out a bubble decoy from the *Pillenwerfer* ejector won't be effective at this depth. We're going to sit her down on the bottom and play dead. It's our only chance."

"Bottom looks to be 250 meters here," warned Chief. "That puts us past the builder's guarantee on the pressure hull."

"Keep going till I say stop. If those warships don't back off soon we're finished anyway. Let's hope the oil slick along with incoming ice will lead them to declare a kill and move out. But it's a long haul till full dark again up there." The boat made a soft landing on the bottom of Hudson Strait.

Winkler listened as the destroyer and corvette coursed back and forth at much lower speed on both sides of them but not yet converging to a point overhead. Hansen speculated that it had a lot to do with the ice conditions above. U-807 was sitting on the bottom pumping out more oil. Then there was absolute silence on the boat, the crew drawing into themselves, those not on active battle stations lying inert on their bunks to slow their breathing. Winkler heard Soldier mutter out loud about the utter helplessness of sitting on the bottom in an iron coffin, and wonder if he could get a ticket back to the Russian front. For another 22 minutes Winkler listened on the hydrophones as the warships probed above, following leads in the ice. Then the boats seemed to converge.

"One would assume they are now assessing our oil slick," the Commander whispered.

* * *

Captain Murphy on the Canadian corvette *Minas Basin* radioed confirmation of the oil slick along the track of the U-boat from its last sighting. No debris could be seen, though the ice could have concealed some of that, depending . . . depending. The two warships worked their way through the ice for another two passes and then turned east to ease out of the ice cover while daylight permitted.

9

August 28: West of Lake Harbour in Hudson Strait

Hansen looked at his watch and ordered "*Auftauchen!*" complemented by the take-her-up nod to the Chief. Same routine, bow up, a low-buoyancy controlled ascent.

What came next were the soul-destroying sounds of rending metal as the rising bow impacted unyielding Arctic ice and was handed a harsh blow to force the bow downward. The Commander yelled out orders to slow their ascent but the rise could not be arrested before the tower followed the probing bow up to slam into the ice anew.

"*Fluten! Fluten! Fluten! An alle Stellen, Schaden melden*! Damage reports from all stations!"

Hansen breathed again when reports started coming in with no indications of serious damage. But the bow fairing would be battered and some of their equipment at the tower bridge could be damaged or lost.

"Chief, how we doing for battery power?"

"We have to make it up next time if we want to control our ascents. After that it's just blow ballast and pop up like a cork, or maybe turn this boat into a pancake on the underside of the ice. He paused, then cursed, "Damn, we came up too fast this time."

"Let's try heading closer to the Baffin coast again."

At 2300 hours U-807 surfaced uneventfully in sparse pancake ice 12 nautical miles from the rugged coast of Baffin Island.

Commander Hansen was on the bridge with the Chief. They watched the undulating ice to the sides of their boat's passage. They had survived the last surfacing attempt though some of the boat's appendages sustained damage. There was damage to their twin 20 mm flak gun. One barrel was bent but Franz reported that the rest of the gun appeared to be serviceable, and he requested test firing at the first opportunity. The other big loss was the observation periscope, pushed back to the point where the optics were hopelessly skewed out of alignment. The attack periscope, somewhat protected in its sturdy housing in the tower, was still functional. Thank God for a little redundancy. The Naxos radar detector, though retracted, was destroyed. Same with their radio direction finder . . . The radio antenna was questionable, while the retractable radar looked like it might still be functional. Railings and stanchions on the raised bridge superstructure, even the purpose-built collapsing ones, were a shambles. Hansen cursed that the upper conning tower did not allow for more shielding to protect the exposed equipment.

The Commander kept the boat on a northwest heading about five nautical miles out from the south Baffin coast. The ice closer to shore was moving in long streams with channels in between for navigation. Mercifully there were no icebergs in Hudson Strait, no calving glaciers ahead giving up their offspring to the currents. It was still varying concentrations of floating pack ice, for the most part last-winter's ice thinned and dispersed by the summer melt. But there was still some presence of old ice too, of the nightmare variety. Most of the ice they were moving through now was less than 30 centimeters thick and generally this was still being pushed up and out of the way by the upward swell of the bow wave.

* * *

Hansen looked over at Chief. "Okay, relax a little bit for now. By the way, what was the outcome of our little consultation process last night?"

"No official response but I have it on good word that the tribal consensus is to turn the boat toward home and take our chances."

"Ah yes, home . . . " Hansen reflected, "The most powerful primal instinct."

Chief continued. "Try for fuel from another U-boat or even from a solitary freighter if we can capture one. The other scenarios, surrender and attacking the Frobisher base, are not popular. Soldier is pissed but he's a professional and on good terms with the men."

"Ha, better Soldier hears it from the men too and not only from me. It makes our differences something more than a leadership and personality issue."

Just then Soldier's voice was heard down the ladder. "Request permission to come to the bridge?"

"Permission granted," replied the Commander.

"Well, speak of the devil . . . Anyway, at risk of boring you both, here in a nutshell is the situation. We're shit out of luck. Low on fuel and low on food." The Commander shook his head sadly and while gazing at the two other men in turn. Both of these men were strong, independent thinkers and he put a high value on that. A First Watch Officer would normally have shouldered much of this valued "second opinion" role but the last one who served him had been one of those transferred to U-494 for medical attention.

"And low on armaments," snorted Soldier.

Commander Hansen ignored him. "Our pursuers might buy our oil slick and think we're blown to bits at the bottom but my guess is that there will still be a lot of air and naval patrols between Baffin Island and northern Quebec for the next couple of weeks just in case, long enough to choke us off in the event we did in fact survive. What to do? Your thoughts, gentlemen?"

Chief noted that the Commander seemed to be wavering in his decision-making, maintaining his democratic perspective. This was unbecoming of a U-boat commander and, friend or no friend, this tendency was beginning to irritate him. Yes, Karl was something of an academic and an explorer in his former life. And, yes, his adoptive family and sister were erased in the enemy fire bombing of Hamburg. Yes, one had to make allowances, but this was going too far.

Chief spoke up. "Well, I want to go home before I die. All my friends are dying."

"Ah, my friend," said the Commander, "dying at home from natural causes is a luxury long denied us."

Soldier laughed.

"Back to our options," continued the Commander. "Attacking the Frobisher Bay base is frankly out of the question. Escaping out to the Atlantic, if the word escaping can credibly be used here, seems remote. Making it back to Germany with no fuel and no resupply on the way home and no secure bases to go to is not only impossible, it is illogical. Surrender is something none of us have the stomach for unless the order comes down from *BdU*. So, what to do, gentlemen?"

Chief winced. "Karl, again this talk of options. We don't need options, we need orders." Chief paused while Hansen considered this, his eyebrows arched.

Chief went on. "The men are willing to put their lives on the line and sacrifice them if necessary for the Fatherland. But they need firm and competent leadership. The men are not used to giving their opinions to superior officers, and they cannot be expected to change their natures overnight. Your experiment with democracy on this boat is dangerous."

Soldier nodded and joined in. "If I may insert a humble Heer opinion here, I would have to agree with Chief. If our troops on the Russian front saw such . . . uncertain leadership . . . it would have meant a bullet in the back for an officer if he were not replaced quickly. I can see it is more challenging to replace an officer here."

Hansen turned from one to the other. "Yes, well, perhaps you are right. Perhaps I am no longer fit to command."

Chief and Soldier exchanged uneasy glances.

"On the other hand, showing the men my human side will perhaps bear me in good standing to command them through the next phase."

"Next phase? And what is that?" queried Chief.

"We don't have fuel for more than another 2000 nautical miles at reduced speed. At the moment that is our most pressing problem. I happen to know that there is a large abandoned fuel cache on the west coast of Baffin Island. It was left behind when a mineral exploration project shut down because of the wartime shortage of icebreakers to assist with shipping through Foxe Basin. In any case we have to lie low for some weeks if we are to outlast our enemy's steel chokepoint in Hudson Strait. In that time, we can fill our fuel tanks with diesel fuel intended for Canadian heavy equipment and power generators. And after that we can get back out to the Atlantic again by mid-September. When ice conditions are actually more favourable than they are right now, and when enemy ships and aircraft are no longer searching for us . . . Over time, we will become that oil slick."

Chief and Soldier looked at each other and back to Commander Hansen and smiled. "Well, why didn't you say so?"

Pond Inlet

Steensby Inlet

Fury and Hecla Strait
Jens Munk

Isortoq Fjord

Igloolik

Rowley Island

Baffin Island

Nettilling Lake

Foxe Basin

Amadjuak Lake

Cape Dorset

Lake Harbour

Southampton
Island

Hudson Strait

PART TWO

10

August 30: Approaching Cape Dorset on
south coast of Baffin Island

Winkler was feeling dread that they were headed further into the
ice instead of toward home, and he knew the other men felt the
same way. The Commander said that the ice was their friend but
that sounded like a lot of crap since the ice had almost done them
in a few times. The water was colder as they went further west
into Hudson Strait, and it was no wonder with all that ice floating
around. Everything inside the boat was damp and clammy cold,
and it was miserable. The good thing was they were on the
surface for a good part of each day as bottom profiles were pretty
much unknown. Also, the Commander had emphasized the need
to make haste to some new destination given the shortness of the
summer season here. Maximum surfaced speed with the twin
diesels was 18 knots as compared to a maximum of 7 knots on
electric power when submerged. And it seemed safe enough to
be surfaced here as there was little likelihood of aircraft or ship
traffic on their heading, and nobody was looking for them in this
slab of Arctic wilderness, supposedly . . . They stayed offshore far

enough to remain unseen by any Eskimo hunters who could be traveling along the coast in their kayaks and small boats.

And on a more upbeat tone, he had added that there were still some good late-summer days coming up yet and they might even get a chance to swim in a small shallow lake near the coast . . . The water would be tolerably cold if not actually warm. They could wash their stinking bodies. Perhaps they could wash and dry their foul clothing as well. And maybe, Winkler thrilled, he could get a better look at Soldier *au naturel*!

* * *

Commander Hansen studied the impressive ship through the attack periscope as it came out into Hudson Strait from the Cape Dorset harbour. The Hudson's Bay Company resupply ship *Nascopie* was a good size, perhaps 80 meters in length and with an ice-breaking bow that explained its presence in such an inhospitable marine environment. U-807's radio crew had been monitoring the ship's radio communications with the Hudson's Bay Company post and the small Royal Canadian Mounted Police detachment in Cape Dorset. The ship had gone as far west as Cape Dorset on the south Baffin Island coast but apparently had not ventured around the heel of Baffin Island into Foxe Basin. Hansen's records revealed that in 1939 the HBC had established a trading post at Igloolik, in the northwest part of Foxe Basin, to buy fur and to trade staples and hunting supplies to the local Eskimos. It was unlikely that even a veteran ship such as the *Nascopie* could make it that far into Foxe Basin in years of heavy ice without an icebreaker. And, with the onset of the war, Canadian icebreakers were much in demand keeping strategic waterways and ports open further south. Was the HBC post in Igloolik still open for business, and was there an RCMP detachment there yet? This was really the only outpost of western civilization in the whole of Foxe Basin north of Southampton Island, measuring thousands of square kilometers but with a population of only a few hundred Eskimos still living a traditional and nomadic life on the land. Hansen knew about the famous *Nascopie*, knew that it also brought medical care and government bureaucracy to the far north with its annual summer sealift to Eastern Arctic communities. He could easily put a torpedo into it and set things back a few years, though that would hardly affect the enemy's war capability. But what a magnificent target! He watched the ship for another two minutes before turning the periscope over to the Chief. "That is a storied ship, Chief. The *Nascopie* was built in England for northern Canada, but it was armed and sent back to carry freight to Murmansk, Russia during World War One. Furthermore, it is credited with sinking a German submarine there. It would be just vengeance for us to send it to the bottom."

Chief nodded. "On the other hand, doing so would make it very clear that this U-boat has survived and is still a threat to be dealt with."

"Exactly. You win the prize, Chief."

* * *

Soldier had calmed down from the Commander's decision not to attack the Frobisher Bay base. It would have been a glorious undertaking but it was true they could suffer heavy casualties. The boat crew were sailors, not trained as commandos. So Sergeant Wolff made an effort to remain sane in the steel coffin. His first priority was maintaining his physical condition with a daily exercise regime including hundreds of push-ups, chin-ups, and deep knee-bends. Beyond that, he played more chess than he had in ten years. And he read books by the dozens, books that were disintegrating with the high humidity on the boat. He talked with the crew, and spent a lot of time with the Commander and Chief. He felt that they were trusting him more as time went by. Yet he felt that Hansen was holding something back from him, not giving him the whole story. He would wait, he had nothing better to do. He enjoyed being up top, scoping the land and the sky for beauty and for threats at the same time. He loved the stark, treeless wonder of the Arctic. Everything was so clean, so uncluttered, so . . . innocent. He felt the pull of wilderness that was something close to the heart of many Germans. He for one was happy to be heading in this direction, into the unknown. He felt the other men would come to enjoy their little respite from the war as well, if they could but tune out that siren call of home . . . Soldier could see the high country behind Cape Dorset, called *Kingnait* in the Eskimo language. Not real mountains like the Alps where he had done some of his training, but still inspiring. It seemed forever since he had climbed mountains.

* * *

Commander Hansen was going over the charts of Foxe Basin. They were rudimentary to the point of being laughable. It was obvious there was little shipping in and out of Foxe Basin, mainly because there was little demand for it at present and no doubt also because of an almost unending stream of ice coming in from the High Arctic through Fury and Hecla Strait at the top of Foxe Basin. The basin itself was shallow, with perhaps an average depth of 100 meters and even less on the east side.

Hansen glanced up at the Chief. "These large islands to our north here are probably only a few centuries old, rebounding from the retreat of the glaciers. The elevation of the land east of the islands is so low that, especially with a low tide, we won't be able to get in very close to shore, for the most part. On some of these so-called maps they don't even appear as islands but as rounded peninsulas."

"So how are we going to get in close enough to get at the fuel cache?" asked the Chief.

"The fuel drums were to be landed on a rise of land above the bank of a river mouth some ten meters deep at high tide. The plan was to float them in on a barge at high tide and individually muscle them up to higher ground. I assume all the able-bodied Eskimos thereabouts would have been recruited to get that job done."

"Ten meters deep! That gives us a very narrow margin for error if there are any high spots or huge boulders down there, which I imagine is often the case with retreating glaciers."

"We may have to move in and out a few times to top up our tanks between low tides."

``And obviously we won't be able to dive if a bomber comes our way!"

* * *

The men's spirits were running high, taking turns to go above to enjoy the sun and the scenery. They were running close to the Baffin coast now where the floating ice was sparse given the prevailing winds and currents. The Commander had allowed Soldier to bag a dozen geese with the shotgun, and he shot them winging toward the boat so that they fell close enough for men on the deck to retrieve them using poles. One bird actually fell onto the deck and the men cheered for Soldier. Cookie was promising a top-notch dinner. Fresh meat!

Hansen suspected that they would see heavy ice again before long. They had rounded the southwest heel of south Baffin Island and were now headed northeast to follow the coastline. He looked at the calendar and they were already into the first week of September. They should be able to make his long-anticipated stop at the river draining Nettilling Lake, the huge freshwater lake on Baffin Island, in just a few days now. Then they would continue on to pick up the fuel and get back out into Hudson Strait before the short summer was over and a new winter fell upon them. From his studies of Arctic exploration, he knew that Parry and Amundsen and the ill-fated Franklin, not to mention American and British whalers, had regularly frozen their boats into the ice to overwinter as a matter of course. That was hardly his plan though. Get in and get back out by mid-September and things would be good. Optimal actually, in terms of minimum ice surviving from the previous winter and just before the onset of new ice as the sun moved its magic to more southerly latitudes. That was indeed a short interval, and you would not want to blink your eyes!

Commander Hansen had learned that one could count on things going wrong, little or bigger glitches that could throw a schedule to the wind and constantly whittle down the safety margin. Yet, he had men to keep happy and he had promises to keep.

Hansen lowered his glasses and consulted with Chief and Soldier before giving the order to bring the boat into the mouth of a river off their starboard bow. The fathometer was showing sufficient depth even at mid-tide. He concluded that this would be the last chance to offer his men the chance to get their feet on land and get some much-needed exercise and a freshwater bath. Moreover, it was a warm and sunny day for early September and a few rays would be good for the pale crew. The Commander had allowed some of the men to wash their filthy clothing in tubs on deck with fresh water, in anticipation of topping up in the river, and hang them to dry on lines running from poles on the deck to the conning tower. If they had to dive quickly there would be a lot of men wearing skivvies on U-807! The boat steered as close to land as looked prudent, still within reach of their water intake hose. A small lake could be seen just to the right of the river. It even had a sandy beach at one end. The *Obersteurmann* quartermaster began to shuttle the men six at a time in the dinghy to a rocky point. From there it was just a few minutes' walk across spongy tundra decorated with some hardy Arctic foliage and what appeared to be low blueberry or blackberry bushes. Soldier had been in the first shuttle with the men, armed against possible threats from polar bears that could be fishing for seals or arctic char in the river. Polar bears! *Nanuk*! What a different kind of adversary, the thought of which brought a rush to his chest.

Hansen was surprised that Winkler, one ear still attached to his headphones, had opted to come up to the *Wintergarten* but declined to join the other men in their swim. When queried about that, Winkler looked rather sheepish but then pulled a sketchpad out of a leather portfolio. Periodically Hansen would peer over his shoulder and marvel at the compelling landscape coming together under the young man's busy fingers. Winkler was talking to himself in accompaniment to his energized strokes. "Look at the colours in that ice piled against the shore . . . must be six different beautiful shades of blue in the different layers, then the whites, the browns between the lower layers. It's amazing . . . look at that purple foliage in the south-facing pockets! Not so bright and lively as what we saw just days ago in Frobisher Bay, but still bold and persevering! And this rocky landscape with patches of green moss turning gold and red as the summer fades . . . " He paused then added, "When I think I can't bear things any longer below I will get out my paints and breathe some life into this. I just have to freeze those colours here so they can't get away." He tapped his finger against his head.

Hansen, pleased at having this serendipitous exchange with Winkler, looked at the sketchpad again and he could see men frolicking in the water, and it appeared that they were all sporting the bodies of Greek gods. Then he raised his binoculars to his eyes and watched the swimming and the horseplay. The small lake appeared to be no deeper than the men's midriffs. It would not be so icy-cold then, as the last few days had been unseasonably warm. Enjoy it while you can . . . He could see the men ducking under the water more frequently and no doubt this was to escape the mosquitos, the last hardy ones that had survived the first touch of frost. The men ran naked back to the shuttle boat, covering their pale bodies with whatever towels or clothing they could muster. He could hear Soldier laughing as he jumped into the last shuttle to the waiting U-boat. When Chief reported that the fresh water tanks were topped up, the skipper gave the order to proceed north.

11

September 2: North into Foxe Basin,
hugging the Baffin Island coast

Commander Hansen was coming to respect this warrior on his boat, this man aptly named Soldier by the crew. There was much he did not know about his past, his personal life, before this war swept away all context in the interests of a common purpose for Germany. Hansen and Soldier were in the conning tower, sweeping the sky and sea with their binoculars to spot any aircraft or ships, even small Eskimo boats that could report their presence. Hansen lowered his glasses.

"Tell me, what was your life like in Greenland? What did you do to keep yourself occupied in a small village, with only a few people who could speak any German or even English?"

Soldier hesitated. He knew that the Commander was not one for small talk, so this was obviously an attempt to socialize and to get to know him better. That was a positive sign and he would cooperate. "I was young and carefree in the beginning, though my scientist father a hard driver in my home-schooling. In my off-time I was out on the land with my Eskimo friends, or with my sweetheart Navarana, the prettiest girl in the village!"

"You said 'in the beginning'. Did things change?"

"My father cursed when he received correspondence from his university's ethnography institute in Germany. He ranted that the Nazi brutes were taking over his research agenda. You can guess how pointless it was to resist."

Hansen smiled and nodded. "Go on."

"They sent him measuring instruments and documents spelling out the physical basis of what they termed Aryan superiority. He was to conduct examinations on a sampling of the 'pure' Polar Eskimos, those with no discernible Danish blood even after several centuries of Danish colonization further south in Greenland."

"Ah yes, the Super-race."

"Exactly. The idea was to establish a scientific basis for the Germanic peoples being chosen by history."

"And?"

"I was enrolled in the effort, pressured to bring my friends and even Navarana into the exercise, presenting it as a game. I got busy taking measurements on a host of variables such as the head size and shape, same for their noses, distance between eyes and nose, ears and chin, their limbs, their reflexes, their response to spatial patterns, and so on."

Hansen nodded again, waiting for more.

"At the end of the summer, when the annual supply ship came in, my father was ordered to move his research to Iceland, where there was a homogeneous population of island-bound Nordic people, pure Aryan stock as they put it. The results of the tests and measures administered to the pure, Eskimo stock in northwestern Greenland were then to be compared with those of the Aryan population in Iceland."

"No doubt in the guise of routine ethnographic inquiry and presumably without the Icelandic authorities catching on."

"The results were much anticipated by Adolf Hitler and Heinrich Himmler, but I gather they were quite disappointed in the findings. In any case, in 1939, I was ordered to board the summer supply ship and report for military training in Germany. I never saw my father again, or Navarana. She couldn't understand why I had to leave her, but I knew that taking her would not have ended well for her, or for me for that matter."

Hansen nodded and gripped Soldier's shoulder before turning to go below. He felt he had a better understanding of the man now, this man who clearly had to come to terms with his role in the loss of a father and a lover.

* * *

When they saw the bomber it was still a long way off and on an easterly heading over Foxe Basin. The boat's Q-tanks were flooded to achieve negative buoyancy with the deck just clearing a rare ice-free surface. Thus they were able to quick-dive the boat to periscope depth using the hydroplanes alone. In half a minute they were under a cloak of black water and surface chop. Hansen guessed that the aircraft was one of those being ferried from the U.S. Midwest or the Canadian prairies to England with a first stop at the Frobisher Bay base, though its apparent flight path was hardly consistent with that route. In any case, it would most likely be unarmed and with a crew not looking for targets, just aiming for a safe place to land. The Commander found the aircraft again in the periscope's optics. The twin-engine aircraft, perhaps ten miles distant, seemed to be flying too low for the Frobisher Bay base, which was still more than an hour's flying time to the southeast. As they observed it became clear that the aircraft was on a landing approach to a point northeast of their position. A point presumably this side of the huge freshwater lake on Baffin Island, Nettilling Lake . . . There were no indications of the presumed landing approach being an emergency one, but perhaps the aircraft was beset with a fuel shortage or some such problem. It was a long haul to the Frobisher Bay base and no doubt many crews got lost in storms heading north, which always had a major impact on fuel stores. There could be a mechanical problem, or there could be heavy fog at the Frobisher base to complicate a safe landing there. But what a bizarre place to build an airstrip, even an emergency strip! Then it dawned on Hansen. No need to build a strip, just have some fuel and emergency supplies stored there strategically . . . His research had told him that there were long gravel eskers in this region left by retreating glaciers, eskers that looked for all the world like excavated gravel runways. This must be where the aircraft is setting down. Well, it's certainly a stray and far enough away that it is not a threat to this boat and crew, he concluded.

* * *

Damn, there was hardly any water here at all. Chief could see they were not going to get very close to the river identified on the map as the *Koukdjuak*, meaning "Big River" in the Eskimo language, according to Soldier. The river appeared to be several kilometers wide at the mouth and a kilometer or so wide in its more than 70-kilometer run from the lake to the coast. The coast hardly looked or behaved like one though, the land being so flat and the water so shallow. The tide no doubt confused things even further, high tide probably running half way up the river to the lake. In other words, this area was a potentially hazardous location for an unsupported submarine in enemy territory. Stopping here seemed to be an unnecessary risk, considering that the fuel cache was still further north! The Commander and Soldier were now talking about a possible reconnaissance of a hypothetical airstrip. That seemed to be asking for trouble.

Chief pulled the curtain closing off the Commander's cubicle from the passageway and peered in. Hansen had asked him to come here and wait for his return from a session with Winkler. He frowned upon the Commander acting as a wet-nanny for that neurotic whiz kid and his sound gadgets. No time for that! Chief looked over the pile of reading material left haphazardly on the Commander's worktable. His English was not as good as the Commander's, but he occupied himself with scanning the titles on the various documents and images. Papers and journals pertaining to Arctic exploration in general and a few focusing on Foxe Basin: Hudson, Foxe, Parry, Hall, Boas the anthropologist, Knud Rasmussen and Peter Freuchen of the Fifth Polar Expedition, Rowley . . . One report by Bernhard Hantzsch had Karl's scribbling all over it, and the word "godfather" inserted before the name. Chief picked up this one and perused it. Hantzsch, crossing Baffin Island from

Cumberland Sound to Foxe Basin, some thirty years earlier . . . He put it down and continued his scan. There were also charts and maps by the Dominion of Canada, the Royal Geographic Society, the Hudson's Bay Company, and modern-day explorers by the names of Dewey Soper and Fleming roaming out of Lake Harbour and Cape Dorset into Foxe Basin just a decade earlier. This reading material must have taken some digging! Some of the maps and charts were little more than hand-drawn sketches with spotty soundings probably taken using weighted ropes. This was a rather impressive library on Foxe Basin and Arctic exploration for a U-boat that just happened to be driven into Foxe Basin . . . Commander Hansen's interest in the Arctic was well known. Chief was aware of his pre-war studies and teaching at the University of Heidelberg, as well as his membership in the Polar Institute there. Then there were the solo sailboat journeys around the North Sea. It was rather an unusual route to becoming a midshipman in the *Kriegsmarine*. Most naval understudies came up through military families and military schools. Hansen, who spent his early childhood as an orphan, did not fit the mould at all. Still, he felt his curiosity piqued by these papers scattered around the desk. Even more, he needed to get the whole story from Commander Hansen, the personal side of the whole story.

The Commander patted Chief on the back as he came in. "What we have to do is poke around and find a hole we can drop the boat into that will cover the boat even at low tide, with at least a meter or two over the tower."

"Yes. Now tell me again why we are stopping here in the mouth of this so-called Big River coming out of that huge inland lake. Oh yes, Nettilling Lake on the map. My God, it's huge . . . truly an inland sea!"

"Well, I spoke with Soldier and he is upbeat about doing a reconnaissance of this supposed airstrip. He is keen to destroy any aviation fuel cached there and possibly even the aircraft we saw on approach, but I suspect it will be gone before we arrive unless it was damaged in landing."

"And would there be any other reason, Karl?"

Hansen paused, a cagey smile gradually lighting up his face. "Chief, I've been trying to think of a way to talk to you about this. We are old friends, but it is still hard. And unprofessional and perhaps even selfish . . . And certainly contrary to my duty as a German officer."

The Chief's eyebrows went up. "Anything to do with an expedition in this area by a Bernhard Hantzsch? About 30 years ago?"

Hansen smiled. "You're making it easier for me, old friend. Yes, my godfather Bernhard Hantzsch and his Eskimo guides crossed Baffin Island by dog team from the east to this very place, then he journeyed further north on this same coast."

"Well, you made it easy for me too, leaving all this reading material on your work table. But tell me more."

"They and their three dog teams pulled a heavy ten-meter wooden boat on a sled, a boat actually contributed by the German navy, from Cumberland Sound on the other side of Baffin Island to the east side of Nettilling Lake. They waited until the ice broke up and then explored the lake. Eventually, they descended this Big River—this *Koukdjuak* River—to Foxe Basin. They headed north along this coast just as winter was falling on them again. They had to continue by dog team."

"Very impressive roots you have. And what became of this wandering troupe?"

"It was extremely cold and there was almost no game to be found, seals or caribou, and the men and their dogs were facing starvation. There is also some speculation that they were weakened by eating polar bear liver, which organ is too rich in Vitamin A for human consumption. Trichinosis is another possibility."

"That is very unfortunate. And how does our being here fit in with all that? I sense there is a connection."

"In Hantzsch's journal, taken by one of the surviving Eskimos to the church mission in Cumberland Sound, and eventually making it back to Germany, he wrote of leaving a container of notes and valuables in a cairn near the northwest shore of the big lake. It has never been repatriated to the Fatherland."

Chief smiled and sighed. "Ah, nationalism and adventure together. A deadly combination!"

"I am proposing that, after Soldier and I investigate the airstrip, I make a little detour on the way back and try to find this cairn. From the notes I have it would not appear to be too difficult, sitting on the highest ground about three kilometers in from the northwest shore of the lake. In from Mirage Bay, an ominous name, but reportedly with some good markers to steer me."

"Ah, just a little detour, after you and Soldier finish up your military mission . . . And what would you have done if this stray aircraft had not come along just now to land at this fortuitous airstrip and warrant a reconnaissance?"

Commander Hansen just smiled and backed out into the passageway.

* * *

Hansen huddled with Soldier and Chief in the control room, looking at a sketch of the lake taken from a copy of his uncle's expedition journal. "Here is the lake and here is the river. We are here. I propose that before high tide we launch the dinghy with us and two other men with our gear. We will run up the river as far as we can while the tide is rising and we have some depth. We will use the outboard motor to get up as close to the lake as possible and then we will leave the men to continue hauling the boat up the river with ropes. It may be less than a meter or so deep there, with plenty of rocks. The men will wait for us at the lake. Soldier and I will hike south overland toward the presumed airstrip. Judging from the airplane's path and rate of descent, the landing strip should not be more than ten or fifteen kilometers from the river." His finger dropped onto the map. "As you can see there are long eskers showing on this sketch, which was made some 30 years ago. That looks to be about where the aircraft was heading. It will be hard slogging until we get out of the tidal range of this river. And after that it looks easier as the land rises, and presumably there are no more rivers in our path. I think it could take us a few hours to get to the landing strip, to see what we can find there. I expect the aircraft we saw will be gone by then. When we are done there we will start walking back north along the lakeshore. The men will bring the dinghy up at daybreak the following morning to rendezvous with us. From there it is a trek north toward Mirage Bay to look for a cairn, a cairn which has German military secrets."

"Military secrets?" Soldier asked.

"Ah yes, highest priority," said Chief.

* * *

Hansen went over the plan with Chief. High tide was expected to be about 8 a.m., so the plan was to launch the dinghy from the U-boat's deck at 5 a.m. The boat would not move in closer to the boulder-strewn river mouth but rather hold its position over a depression in the basin's bottom that offered sufficient depth to cover them at low tide. The Evinrude outboard was going to have some work pushing the dinghy with four men and gear up the huge river, even with the tide running up against the current.

The full moon would do wonders to launch the dinghy with a high tide. It could also work against them in the unlikely event that another aircraft would fly over when they surfaced in the evening for recharging. And while this whole coast was reportedly uninhabited, seasonal Inuit camps and local hunting or fishing boats could not be ruled out either. All the more reason to keep the boat on the bottom as much as possible.

"Look for us in three days, Chief. Have a man on the periscope at high tide starting in two days, but we may need three."

The Chief nodded to Hansen and thought to himself that they better be back in three days so they could continue north to get that diesel fuel and get the hell out of this cursed submarine trap with its shallow water, no decent charts, and tides and currents that had not yet revealed their secrets to them. On top of that, the abundance of ice coming down through the northern strait was variable, and fickle Arctic winds could blow the ice away one day and right back with a vengeance the next. A submariner's nightmare!

12

September 3: Up the Big River to Nettilling Lake

The dinghy went up the river keeping as close as possible to the south shore while still maintaining running depth. The quartermaster was proficient with the outboard motor and knew when to tilt it up for more clearance from the rocky bottom, and how to quickly install a new shear pin when the propeller banged into a rock too hard. They made it to within 15 kilometers of the lake by the time the tidal effect diminished and they were left with hardly a half-meter of water, putting the dinghy and motor at risk. Hansen and Soldier hopped out with their gear to lighten the load and left the other two men to rope the dinghy the rest of the way to the lake. They would meet up again at a point near the lake's southern narrows bright and early the next morning.

The commando and the U-boat commander were wading fast in the icy cold river and hopping from rock to rock where they could. The sky was overcast and there was some drizzle but their spirits were high and they felt strong. It was good to be out of the boat and stretching their legs and inhaling fresh air. It was twenty minutes before they were far enough away from the reach of the river that the ground was firm and dry beneath their feet. They stopped to take a breather, wring out their socks and munch on a snack prepared by Cookie. They had their first taste of fresh Nettilling Lake water from the canteens they had filled before leaving the dinghy. It was delicious, as was the nature show from their resting spot. It was obvious from the abundance of geese in the air that they were in a major nesting area. Snow geese, blue geese . . . everywhere. And caribou could be seen in every direction!

* * *

Lieutenant Ernie Jones flew the twin engine C-47 Dakota north over Amadjuak Lake at only 500 feet, but he knew where the airstrip ahead was. He had landed there twice before with drums of aviation fuel for just such a situation, an aircraft needing an alternate landing strip instead of the Frobisher Bay base for one of a number of reasons. Yesterday the Frobisher Bay base was totally socked in by fog and this emergency strip was the best alternative for this aircraft at this time. They also had a mechanic onboard to look at one of its engines that was performing below par. This strip was not the place to have less than full thrust on takeoff. Jones looked down at the rapids in the Amadjuak River and wondered how the fishing for arctic char would be there. His co-pilot pointed at the long esker lying off their nose about ten miles away. Damn, it seemed that you could see forever across this flat tundra and in this clear Arctic air. Presently they could see the light bomber at the south end of the airstrip. Nearby was the small fabric-covered Quonset hut on the left side to keep the men out of the wind and the mosquitos. Hopefully the shelter was not ripped to shreds by a bear again, though on the last trip in they had left some tinned and dehydrated food stored in an anchored and locked steel box some 200 yards away. The plane shuddered as the landing gear went down. Two men came out of the shelter to watch them approach. They would no doubt be happy to see them. Lieutenant Jones noted that the aircraft below had a distinctly menacing look to it, even on the ground. And the pilot must have known what he was doing to get this aircraft type safely down on this crude strip, even at the best of times. Some fuel drums lying on their sides indicated that the crew had already pumped additional aviation gas into their tanks. Not too much, given the additional weight for taking off, but enough with a safety margin to reach the Frobisher Bay base.

* * *

Commander Hansen and Soldier watched the C-47 with USAAF markings taxi to the Quonset hut and the crew disembark. A man was quickly uncovering one of the plane's engines, obviously a mechanic. The pilot, who appeared to be a woman[3], was assisting. Hansen saw that Soldier's views of what to do were quite different from his own. He wanted to get close as possible by taking advantage of a low ridge and large boulders west of and parallel to the airstrip. Then attack! He claimed that he could get close to the shelter undetected, just lob a grenade through the entrance and then shoot any survivors. After that he would pick

---

3   Female pilots were not uncommon in the ferrying of aircraft to the
    war in Europe

off the mechanic and pilot, permanently disable the aircraft, and de-bung the fuel drums and push them over. Soldier was well equipped for this task. In addition to the big assault rifle he had his Walther P-38 sidearm, two grenades and his dagger. Hansen could also see that under his rain gear Soldier was wearing his German infantry tunic.

"Why attack?" questioned the Commander. He fully expected this aircraft to be gone by the time they arrived on their reconnaissance, but now he had to deal with it.

"We will remove these planes and men from the war with Germany, saving German lives."

Hansen wanted to ask why not capture them instead of killing them, but he knew right away that was a non-starter because what would they do with all these witnesses to the enemy in their midst? Best thing to do was stay hidden and observe, as they were doing now.

"Sergeant Wolff, if that C-47 does not show up back at Frobisher Bay the Americans will investigate. They will have a look at the wreckage and carnage here and put two and two together. An escaped German U-boat now in Foxe Basin will become the logical explanation."

Soldier was listening, though clearly conflicted between doing what he saw as his duty to destroy his enemy`s war assets and the passive observation option promoted by the Commander. Yes, attack could impact the U-boat crews' prospects for survival, at least until they could escape this shallow ice basin and then the chokepoint on their return path to the Atlantic. But damn, he could do this. Two enemy aircraft, 30 drums of fuel, and five skilled men. Not a bad score. But in the end Soldier knew that Hansen was right, and that he had to capitulate to the Commander's will. Even in the absence of a direct order . . . Soldier thought it curious that, back in the boat, Hansen had gone along with the idea of destroying the aircraft. Now he was backing off . . . Strange.

"All right then, they fly out of here and then we eliminate the fuel stores and shelter, and roll some big rocks onto the esker. We can stop this from happening again soon."

Hansen smiled. "Excellent strategy, Sergeant Wolff. I totally agree with you. And we can perhaps find some supplies and food stores that are worth looting. They will think all this was the work of some naughty Eskimos." Hansen was relieved. He had already decided to use his knife on this warrior if he disobeyed a direct order to desist, if it went that far.

As it happened, the two American aircraft were warming up their engines for takeoff within the hour, and the two Germans were waiting only 50 meters behind the Quonset hut, hidden behind a six-foot-high boulder. Hansen recognized the light bomber as a Mosquito, obviously one of those built by de Havilland in Canada. Very capable, but with insufficient range to fly direct from Gander, Newfoundland to England . . . He wanted to tell Soldier this aircraft type had already this year sunk more than its share of U-boats in the Bay of Biscay, as they ran for sea out of their harried bases. The Mosquitos were extremely fast, had excellent radar, toted up to four 500 lb. bombs and some sported a deadly 57 mm cannon in the nose along with the machine guns. And they were made of damned balsa wood and Sitka spruce, which dramatically reduced their signature on German radar. The Mosquito pilots were trained for night fighting, so pouncing on U-boats in the dark came second nature to these bastards. A German fighter pilot who managed to down a *Mossie* was awarded two kills instead of one. Hansen would have loved to give the nod to Soldier to destroy this aircraft, but he kept his mouth shut.

* * *

Where the *Koukdjuak River* runs into Foxe Basin lies just north of the Arctic Circle. That day in September brings sunset shortly before 8:00 p.m. That was the time of day that Chief gave the order for U-807 to surface to charge batteries and give the crew some fresh air. If there was a *schnorchel* fitted the boat could continue resting on the bottom with a veil of water over the conning tower and fire up their diesels to charge the batteries without surfacing. Still, in balance, the Chief for one was just as happy they did not have one fitted. Besides the potential for hitting ice or getting picked up on enemy radar, there was the risk of air intake and exhaust valves being blocked. Popped eardrums and asphyxiation were the outcomes of that.

When U-807 surfaced off the mouth of the river, Chief would send the men up six at a time for a smoke and to look at the stars. If they were lucky they would get a good light show from the aurora borealis. Summer was still holding with a tenuous grip but the men could feel a wintry nip in the air now as the sun slipped over the horizon. For Chief, there was always tension owing to the unpredictable winds and movements of ice. What would they do if heavier ice blew in and threatened to cover the boat when submerged? They did not have sufficient depth to dive under the ice and escape, even if they knew where to surface. So Chief and the Second Watch Officer were very attentive to the wind direction when topside. Throughout the day they raised the periscope briefly to check on ice conditions. Ice could be seen drifting south only a few kilometers west of them but it did not appear to be sufficiently packed or thick enough to be an immediate threat. With the wind from the north it appeared that the large pancake islands that lay in that direction were acting as something of an ice barrier as well, but a sudden west wind could change all that, fast. Chief would be damned glad to get out of this location when the scouting party returned to the boat.

* * *

Hansen and Soldier were hungry and the first thing they did after the aircraft departed was to search the shelter for loot. The shelter had only a table with a few folding chairs. There were six steel bunk frames with some blankets in a wood box. Next stop was the metal food box outside, and it took Soldier only ten seconds to break off the lock. In addition to the standard GI rations, there was a fair selection of canned ham and bacon, beans, bully beef, and some bags of oatmeal, sugar, flour, coffee and tea. Most of it was crammed into their packs. Hansen glanced at his watch. It had been a good day. The two men could now relax, take advantage of the shelter, and have a good meal at the enemy's expense.

After dinner the two took a stroll. First they walked down the improvised landing strip. They could see where shallow trenches running across the strip and a few other depressions had been filled in and smoothed over. They could see tire tracks from a vehicle, probably a Willys jeep that could have been brought in by a C-47. They saw other marks that appeared to be from a weighted drag pulled behind the vehicle to groom the strip as much as possible without benefit of heavy equipment. Then they turned to walk down to the lakeshore. Soldier saw it first, partly obscured as it lay overturned in a trench with rocks piled on top of it, presumably to keep it from blowing away in high winds. A canoe! It was a small one that could be maneuvered through the C-47's cargo doors but still big enough for two men to go fishing in the lake, which was no doubt why it was here. Ah, Americans and their happy-go-lucky approach to war . . .

"We have some time before dark. Let's get this canoe in the water," said Hansen. "Maybe we can have fresh arctic char for dinner. I hear it's even better than salmon!"

"It definitely is," said Soldier.

* * *

Next morning Soldier and the Commander loaded their gear into the canoe and in no time they were making a small wake paddling up the lake toward the narrows. Soldier had mastered the technique of kayaking in Greenland, and Hansen, being athletic as well as clever at all things nautical, picked it up quickly. They crossed to the other side of the narrows, which had a span of only 200 meters. On the way, a seal popped up beside them and circled the canoe, watching them curiously with very large eyes. Soldier told Hansen that Nettilling Lake derived its name from *netsiq*, the seal. Obviously the seals came into the lake from the ocean, following the arctic char as they migrated up the river during the summer to over-winter in the lake. As they neared the shore there was still no sign of the dinghy, though it was early yet. The canoe was faster than walking along the shore, at least in calm water like this. Hansen looked up and the sky this morning was like an inverted bowl over them, blue sky with puffy cumulus clouds. Ah, what a paid holiday this was! With some time to spare, they pulled the canoe up on shore and decided to explore a little on that side of the small bay. But first a little break . . . Hansen sat on a rounded boulder and beckoned Soldier to take the one next to him.

Soldier accepted the flask from Hansen, taking it as a sign that good will and pleasantries were in order. Time out! The Old Man was trying to shrug off, at least momentarily, the heavy responsibility riding on him for the boat and especially for his men. And ease the tension that had so recently come to the surface between the two of them . . .

"Ah, for one of your Cuban cigars right now, Helmut, and some dark rum."

"Yes, that would be just the thing, Karl."

"Are you enjoying your complimentary cruise and related adventures, or do you still wish for a return ticket to the Russian front?"

"This is hardly a pleasure cruise in the South Seas, what with the ice and the occasional blessings of the bombs, but no, I would not wish to go back there."

"It's hard for me to imagine combat on land, fighting an enemy so close you can see into his eyes. Tell me about it."

"It's hell, and I don't want to talk about it."

"Try, it will do you good. Catharsis and all that . . . First a happy story, then a sad one."

Soldier went quiet for a minute, weighing his thoughts. "There are a few happy stories among the bad. Here is one of them. One of our *panzers* was pinned down, a track blown off. The men inside kept fighting. They managed to blow up two Russian T-34 tanks attacking them before they ran out of ammunition. They wanted to get out of their crippled tank and back to our lines before more Russian tanks arrived. A squad of Russian infantry with a light machine gun had them pinned down inside the tank. I managed to kill them all and get our own men back to our lines unharmed. The oldest one of them was 21. That was a good day for me."

Hansen pondered that and smiled grimly. "Okay, that was your good day. Now tell me about a bad day. Something that might have pushed you to abandon all hope for the cause. Were there any of those?"

"Plenty, but those ones are even harder to choose between." He closed his eyes for a longer time. "I was with a sniper in Stalingrad, spotting for him and also evaluating our new STG 44 assault rifle." Soldier paused to pat his rifle. "For three days we were stopping a lot of Russian infantry trying to move through our position. There were still a few civilians in that fringe part of the city and we could see that a mother and two children were pinned down in the shell of a house. We knew they were starving but were too afraid to move out of the house. I wanted to take them food and water. The children must have been about four and six. I couldn't do it until we could take out a Russian sniper sent in to target us. We took shots at each other for another day and a half, shifting our positions as necessary. I scoped the house where the mother and children were holed up and I could still see occasional movement. Finally I decided to take a chance and asked the sniper to cover me while I worked around to get to the house with some food and water. I made it, dodged a few bullets . . . But I was too late. I found the mother and her two children in a death embrace, rats eating them."

Hansen could see tears forming in Soldier's eyes, and his regard for the trooper went up considerably.

Soldier was not a man to cry, catharsis or not. He pushed the soul-searing thoughts out of his mind and brightened up enough to counter the Commander. "Now it's your turn. Try it. It's good for you."

Hansen sighed. "Yes, well . . . a happy story? We made it back to our base four times after extended war patrols with no casualties and enough tonnage figures to hold up our heads, even if not enough for medals or promotions. For me, that is a very, very happy story."

"Yes, I can see that. And now a sad story . . . One that that pushed you, as you say, to the brink of abandoning all hope for the cause?"

Hansen closed his eyes in thought, then came back from a long ways away. "I was First Watch Officer on the U-boat that torpedoed the liner *Laconia*. It turned out that it was not an enemy troop carrier after all. It had more than two thousand Italian prisoners of war on it, our allies. And many women and children, mostly British. We rescued as many as we could, helped swimmers get into their lifeboats, took others on board our own boat. We called in other U-boats in the area and alerted the French Red Cross to mount a rescue operation and arrange a cease-fire so we would not be attacked on the surface. The Lion Donitz himself approved of our action. Then we were attacked by a B-24 bomber, British or American, we're not sure, but obviously the result of a communication failure. Fortunately the bomber's aim was off, probably thanks to the lifeboats and rafts in the water near us. Our U-boats escaped but at least one lifeboat full of women and children did not. After that, orders came down from *BdU* to not rescue civilians, and we were told that the surviving crew of sinking enemy warships and downed aircraft are to be considered enemy war resources, and thus more deserving of a bullet than a helping hand."

"Hmm, that started out as a sad story, then a happy one, but ended as a sad story after all."

"Yes, and that was when I lost my enthusiasm for participating in this war. You see, Helmut, at that early stage of the war, *U-bootwaffe* still considered themselves akin to fighter pilots, fighting worthy combatants with honour and chivalry, not murdering civilians. The first heroes of this war were U-boat commanders. Gunther Prien of U-47 snuck into Scapa Flow in darkness and fought vicious tides to sink the British battleship *Royal Oak.* Otto Shuhart of U-29 sank the British aircraft carrier *Courageous.*"

Soldier nodded, pondering the Commander's words.

"Thus inspired, I often failed to meet my tonnage expectations for freighters and troopships. But, even so, with the escalating loss of U-boats and trained crews after *Schwarzer Mai* in 1943, the Lion decided to promote me to Commander. An offer I could hardly refuse . . . "

Soldier smiled and nodded again.

Hansen stretched and then pushed himself up from his rocky perch. "And that, Sergeant Wolff, is enough catharsis for one day."

They walked easily for ten minutes before Hansen suggested that they shoot two caribou to cut up and send downriver in the dinghy. While the boat's crew was waiting a day or two for his return from the cairn at the north end of the lake, the cook could make some hearty soup for the men. Hansen would take the canoe, leaving more room in the dinghy on the easier downstream run. Soldier patted the assault rifle slung over his back and smiled in agreement with the hunting suggestion. And he had understood immediately when the Commander announced he wanted to go alone to the cairn, it being a very personal journey for him. They were lost in their own thoughts as they walked unhurriedly along the shore, then started up a gentle slope to a shorter esker on that eastern side of the narrows. They were approaching a point with water on three sides. They could see a rough line of rock cairns running perpendicular to a long narrow inlet. Soldier looked over the vertical constructions of rock, obviously made by man and not nature, and mumbled "*inuksuks*". Then he explained to Hansen that the Eskimo word *inuksuk* translated as "in the likeness of a man". They had different purposes: markers, directional aids, a funnel for herding caribou and blinds for the hunters, and sometimes just an assurance for lonely travelers that man had been here. These ones appeared to be of the caribou-hunt variety. Presumably caribou walking along the inlet ahead generally moved west to the narrows of the lake to swim to the other side. A hunter, aware that caribou were moving toward him, would just hunch behind this rock-pile and bide his time. Soldier speculated that these cairns, from the lichen and moss growing on them, were perhaps hundreds of years old and were more suitable for hunters using bows and arrows or even spears.

From their position the two hikers could see to the end of the point they were approaching. They could see caribou moving along the shore. There was a rise that could be hiding more caribou as well. They decided to walk to the end of the point and shoot a couple of them nearer to the shore. When the dinghy came down the lake toward the rendezvous point, they would get their attention by waving their jackets. The men walked along quietly watching the caribou. They also observed numerous flocks of geese, forming up for their migration south from their nesting grounds in the huge plain to the west of the lake. Soldier paused and raised his binoculars. He saw some smaller caribou but wanted to hold out for two larger ones with more meat. Hansen saw Soldier's hesitation and whispered, "No trophy antlers to be appended to the conning tower!" Then, hearing the sounds of an outboard motor, they looked up the lake to make out the dinghy moving slowly toward them down the opposite shore. Obviously they had heard the two enemy aircraft taking off and were not concerned about making a little noise. The dinghy was still a few kilometers away but would be less than half a kilometer from them as it approached the narrows. Soldier and the Commander resumed their walk to the point.

13

September 4: Eskimos!

Joanasie and Sila were very frightened, more so for *Anaanattiaq* than for themselves, as their grandmother could not run well and her vision was poor. At first she was intrigued when the two airplanes dropped out of the sky the day before and landed beside the lake not an hour's fast walk from their *tupiq*. They had seen airplanes flying high over them before, and even on the ground in Igloolik and *Kingnait*, mounted on skiis or wheels. But they had not had one land so near their own camp! They had heard from other Inuit that the Americans building the new air base at Iqaluit were armed against possible attack by the Germans. Maybe these airplanes were going to Iqaluit to drop bombs on them. And then they observed two other armed *qallunaat* stalking the men from the airplanes! It looked very much like these ones were intent on killing the ones from the airplanes. And where did the two stalkers come from? It seemed that the *qallunaat*'s war being waged overseas and further south had come now to their own land. This was very disturbing, but gradually curiosity got the better of them. Sila and Joanasie had reluctantly given in to grandmother's urgings for a walk to the east of the narrows where they might be able to get a peek at these unexpected visitors. That idea had backfired on them. When they saw the two stalkers coming up the lake in the strange kayak they scrambled to make themselves invisible. But when the stalkers came ashore at the narrows and walked east across the land to the other inlet they were quickly cut off from a retreat to their camp. When next they saw the two interlopers commence walking north toward the point, the fleeing three took advantage of a line of gullies and ridges to keep out of sight. Before long, though, all they could do was huddle behind a large boulder on the shore and hope that the approaching *qallunaat* would turn back before they reached the point. And now they could see a strange type of boat with the sound of a motor coming from behind them down the lake! They were feeling very exposed and very frightened. Joanasie tried his best to calm Anaanattiaq and his sister, a young woman who was not easily frightened. They melted into the ground at the base of the boulder, trying to make themselves as small as possible. Their grey and black seal-skin clothing at least helped them blend in with the rocky terrain.

* * *

Soldier could see that two caribou moving toward the point stopped abruptly, as though alerted by something. The boat? Unlikely, as the animals had probably had no previous experience with a motorized boat, and hence no fear. He raised his binoculars again and scanned the terrain, nothing to see as far as some big boulders by the shore. The caribou began to run across their approach to the point where they would no doubt leap into the lake and swim to the other side. The dinghy was now only two kilometers away. Soldier decided to take the shot. The range was over 250 meters and the first bullet dropped the lead caribou like it was hit with a poleaxe. Another shot dropped the second caribou almost on top of the first one.

"That was some shooting," Hansen marvelled.

* * *

Joanasie knew his bow and arrows would not win a contest with the *qallunaaq* carrying that rifle, the likes of which could spit out two bullets so close together and drop caribou from such a distance. Still he would defend his women to the death. He wished now that he had not used his last three bullets to put caribou meat in their hungry bellies, wary animals that had managed to stay out of range of his arrows. Ever since the trading post had shut down in Igloolik the year before, it had been difficult for the Inuit in the region to trade fur for ammunition and other supplies. So for Joanasie it was occasionally back to his bow and arrows until he could manage a dog-sled trip to one of the more distant posts at Pond Inlet or Cape Dorset or Repulse Bay. Joanasie peered around the boulder from his prone position and saw that the two *qallunaat* were very close now. Grandmother's breathing had become laboured but she had been keeping quiet and still, in spite of the panic showing in her eyes. Sila moved closer and was speaking softly to her, holding her hand. Joanasie drew back his bowstring and prepared to put an arrow in the chest of the caribou-shooter. When grandmother started hacking and convulsing the two tall *qallunaat* suddenly stopped. Then they conversed and began to cautiously approach the boulder with their weapons in ready position. The other man accompanying the caribou-shooter had a small gun in his hand, the kind sometimes carried by the *paliisi,* the Mounties. Joanasie came around to face them, not wanting to be the first to let loose but to let them know he would fight like a man.

Soldier kept his eyes on the young hunter with the bow and slowly positioned himself to take a look behind the boulder. He took it all in immediately, saw that these Eskimos had been cornered on the point and were overwhelmed by what was happening here. The young male looked to be about 17 and the female crouching now by an older woman was perhaps a year or two older. Soldier looked into the young man's tense face and fixed stare, before speaking "*Qanuippit?*" He registered an initial startle response on the Eskimo's face, followed by a more appraising expression and then his response, "*Qanuinngittunga*". Soldier leaned his rifle against the boulder and showed his palms. After a measured moment he moved toward the old woman and knelt before her. He paused to make a quick assessment of her condition and began emergency medical procedures on her. The young hunter's initial alarm subsided though he continued to watch warily while the stranger from another land ministered to Anaanattiaq. The young woman stared too, uncertain whether to assist or to push him away. He seemed to care, and to know something about what he was doing. The Inuit watched as the other *qallunaaq,* now holding the big rifle, called out to one of the men getting out of the dinghy beached on the sandy shore. The new man hurried over to the big boulder, obviously baffled by events, and squatted in front of the elderly woman. The young hunter watched as he demonstrated the same practiced moves he had observed with the doctors and nurses on the *Nascopie* when it visited in the short summer to attend to the sick Inuit.

Soldier was happy he had requested the sailor with medic training to be one of the dinghy crew, should he or the skipper be wounded in a possible skirmish with the Americans. In a few words Soldier told the new German arrivals as much as he knew about the Eskimos they had found here. The young man and woman were both physically impressive people, possibly brother and sister from the look of them, and there being no baby packed on the female's back in an *amauti*. After watching them for a few minutes Soldier walked over to the downed caribou with the second man from the dinghy and they began to quarter them for transport. Joanasie saw that they were crudely competent but clearly not practiced butchers. After watching a few minutes, he summoned up the courage to join them. He pulled out his knife, smiling reassuringly when he saw alarm on the new face from the dinghy. Then he quickly took over the butchering and in a surprisingly short period of time had the meat cuts wrapped up in the caribou's own skins for easy transport in the dinghy.

"A word with you," Hansen murmured to Soldier. They moved away from the others. "Seems like a wasted effort helping the old lady."

"Yes, I know what you mean," Soldier responded. "I guess what it comes down to is, will these people talk with others in the next two weeks so that the word gets out before we can get back out into the Atlantic?"

"We have to assume they will, and they will know the language we are speaking is not English. And they will know we did not arrive here by plane, and that we are not friendly with the Americans."

Soldier nodded. "Not many options, I'm afraid."

"Not at all. I want you to take care of it, quickly and efficiently. No signs to tell stories."

"Why not make it look like the Americans did it, perhaps because they stole their supplies at the airstrip."

Hansen chuckled. "It's worth a try, but who would believe that the Americans would do such a thing?"

Soldier nodded.

"I suggest in any case we all move back to the shelter at the airstrip. We have heat and a cooking stove there so we might as well use it. Tomorrow is a new day."

"And maybe I can see what we can learn from these Inuit."

"Inuit?"

"That is what they call themselves . . . it means "the people". *Eskimo* is an Indian word meaning "eaters of raw meat".

"I see. Yes, let's tow the canoe behind the dinghy. Put the old woman in the canoe with the other Eskimos, if she is still alive. Take their paddles. And the bow and arrows, and their knives."

* * *

Sila was weeping again for Anaanattiaq. Her frail grandmother had been carried into the *qallunaat's* shelter and was now lying on a caribou skin on the wooden floor between two metal bunks. It seemed she would not last much longer, the ordeal of the past two weeks having ground her down. First, losing four of her dogs to wolves when they were left secured near their *tupiq* for the day while the three were out hunting caribou. Then the airplanes, and now being captured by these strange *qallunaat* . . . The uncomfortable trip down the lake in the towed canoe was almost too much, cold water splashing over the sides to keep them wet and shivering. Joanasie came in and asked Sila to cook caribou. He helped her put fuel in the primus stove and brought up some water from the lake for the stew-pot. Then he went to the steel box with one of the *qallunaat* and came back with wooden matches, tea bags, flour, sugar, a can of strawberry jam, and salt. Things she had not seen for more than a year . . . She and her brother had been tempted to approach this shelter earlier to see what they could find but they were afraid of the people in the airplanes and besides, stealing did not come easily to her people, unless it was a matter of survival. Sila cooked caribou and made bannock and tea. She set aside some choice pieces of meat for Anaanattiaq, herself and Joanasie to eat raw. It was getting hot and steamy in the shelter so she opened the door and two small windows to let in some fresh air. There was a wooden box in the corner containing cutlery, dishes, and some pots and pans. She set out some dishes and mugs on the table at the end of the shelter. She was glad that the strange men were talking and smoking outside, outside where they couldn't stare at her as they had before. But she wished Joanasie would come back in so she could talk to him about what they would do, how they would get away.

Down by the lakeshore, a *qallunaaq* offered Joanasie a cigarette, which he quickly accepted. It had been a long time since he had tobacco to hand-roll his own cigarettes. Joanasie observed the strange men. They were mostly young, tall and slim, and they appeared to be in good physical condition. They looked similar to the *paliisi*. They were pale though, and it appeared they could use some fresh air and exercise. These men looked all business but were not unkind. They had taken his bow and knife from him, and kept an eye on him as though they thought he might try to attack them, or flee. But how could he leave his sister and grandmother? He would wait until he could find a way for all of them to escape.

14

September 5: Nettilling Lake

When the sun was about to make an appearance from the east side of Baffin Island, Hansen was already preparing to leave for the northern part of the lake. The peaceful sleep on the bunk with fresh-smelling blankets was a nice change, and the primus stove had kept the overnight chill from the air. He had slept well in spite of the old woman's moaning and the Eskimos' fussing over her. Outside, he noticed that there was skim ice along the shore of the lake, a reminder that they were hovering at the Arctic Circle with the summer rallying for retreat. He took some solace in knowing that the fresh water in the lake would freeze over much earlier than the salt water in the ocean. The caribou meat and the ten arctic char they had caught last night in front of the shelter were partly frozen, better for storage and transport. The quartermaster would take him up the lake in the dinghy. And they would tow the canoe so he could make his way back to the U-boat on his own. Hopefully after finding the cairn . . . The dinghy would head back immediately to the shelter to pick up the cargo and passengers, and the passenger manifest to the boat would not include the Eskimos. Hansen preferred not to be around when Soldier attended to that unpleasant but necessary business. Then they would be back at the U-boat only one day late. Chief would be fretting like an old hen.

* * *

Soldier was watching the dinghy as it made its way north along the shore of the lake, towing the canoe. Sila was making tea and bannock to go with the fried char and boiled caribou. All in all it smelled delicious. Joanasie was down by the shore, watching the sky. He looked up as Soldier joined him. He was curious about this *qallunaaq*'s Inuktitut ability, his knowledge of their language. The dialect was different but for the most part they could understand each other, sometimes dropping some expressions and taking another tack to get their meaning across. They discussed the lake and the wildlife in the area. Joanasie explained that very few Inuit lived on this western coast of Baffin Island, but sometimes they would come to hunt caribou for meat and for skins to make clothing. And for white fox and wolves whose skins could be traded at a trading post . . . He explained that they would return further north along the coast to their extended family camp when there was enough snow and ice again for their dog sled. His grandmother had insisted on coming to this place before the snow melted at the end of last winter, to this place imbued with so many happy memories from her childhood. To stay through the summer season with plenty of *iqaluk*, the arctic char, seals, geese and their eggs, and caribou . . . Now they had only two dogs left, one still mending from the battle with the wolves, so it would be slow going on their return journey with the two of them walking and pitching in with the dogs to pull the sled. Maybe they would encounter some of their people along the way and borrow a dog or two from them.

Joanasie's face clouded over and he just shook his head to Soldier's query about the old one's prospects for recovery. After a short period of silence between them Joanasie stiffened as he looked to the south along a ridge that ran parallel to the shoreline. Then he touched Soldier's shoulder and pointed at a ghostly movement along the ridge, an animal at a steady lope. Then a halt, a slower trot, and another halt.

"*Amaruq,*" Joanasie whispered. Wolf!

Soldier retrieved his rifle, which was never far from him. He looked through the scope and watched the animal move along the ridge. It was a large adult, likely a male, and almost pure white. It seemed to be looking at them when it paused its trot.

"*Amaruq* is curious about us, and he smells the food. But he is wary. Much too far for my bow."

Soldier held the rifle over an empty fuel drum and beckoned for Joanasie to take a look through the scope.

"Ee," he exclaimed. He looked at the scope and the rifle in wonder, touching the magazine holding 30 bullets.

Soldier shouldered the rifle and nestled his hand underneath it and on top of the fuel drum. He quickly acquired the wolf again and saw that it was changing direction, now loping away from them. It did not appear that the wolf would halt again. Soldier estimated the range at almost 300 meters, and observed that there was only a light breeze. He quickly determined how much lead and elevation were required at this range and squeezed off a shot. Then another, quickly. The first shot missed but the second one did not. The wolf was on the ground but alive, nipping at its shattered hip. Soldier raised the rifle to finish it but Joanasie signaled against this and was quickly running along the shore with a knife and a stave he had whittled from a piece of scrap lumber found by the shelter. Another bullet hole would only lower the value of the skin. Soldier watched as Joanasie made quick work of the wounded wolf, strangling it.

It was not long after this that the old woman finally gave up the ghost. Sila was crying while Joanasie moped around the shelter looking for things to do. Soldier knew of their pain, remembering how he had felt when his own grandfather died, so long ago it seemed. He left them alone with the body in the shelter and went out to join the sailor down at the lakeshore. It had stopped drizzling and the sun was stronger now. Soldier was skipping flat stones on the lake surface when Joanasie approached him and spoke to him in his language. "We wish to leave now to take grandmother's body to our camp." He pointed south down toward the bottom of the lake. Earlier he had indicated their camp was not far from their present location, near where the smaller river linked Nettilling Lake to Amadjuak, the other large lake to the south.

Soldier did not reply immediately, stumped for an answer. He could not let them go. They obviously wanted to carry the woman's body along the shore. He saw the two rounded staves Joanasie had carved from scrap lumber, lying beside the tent. They would carry her on a stretcher, which would not be too difficult as she could not weigh more than 40 kilograms. In a flash Soldier made his decision that they would all go together.

He would help them by carrying their other gear and some of the fish they had caught and dried at the shelter. Then and there things would have to be sorted out, and it was only fitting that it would be away from this wartime hut and at their own camp by the river. He could do this and be back by the time the dinghy returned to pick them up for their descent down the river to the boat.

The three made good time walking along the lakeshore. There was a shallow river in their path that they had to wade across up to their knees, and they had to be careful with their precious cargo. As they approached the camp Soldier could hear a dog's mournful howling, yet he could almost feel the Eskimos' mood brightening. Yes, they would have to leave their grandmother here but she would rest easy in this place so special to her. There were many memories and good spirits to keep her company. The seal-skin tent was simple, built over a framework of scrap wood and bone and antler. Caribou sinew was used as well as lengths of twine traded for years earlier. A flattish soapstone lamp, the *qulliq*, was at one end of the tent on the ground. It burned seal blubber and was used both for cooking and for warmth. Caribou skins were arranged over moss for sleeping. There was a pot for cooking and a kettle and a white enamel washbasin. A *kakivak* fish spear stood upended from some spongy tundra. There were two dogs, one of which was lying down licking its wounds. The other dog was not injured but stayed close, occasionally licking the other's wounds as well. Soldier felt a strong wave of nostalgia, having spent some wonderful summer breaks during his untroubled youth in such camps in Greenland. Lots of fresh air and food from the land, and the camaraderie of the people. They were precious times to him, and at that time being away from his father was no great burden as they had started to drift apart, as the youth learned more about the father's research.

Sila and Joanasie gently lowered the body, wearing an old faded and mended calico dress, wrapped in her bedding, onto a bed of moss. Then they began to carefully arrange rocks of various sizes and shapes over the body to build a respectable grave they could visit on a future journey to this camp. And to keep animals away from the body . . . When that task was completed Sila smiled as though a great burden had been lifted from her. When she smiled she was absolutely radiant with beautiful white teeth that contrasted with her sun-browned face and raven black hair that fell to her shoulders. Joanasie too was moving more vigorously and his face was more animated as he showed Soldier around the camp, while Sila made tea and bannock from some of the supplies found at the American shelter.

Joanasie called out to Soldier with excitement and pointed at what appeared to be a side extension of the river, a parallel stream with rocks forming a barrier, obviously man-made. *Iqaluk*! Fish! Soldier could see sleek fish darting back and forth in the water, splashing as they turned at the edge of their enclosure. Joanasie ran for his *kakivak* and then dashed into the shallow water in the trap. He sidestepped and thrust the spear quickly into the water and raised it back up holding a thrashing arctic char as long as his arm. The salmon-like fish was impaled upon a steel point and held in place by two caribou-bone prongs. Joanasie flicked the spear and the gleaming char was tossed onto dry land safely away from the water. Then he thrust again and flicked another beauty over the bank. Laughing infectiously, Joanasie tossed the *kakivak* to Soldier who had done this himself years earlier, a lifetime ago it seemed. He laughed too when he speared a good-sized fish after missing a few times. In no time they had a dozen fish on the bank and Sila was already busy filleting them to hang on a line. It would take a few days to air dry them to a good consistency and flavour. When they had caught enough fish Joanasie and Soldier sat on a big flat rock and lit up cigarettes. Sila brought them tea and bannock and some thinly sliced raw char. It was delicious.

15

September 5: Nettilling Lake

North of the narrows the immensity of Nettilling Lake had become more apparent. It was truly an inland sea. There was drizzle again now but no wind and the water was calm, which was a blessing with the towed canoe slaloming on its towline. As they motored north along the shore they noticed more stone cairns, *inuksuks* Soldier had called them. Some were on small islands as well. These cairns had the appearance of being markers . . . even navigation aids, and Hansen would have bet that is exactly what they were on this landscape that would be even more featureless in winter. Joanasie had informed them that Eskimos had long moved back and forth between Cumberland Sound on the other side of Baffin to this lake, from Cape Dorset and Lake Harbour in south Baffin, and from Igloolik as well. By dog team mostly, but likely there had been kayaks and *umiaqs* on this lake too. The lake had arctic char and seals, the plain to the west had huge populations of nesting geese and the endless bounty of their eggs. There were wolves about for fur, and plenty of caribou. Hansen observed then that the dinghy had less than a meter of water under it here so he was in the bow watching for rocks and calling out when the quartermaster had to turn or tilt up the outboard motor.

By mid-afternoon Hansen was dragging the canoe above the rocky beach and watching the quartermaster point the dinghy southwards for his return trip to the narrows at Burwash Bay. He reviewed the notes and sketches in his notepad for the hundredth time, and then he took a compass reading. Shouldering his pack, he commenced walking inland. He was not confident his compass heading would correspond with the track Hantzsch had taken more than 30 years earlier when he passed through here with his Eskimos on his daring, if not reckless, journey. The land was flat and almost featureless but Hansen held to his course to the northwest. Before long he could see a line of low-silhouette cairns just three rocks high running on his heading. Following this for another ten minutes brought him to a low rise where he could see one cairn noticeably higher than the others. It was in a depression and it could not readily be observed from any other position than this one. He felt his pulse quicken as he picked up his stride. He knew where to look, 25 paces west from the cairn. The *inuksuk*'s right arm pointed to the spot. Hantzsch had found it necessary to construct the cairn himself before he fell ill, jealously guarding its whereabouts from even his most trusted Eskimo guides. It was those same guides who carried back the veiled whereabouts of this cairn, in sealed German script, to the church mission in Cumberland Sound on the other side of Baffin Island. And, with the help of the missionary, the message was sent on to Germany where it was presented to the explorer's surviving family. Hansen stopped and stared. He knew in a heartbeat he had found the "big flat rock", almost a meter square with round rocks at each corner. He pried up one corner of the flat rock and put his weight into it to flip it over. There was a depression under it revealing some clever drainage, and in the center were two canvas-wrapped bundles. His trembling fingers quickly peeled off the oiled canvas from a heavy compact object. It was an automatic pistol, a Mauser! Hansen remembered from Hantzsch's journal that he had taken two of these fine large-caliber automatic pistols with him from Germany, one of which he had presented to his favourite Eskimo guide for loyal service before he died. Then Hansen unwrapped a brass cylinder, presumably waterproof. His hands fumbled as he worked to get the top off the cylinder. Then he was in, and could peer into its still-dry contents. He could see some small objects as well as a number of rolled and sealed documents.

* * *

Chief was sitting in the saddle of the attack periscope, scanning first for ice, then sweeping back to the river mouth watching for movement. Damn, where are they? A day late already and a few snow flurries this morning . . . Madness, they had to get out of here! They had been lucky with the drift ice, which was still patchy and thin at this tail end of the short Arctic summer. But new ice was just around the corner, of that he was sure. Just then he saw the dinghy coming down the river, floating in deeper water now with the tide and the pilot obviously less concerned about hitting rocks. *Auftauchen*! Take the boat up! He passed the word for the crew to hustle and get the arrivals and dinghy aboard so they could get underway as soon as possible. As the dinghy approached Chief became puzzled by the image in his glasses. There was Soldier in the bow with a paddle and the quartermaster at the outboard motor and their other man there in the middle. But who were the other two passengers, who appeared to be dressed in unusual clothing of some sort, perhaps animal skins. And where was the Old Man?

* * *

Hansen looked up at the sky and then at his watch. It was going to be dark inside two hours so he would spend the night wrapped in two U.S. army blankets under his overturned canoe and head downriver to the boat at first light. He was still overwhelmed by the findings inside the cylinder. He had put everything from the cairn into his pack with care bordering on reverence. He felt a strange quiet as he shouldered his pack and began a slow jog back to the canoe. The canoe was small but he managed to get himself and his gear under it. He lit his candle and looked at the articles again, and found them referenced in the first page of the accompanying journal. "To my dear family." My God! He read on with growing excitement.

> *I wanted you to have a few mementos from me, to remember me and even share my journey a little bit. The polar bear tooth and claws are from a large bear that came to our camp after some seals we managed to kill in the morning to ease our growing hunger. The nail is from the heavy ten-meter wooden boat that we and our dogs*

hauled and cursed all the way to this coast from the other side of Baffin Island. The cartridge shell is from the bullet I shot my first caribou with. The bone comb is a gift to me from one of the two Eskimo women in our party, and the snow goggles designed to prevent snow blindness were made from bone by my most trusted guide Ittusakdjuak. The cartridge shell is for Karl, and the Mauser pistol as well if he wants it.

To all of you, I wish I could say that I will still be of this world to swap stories with you in person again, but I fear there is little chance of that.

Yours, Bernhard.

This was all too incredible . . . a German explorer and scientist, his own godfather, leaving a capsule on the other side of the world, and the capsule found and opened by one of those it was intended for. Yes, incredible . . . even if he were one of the very few with the background information to look for the capsule in the first place, and even if he did have at his disposal a U-boat to get around in . . . He chuckled at this. This journal in his hands now and these articles were personal ones for his family, not for academic societies that the other journal was styled for. There were notes on various subjects, written and dated at various times during the journey, but more of them only months and weeks from his tragic end. There was more scribbling, some hardly legible, and some sketches, even a poem. Reading this in the darkened shelter of the canoe was hard on his eyes, though it was even more telling on his emotions. He was actually near the geographical location where Hantzsch had explored and endured and triumphed and perished more than three decades earlier. Hansen stretched as best he could in the narrow confines of the overturned canoe. The rest of the journal would have to wait until later. For now, he needed rest, but the fantastic journey of his eccentric mentor continued to stir his mind.

16

September 6: Koukdjuak River

Chief was at a loss for words when the dinghy bumped up against the boat's steel hull and Soldier jumped onto the deck, tossed off a sloppy salute, and turned to help his passengers aboard. Chief's mind was spinning as he tried to make sense of these two oriental-looking, animal-skin wearing . . . Eskimos, they must be. What the hell were they doing on his boat?

The Chief's confusion was nothing compared to the mental state of the exotic pair now standing on the deck of his boat and looking up at the conning tower, trying to make sense out of it. The young woman appeared to be trembling and wringing her hands. The young man appeared equally tense as he looked back and forth uncertainly between Soldier and Chief. Both of them looked the boat over from one end to the other, holding their bodies in the manner of a wound spring, ready for fight or flight. Their faces were tight and expressionless. They had never seen such a strange-looking boat. The waves that were now lapping against the hull could wash right over it with any wind at all. They did not feel safe on this boat, yet they knew Soldier was no fool.

Still wearing a mask of disbelief, Chief turned back to Soldier and asked the question, "Where is the Commander?"

"He chose to travel solo up to the north end of the lake to find the cairn that was obsessing him, so he left me with these Eskimos we stumbled upon near the site where the American plane landed. He should be here by tomorrow."

Chief raised his eyebrows in his characteristic way. "You have a lot to explain, but for now just one question. Did the Old Man want you to bring these two to the boat?"

"Not really, but it dawned on me that bringing them along with us until we get back out to Hudson Strait will serve well enough to button them up. Meanwhile, Joanasie and Sila here can help us survive until we can refuel and get the hell out of Foxe Basin." He felt no need to add that he simply could not pull the trigger on innocent civilians.

Chief reflected on this. "And what do your Eskimos think about being on this boat with us, or do they think this is a just a visit for tea and cookies? Do they think we are some kind of modern-day whalers?" He glanced at Joanasie and Sila who were now talking excitedly and pointing at something on shore. "*Qimmiq! Isuraqtujuq!*" the young woman shouted with excitement.

Soldier raised his binoculars and looked toward the southern side of the river mouth. *Scheisse*! It was the dog he had insisted they leave at the camp, as an alternative to using a bullet then and there. The other injured dog must have died. This one, the lead dog, which had been unleashed to enhance its survival prospects, had obviously followed them in the dinghy, along the shore of the lake and down the river. The forlorn creature looked to be a soggy, muddy mess.

* * *

It took Commander Hansen four hours of paddling with the wind at his back. There were waves now and he was nervous in the tippy craft. He stayed close to shore, though it was a little shallower there. Around noon the north wind and accompanying waves were so menacing that he went ashore and huddled behind the canoe on the beach. The water calmed down later in the afternoon as the wind lost most of its heft, and he was able to resume paddling to the Big River. He came within 20 meters of caribou along the shoreline, and once he came upon a seal swimming in water so shallow that it could not dive. Hansen smiled grimly. That was a lot like his boat's present situation in Foxe Basin. Finally, in the fading light he could see the narrow island above where the lake poured into the river on its journey to the ocean. The island looked about a kilometer long and was just a few meters above the water level. It was now too late to start down the river as he would be caught in the dark before reaching the mouth, and the tide was not right for the descent. He decided to stay the night on the island and occupy himself with the journal, and get away at first light.

Hansen stretched out as best he could under the upturned canoe and was soon in an exhausted state of rest, a fitful place between sleep and not-sleep. A continuous stream of thoughts and dream shadows flooded through his unconscious, just as the water circling his little island camp flooded the sloping plain before its final descent to the ocean. The central figure in his ruminations was Hantzsch. Somehow he felt a strong bond with him. His mind played over images and events described in his godfather's academic journal, which he had read years ago in Germany, and then the newer, more personal, renderings in this one. The ornithologist *cum* explorer was determined, probably obsessed. Perhaps he was even a self-centered bastard who used people, including his Eskimo guides, to further his own ends. As he came to know his godfather better it appeared that this strength of character, this obsession, was precisely what was needed to get him through his amazing personal journey. Bernhard had been driven by the dream of sledding or boating along the west coast of Baffin Island to Fury and Hecla Strait at the top of Foxe Basin, and then crossing Baffin Island again to Pond Inlet where he hoped to catch a ride home on a whaling ship.

Hantzsch's journey was plagued with hardship from the beginning and only his tenacity and the Eskimos' loyalty and extraordinary labours enabled them to keep going. First, the ship *Jantina Agatha* carrying him and the supplies for the expedition was shipwrecked in Cumberland Sound. All hands made it into the lifeboats and to shore, but the stores and supplies needed to sustain his project through the next two or three years were much depleted.

After over-wintering with the Reverend Greenshield at his church mission on Blacklead Island, Hantzsch set out with three recruited Eskimos and their families toward *Kangianga*, at the head of Nettilling Fiord where salt water ended. Here the three dog teams were put to work hauling the boat and other gear over the height of land following frozen rivers and a chain of lakes, finally arriving at the eastern shore of Nettilling Lake. By late September, the time of year only a few weeks advanced from the present date, they had descended the river to Foxe Basin. The land-fast ice made it necessary to cache the boat and much of the equipment and supplies above the high water line of the river, and carry on north along the west Baffin coast by dog team. At first there was food but soon there was a scarcity of game including the seal, which was much needed for its fat to sustain the men and the dogs, and to give heat and light in the lamps. When Hantzsch first became ill, the Eskimos did everything they could to nurse him back to health. When he was eventually on his deathbed, he bade them farewell and beseeched them to take his journal and specimens back to Cumberland Sound. And now, perhaps 200 kilometers from where Hantzsch was buried and some thirty-three years later, an exhausted Karl Hansen closed his eyes under an overturned canoe and eventually slept the untroubled sleep of a contented man.

When Hansen awoke, stiff and sore from his cramped posture on hard ground under the canoe, he could see a bare sliver of light on the horizon. He unwrapped the blankets from his body and stumbled down to the water to splash icy water on his face. Shivering in the cold, he waited impatiently until there was enough daylight to make out some features on the other end of the island. He quickly put the canoe into the water and headed west toward Foxe Basin. The tide was right and he paddled hard downriver to get back to the boat. He felt a new urgency about it. He felt that he had come to terms with a nagging vacuum in his sense of identity. For now, he missed his men and his boat. They were his family and the boat was his home.

17

September 6: Koukdjuak River mouth

Joanasie and Sila were in the *Wintergarten* looking through Soldier's binoculars at a group of walruses moving past the boat. The perspective was much better up here compared to the deck, which was now taking waves over the bow. Chief looked through his own binoculars up the river for a sign of the canoe with the Commander. Nothing yet! The sun, though covered by cloud, was inching a little higher into the sky. Time to pull the plug and sit on the bottom again till dark. And hope that the wind would not blow a ceiling of ice over them in the meantime . . . They would still be able to keep an eye out through the periscope. Chief looked over at Joanasie and Sila. Soldier had made the right call in his opinion, and in any case the other option was unpalatable at best. Clearly these Eskimos were at home in this God-forsaken country and would be an asset in these cursed waters, for which no decent maps or charts existed, and with winter just around the corner. Chief smiled as he played back in his mind the very first time the two Eskimos had to go below for diving the boat. They were naturally very frightened, and his attempt to calm them by signing that the boat was going down in the water did not help matters. Chief heard Soldier speaking to the Eskimos soothingly in their language. He was making up and down signs with his hand, akin to the motions of a whale, and Chief realized sheepishly that he himself had indicated only the down motion. Hmm, yes, he had some way to go in communicating with these people. Prior to the first descent to the bottom, Joanasie had positioned himself to follow Soldier through the hatch and down the ladder into the boat. He looked nervous but somehow excited too. Sila was still trembling and breathing fast, but she trusted enough to follow her brother down the ladder. She probably thought she would soon be joining her grandmother though, and she and her brother later agreed that grandmother would never have survived this. At the bottom of the cold and wet steel ladder in the control room were some of the crew crowded around hoping to sneak a quick look at the exotic newcomers, fascination showing on their pale features. One of them, a slightly built young man wearing glasses and strange coverings over his ears, was staring at them in open wonder. Chief had shooed them all away.

Chief recalled his comment to Soldier. "I'm surprised the Eskimos agreed to board the boat and to come down the ladder voluntarily. I thought they would have to be dragged down."

Soldier had smiled. "These people are very curious, and also very quick to make judgments as to whether strangers can be trusted or not. Their survival depends on it. But I would say they trust me more here and now on this boat than they did back at their camp, when they saw me holding my rifle and watching them pack up to return with me. They weren't too happy about having to cache some of their things there, but the girl insisted on bringing the old one's soapstone lamp, the *qulliq,* and I gave in to that. They were pretty pissed about abandoning their dogs, which stood a chance of surviving if they could chance upon Inuit journeying to the lake after freeze-up. But, on the other hand, the Eskimos were happy to hear that we could drop them off at their family camp up the coast."

Chief had prompted him again. "I am still surprised that they came down into the boat without being dragged down."

Soldier had shrugged. "Some of their people have boarded the *Nascopie* and other ships in the past without coming to harm. And going further back, they had heard about Parry from stories handed down to them, the explorer who over-wintered his ship in Igloolik. But these Eskimos in this region have generally not had the same experience with whaling ships, the good and the bad, that some of their people in other regions have had." Soldier had paused, then went on with a smile. "And besides, some of their people have travelled to the moon and to the bottom of the ocean before, I mean their *angakkuqs,* their shamans in their quests to appease evil spirits. So what's a little ride on a tin boat under the waves compared to that?"

At that, Chief had raised his eyebrows with an expression that said, "Cut the shit!"

"And by the way, I had to tell them we would pick up their dog on the shore and bring it aboard. The poor creature comes back down at each low tide to watch us. It must be miserable and starving by now. We can muzzle it and tie it on the deck."

Chief had grimaced, definitely not amused with this trooper taking such liberties on his boat. "And if we have to dive again here, should the Commander not make it back by tomorrow?"

No response.

"I will defer on that question to the Commander, who will demand a lot of answers when he is back on the boat." Chief could not help winking at the young trooper, sharing the certainty with him that he would be shot immediately for his actions, at least in any other place and time but here and now.

Chief had turned away and then paused. "And by the way, are you really proposing we drop these Eskimos off at their camp up the coast, after we find the fuel cache?"

"No chance, but I think it would be safe to drop them off near a settlement on our way back out to the Atlantic, perhaps near Lake Harbour on Hudson Strait. We can make sure they are a few days' walk from the nearest radio set."

As recommended by Chief, Soldier had led Joanasie and Sila to the aft crew quarters he shared with two others. It had four bunks. The two seamen he had been sharing the space with were obliged to move to the forward crew quarters. The only real grumbling at this came from the displaced torpedo mechanic, who was a surly individual with no friends on the boat. For now Soldier was bunking with the Eskimos, as he could passably communicate with them in their own language and generally keep an eye on them while attending to their needs. And, most importantly, maintain their calm while keeping curious others away from them . . . He stowed most of the Eskimos' possessions under the bottom bunks. Some of their outer clothing and a roll of seal-skin accoutrements had a distinct aroma yet proved an interesting contrast to the heavy diesel fuel smell that had pervaded all nooks and crannies of the boat. Soldier had taken his charges on a little tour of the boat to show them where the two heads were for relieving themselves, and where they could get some food from Cookie and sit down to eat. Joanasie and Sila had grimaced with disapproval when everything they touched was cold and wet and clammy . . . the walls, pipes, gauges, machines, valves. And they frequently wrinkled their noses in disgust at the diesel fumes and stench of bilge water, exhaust fumes, and the foul body odours and unwashed clothing of these *qallunaat*. "*Mamanngittuq!*" Sila had complained on several occasions. The only good smell was the caribou and fish being prepared by Cookie in the galley.

Joanasie and Sila had been sitting down at a cramped table drinking tea and trying to make sense of their present situation. Then the boat moved! Soldier and Chief had watched their captives intently to see how they would take the boat's brief positioning movement with the electric motors on the surface, followed by the short descent to the ocean bottom. To the Eskimos, the sounds of slamming hatches and clicking valves and flooding ballast tanks were the sounds of approaching doom. Their eyes swept the room as they felt the boat shudder and creak, and they tried to comprehend the reality of the boat dropping below the surface with them in it, whole and unharmed, as Soldier had motioned to them. Finally, Joanasie and Sila felt and heard the boat's steel skin scraping and bumping before settling onto the bottom. And all became quiet except for Sila's accelerated breathing as she clutched Joanasie's arm.

* * *

Commander Hansen was back on the boat shortly after noon, his bright mood darkened by the news of their new company on board. And he was at first scandalized at being one-upped by the trooper. Nevertheless, he could not argue with the logic of kidnapping the Eskimos and benefiting from their knowledge, as an alternative to shooting them and then hiding the evidence. He knew he did not have the stomach for unnecessary killing, particularly of civilians. Unless the crew's own survival was at stake . . . That fucking dog tied up on the deck in its little shelter was going to drown though if they had to make an emergency dive. Already there were overtures from the crew to move it up to the *Wintergarten* so it wouldn't get its feet wet! He had to acknowledge that already they had received good information from the Eskimos, that this time of year it was futile and dangerous to go up the inside of the large islands immediately to the north, big pancake islands just above sea level that would soon have land-fast ice shutting down any movement along the coast by sea. Then there was the shallow water with unknown bottom complicated further by the tides. The only safe route was to go west on the outside of the big islands and then come back in to the Baffin coast further north and east of Rowley Island. Joanasie had also informed them that the fuel cache that was reportedly in place two years before was in fact offloaded short of its destination of Isortoq Fiord due to heavy ice that year. The Eskimo had pointed to Rowley Island on the map, calling it *Qikiqtaarjuk* in their language, as the probable place to find the fuel. And if they could not quickly find the fuel cache they were in real trouble. He knew that as a Commander he could quickly lose any credibility and respect that he once enjoyed. Even Soldier and Chief might turn on him if they concluded that he had further squandered their diminished fuel and other supplies for a personal mission having nothing to do with the war effort and thus detracted from their own prospects of survival. Mutiny hardly posed a real concern though. That was pretty much an overblown British thing, as in the case with Henry Hudson whose crew cast him and his son adrift in a rowboat, but which action nevertheless left the Hudson name on the strait and the large bay to the south of them. In the German military machine, in the absence of a more senior officer, it was more likely that a wayward commanding officer would be removed by someone who could assume the role of a political officer. But on U-807 those safeguarding the extreme ideological perspective, the likes of the late First Watch Officer, were among those stricken with food poisoning and transferred to the *Milchkuh*. Hansen looked at his watch and passed the word to Chief that they would spend the remainder of this shortening day here, and head north at dawn.

The last evening on station off the mouth of Big River draining Nettilling Lake was a tranquil and beautiful one. The men had enjoyed a top-notch dinner of caribou stew with dumplings and fresh bannock, a collaboration between Cookie and Sila. Cookie babbled about how nice it was to have Sila around to help with cooking and to take on some of the departed steward's duties. Then the men rotated above in groups of six for cigarettes and steaming cups of tea. The Eskimos pleaded to stay up top longer, faces to the sky. "*Aqsarniit!*" they exclaimed.

The aurora borealis was putting on a spectacular display of shimmering purples and yellows and greens overhead. On the land, a fresh dusting of snow added to its haunting beauty. Underlying this siren scene was a faint whisper of caution that these visitors should ponder such things as season, location, and heading as they departed their perch on the Arctic Circle to press even further north.

PART THREE

18

September 7: Heading North in Foxe Basin

As the boat headed north into unknown territory and an uncertain future, crew confidence in the Commander was running high. The radio antenna was repaired to a point, and Winkler tuned in to radio transmissions from southern Canada, from Europe, from Greenland and from the other side of Baffin Island. He would signal the Commander, who would often listen in if not otherwise occupied, and he in turn would selectively share the news with the crew. As usual, radio transmissions originating from the boat were nil to prevent the enemy from locating them with their direction finders and from decoding their messages. All the reports received, except those coming from Germany, indicated that Germany was losing the war. By the law of averages, the boat and crew would have long ago been listed among the *U-bootwaffe*'s estimated 80% casualty rate. Yet here they were growing blissfully older at the top of the world. It was a surreal experience of Arctic landscape, wildlife and Eskimos . . . and an almost total absence of warfare. Some of the men confided to their best friends that they felt a strange unwinding in their psyches, a new calm at the center of their beings.

Shortly before sunset the boat entered a narrow bay on South Spicer Island. In the evening the men rotated up top again to have a smoke and enjoy another spell of unseasonably tranquil yet crisp Arctic weather. Presently there was another majestic light show overhead. The ocean seemed to undulate in rhythm with the shimmering heavens. Yes, the men agreed, the ocean could be a thing of rare beauty. When it wasn't threatening to devour them . . . The Old Man was being generous with another grog, which served to steel them against the chill while seeming to draw the aurora borealis around them like a blanket. When they retired to their bunks at day's end they slept the sleep of contented men.

The next morning the boat was headed north on a bearing to the south coast of Rowley Island. As their location became more remote the Commander thought he would be less anxious about things, but he was not. He was happy with the fathometer's confirmation of deeper water under their keel in the event they would have to dive. Winkler was their main man for identifying non-visual threats, glued to the hydrophones and Naxos set. At the tower bridge the Second Watch Officer, the Commander, Soldier, and Franz the gunner took up a constant vigil with their binoculars, scanning the horizon for aircraft and for any smaller vessels used by Eskimo hunters. The "damned dog", as called by the Commander, was now tied and muzzled in the *Wintergarten,* secured to a crude shelter consisting of a wooden pallet with an old caribou skin to lie on and a canvas roof overhead to keep the rain off. The crew had adopted their passengers' term for the wolf-like animal: *Qimmiq,* which Soldier explained was simply their word for dog. Hansen was more positive about the dog now than he had been before, having observed how the animal heard and smelled marine mammals and seabirds much earlier than the men up top could. Presumably it would detect other threats as well, from the air or from the sea. The dog's reward for detecting a threat, sadly, could be rapid immersion in freezing water as the boat plunged below the surface. Well, they would have to see about that when the time came. There was no more rain now, which would have been brutal for the dog even with his shelter. He seemed to take the chill wind and occasional snow flurries in stride.

Soldier had taken the two Eskimos under his wing. In fact, looking after them became his principal duty. Hansen admitted to a kind of detached academic interest in them, but was content to stand back and observe Soldier and the crew interacting with them. As the Commander, he was concerned more than anything else about the potentially destabilizing effect of bringing a beautiful woman on board a boat full of single men too long separated from women . . . lovers and wives. But they were also missing their sisters, mothers, and daughters. Hopefully those memories would maintain their civility. Sila was hardly Nordic in appearance. Her hair was straight and raven-coloured, her exposed skin was a brownish gold hue from exposure to the sun during long summer days. Her skin that was normally covered was almost as white as a German woman's. All in all she was definitely an exotic package with a brilliant engaging smile and a voluptuous body. A recipe for trouble, Hansen mused. He was confident that Soldier would keep the men at bay, most of whom were not much older than Sila. But would Soldier behave himself? As for Joanasie, he was indeed Sila`s brother and not her lover. He too would watch out for his sister. Already Hansen had seen lustful glances at Sila from some of the men and on one occasion had overheard a ribald comment pondering Soldier`s activities behind the curtain where he spent his sleep-time with his two charges. He would need to have a word with Soldier about how to handle this. He would have to get some rules laid down for the Eskimos as well, starting with forbidding Sila from moving at will around the boat wearing nothing up top but that skimpy man's undershirt given to her by Winkler. That she had no idea about the effect this had on the men didn't matter. Hansen had passed the word to keep traffic through the aft crew quarters to a minimum—no sightseeing. This was not easy to enforce as the passageway ran right through the crew quarters strung along the length of the boat, bunks on the side with only curtains providing a small measure of privacy.

* * *

The Chief smiled as he contemplated Joanasie`s fascination with all things mechanical on the boat, a man after his own heart. The young Eskimo had gradually increased his orbit from his sleeping space. First Soldier, then Chief and eventually Lutz the *Obermaschinist* took him under their wings to show him how things worked on the boat. In spite of the language barrier, but with a lot of sign language and gesticulating, Joanasie soaked up things in the engine room and the machine shop like a sponge. He liked to handle things, and to see how parts of a whole worked together to achieve some desired end. Through direct observation and crude sketches, he learned how explosions above the pistons of the MAN diesel engines caused them to plunge in ordered sequence to drive the crankshaft and which turned the screws and propelled the boat forward. He was awestruck. More puzzling to him was how the diesels breathed new life into the banks of storage batteries under the floor to drive the electric motors for underwater propulsion. In this case he could not visualize moving parts in a causal sequence. Outside of the engine room there were yet more wonders. When Joanasie was first invited to look through the periscope, and when Winkler pulled his headphones down over Joanasie's ears, he was speechless. The young Eskimo felt that what he was seeing and hearing and experiencing was all about mastery of the other world. When the boat dived into the underwater realm of *Nuliajuk*, he felt the euphoria of an *angakkuq* making a spirit flight. At the same time he felt a foreboding that he was intruding into a world where he didn't belong.

* * *

Soldier felt a stirring when he talked with Sila, and he did his best to beat it down. He found her absolutely bewitching, even more so because she seemed unaware of her beauty and her effect on men. He wondered if Inuit men reacted in the same way to her. She thought she was 19, not quite *avatiit*, the sum of her fingers and toes. But she was the real thing. She had the same quick intelligence as Joanasie, and a direct smile so dazzling that he had to turn away. When she wore her seaman's undershirt behind the blanket, while resting on the bunk underneath his own, she hardly looked like a man. She had never heard of a brassiere and her firm breasts and poking nipples were hard to ignore. Nevertheless, Soldier conducted himself admirably well. He had spent time in Greenland and he knew that sexual relations between men and women there were much less restrained and less complicated than in Germany. But he owed it to the other men to keep things orderly with Sila, and he knew there was no point in bonding with the woman as it would be all over for them soon, one way or the other. But more telling were the haunting memories of another girl who had looked a lot like Sila, a girl from another life and time . . .

Soldier got up to empty her "pottie" in the head. He had frowned upon her urinating off the *Wintergarten* into the waves below, as the men routinely did. He smiled as he pictured her hanging onto a railing, seal-skin pants down to her knees, hair blowing in the breeze, and the Old Man barking "eyes front!" to the surprised men. Soldier knew that it was much better doing it that way than in the smelly head, the toilet that so disgusted her, or even in the covered potty under her bed. But some things just had to be.

* * *

By mid-afternoon of the second day after leaving Big River, U-807 had covered only 200 nautical miles at a speed of eight knots. The relatively low headway was an outcome of running on only one main diesel to conserve fuel, while providing Lutz the opportunity to maintain the engines on an alternating basis. The starboard diesel engine was becoming a problem.

Commander Hansen plotted the boat's position with the sextant, his own that he had used to navigate with in his sailboat in the North Sea. To the west there was heavy ice drifting south with what must be a main current. It appeared there was less ice to the east as he kept the boat headed north to the southern point of Rowley Island. The day was clear and cold with occasional snow flurries. The sun was looking pale and weak. The wind was light from the northwest and whitecaps at least gave some colour to the forbidding black sea. Waves sloshed with minimum violence over the deck below. The Second Watch Officer suddenly pointed out to starboard. There were six narwhal swimming parallel to the boat's course and maintaining the same speed. The dog had detected them first, sniffing and growling, ears erect and gazing intensely at a point in the ocean. As the men watched the whales they swam nearer to the boat, holding off no more than 200 meters away. The Commander passed the word down for Soldier to bring the Eskimos up. "*Allannguaq!*" they exclaimed. Their pleasure at watching the graceful animals cavorting was infectious. The seamen were allowed to come up in groups of six to have a look at these fabled unicorns of the sea. Some of them had already observed narwhal, but not so close up. Joanasie told Soldier that he found it very strange that narwhal would approach a ship like this with all the noise from its engines and propellers. Sila watched the whales contemplatively, her eyes sparkling. Suddenly she pointed off in the distance, in the wake of the whales. "*Aarluk!*" Soldier and Commander Hansen spotted the tall dorsal fins of the two killer whales following some distance behind the narwhal. It appeared that the pursued narwhal sensed a form of protective veil around the U-boat, or at least that the boat was the lesser menace for the time being. Ten minutes later the killer whales were gone.

* * *

Soldier and Hansen were picking Joanasie's brain about the fuel cache at Rowley Island, the island the Eskimos called *Qikiqtaarjuk*. Joanasie had heard about the cache but had not actually seen it. From the way he had heard it, there were "many" fuel drums lined up on a raised gravel beach safely above the high water mark. Soldier and Joanasie then went through some comical exercises to put a numerical value on "many". The estimate derived was something between 600 and 800 drums. Good! The boat needed at least 600 drums to get home. A little more would provide a reserve. The fuel cache was apparently awaiting the mineral exploration to resume, come peacetime. The drums had been dumped at Rowley Island by the last sealift into Foxe Basin, as it was conveniently along the shipping path to Igloolik and a good departure point for the final destination of Isortoq Fiord. Isortoq was pointed out on the map. It was in the northeast reaches of Foxe Basin, on the west side of Baffin Island, perhaps 70 nautical miles from Rowley Island. Hansen had a look through the binoculars and then another brief go at the map with Chief and Joanasie. It appeared that there was a sheltered harbour on the southwest coast of Rowley Island where they could spend the night. They would continue up the west coast of this island, ice permitting, and look for the fuel cache with the morning light. Joanasie assured him there were no permanent Eskimo camps on the island, calming the Commander's constant anxiety about detection when surfaced. When U-807 approached land behind a protecting peninsula it was darker than usual with no moon or stars, no aurora borealis either. Darker than Hades, Chief had quipped. For the first time they had to use searchlights on the conning tower for their approach to a harbour.

19

September 7: Onward to Rowley Island

It had become a habit in the evenings for the men to gather in the forward torpedo room/crew quarters for group entertainment. Some of the men were skilled singers and musicians, and the instruments available included a guitar, a violin, and a few harmonicas. There was even a trumpet. War booty! One man was a fair magician. Another, Winkler's understudy, was a skilled gymnast who could perform circus-style feats even in the cramped space available in a U-boat. Hansen approved of this diversion on the basis it was good for morale. Joanasie and Sila had begun sitting in on these evening sessions, always in the company of Soldier as the Commander did not want them in the forward crew quarters on their own. The pair enjoyed the performances to no end. On this occasion the men inquired as to whether the Eskimos might want to take a turn at entertaining, hoping for a cultural exhibition of some kind. Joanasie and Sila conferred with Soldier and came up with a few ideas. Soldier smiled when he understood what they were up to, and he knew he would enjoy it as much as the rest of the crew. While Sila hurried aft to get her accoutrements, Soldier sent a request for Commander Hansen to join them. Karl should see this! It might take his mind off such mundane matters as finding enough fuel to keep the engines running and getting home!

The assembly typically started off with a spirited chorus of *Lili Marlene*, to get the blood flowing and the hands and feet moving. Then came a guitar solo of some Spanish flamenco music, while a slim youth dressed up as a Spanish tart pranced and clicked heels to howling appreciation from the audience. Winkler played his harmonica competently and somehow provided spirited accompaniment to his radioman playing out his acrobatic routine. Soldier picked up the trumpet and belted out a couple of tunes he had learned in Paris and Montreal before the war. The men stared at him in wonderment, a few of them with expressions of unease. This was jazz, the Afro-American "jungle music" that Karl Donitz, their leader in the *U-bootwaffe*, had warned them against as a clear sign of cultural decline. But it appeared that Commander Hansen did not take exception to it. Sila watched and listened as Soldier played, strangely moved by the notes.

When Joanasie and Sila stood up for their turn there was some hushed anticipation. Joanasie began to gyrate while banging on a crude drum fashioned from a galley container wedged between his legs, while Sila sang out in a hypnotic chant with undecipherable words accentuated by frequent insertions of *ajaa-jaaq ajaa-jaaq* . . . Then the brother and sister put noses together and started taking in breath, fusing and expelling it in a guttural mode that sounded like bruised grunts and wails. The overall effect was spellbinding. An exhausted Joanasie collapsed onto the floor convulsing with laughter, followed shortly by his sister.

"That was throat-singing," Soldier chuckled. "This is something normally done by two females. Sila must have threatened to make a permanent woman out of Joanasie if he declined the role."

Jumping up, Sila quickly pulled a roll of twine from a seal-skin pouch.

"And next we will have some Cat's Cradle," Soldier whispered.

Sila splayed the string across the fingers of both her hands and deftly commenced to make shapes. At the same time Joanasie was rapping a beat on his drum. Sila made an animal first. "*Qimmiq,*" she smiled, nodding her head as if to indicate . . . yes, the dog up above. Then she made a little howl and laughed. Soldier watched the men and saw that these exotic performers definitely held their attention. Then Sila flexed her fingers and concentrated. The dog was walking! The next creation in her repertoire baffled the spectators. Then it was revealed to the men through Soldier that it was obviously a walrus's asshole, and raucous laughter filled the spaces of the fore torpedo room.

The captive audience watched as Sila unraveled the strings and started anew with great concentration, whispering to Joanasie who pounded a new beat on the drum. This one was a challenge and she had not practiced the art and science of the shapes and sequences before. But gradually it came together, and to a pulsing crescendo from the drummer, Sila's magic fingers somehow wove the shape of their boat. Winkler saw it first and shouted it out, to the amusement of all. It was their boat, U-807! First it was stationary, then it was moving. Joanasie's drum beats were mimicking the sound of a diesel engine. It was overall a hypnotic effect, an illusion, and the men were not sure they had not been somehow bewitched by this clever duo. Even Soldier did not know how they pulled that one off.

Social hour over for the evening, the gathering disassembled in high spirits as the crew and passengers went back to their bunks to read, or aft to get tea and a cookie. Krause, the torpedo mechanic, was not impressed at all with the Eskimos' performance. He thought they were cunning but dangerous sub-humans who should be treated properly as prisoners. Shackled to a torpedo, for example . . .

* * *

Soldier's eyes were only half closed that night after he and Joanasie turned into their bunks. Their reading lamp was out but some red illumination came in over the top of the curtain from the passageway. He could make out Sila pushing out against the curtain to make room. Dropping her seal-skin pants, then taking off the outer shirt he had asked her to wear around the boat, now donning only her flimsy undershirt that did so little to hide her body. She looked at him and smiled at seeing his sly gaze. She seemed to hesitate a moment before pulling off her undershirt as well. Soldier groaned inwardly and shut his eyes tight. He could feel Sila's eyes on him but he persisted in his forced slumber until he finally drifted off into troubled sleep. And as he tossed and turned in the currents of his dreams, the face and the whispered words of another girl from another life filled the elastic spaces of his mind.

Soldier shuddered and awoke with a start. His body wore a film of sweat, though it was cold in the boat with both main diesel engines shut down temporarily for maintenance. He sensed that he was being watched, and then he felt the weight of someone climbing up to his bunk. Soldier peered through one eye to see Sila move her head closer to rub her nose beside his and inhale his bodily essence, in the Eskimo manner of a tender kiss. She was still without the undershirt and he could feel her shivering. Soldier drew back his blankets so she could join him in his bunk. It was a tight fit and the only way forward was vertical.

* * *

At first light U-807 was cruising north at ten knots following the west coast of Rowley Island. Commander Hansen was up on the bridge with Joanasie and Soldier, scanning the indented shoreline for the fuel cache. From the crude map there appeared to be a number of possibilities for the fuel cache site, harbours offering some shelter from wind and ice and likely water depths on this side of the island that would have accommodated the sealift ship.

Joanasie pointed. Hansen moved his binoculars to the left and picked out the drums that Joanasie had made out with his bare eyes. How many? He could make out two rows . . . there were perhaps 35 of the 45-gallon drums. Some more were on their sides, possibly drained. Thirty-five drums! *Scheisse*! There damn well better be more behind one of those ridges. They would still need 570 drums more to top up their fuel tanks sufficiently to get home, more if they had to keep chasing this fuel around Foxe Basin! His own intelligence gathering had indicated that at least 700 drums had been delivered to Foxe Basin for the exploration project, which corresponded well with the convoluted estimate from Joanasie and Soldier. But where were the rest of them now?

A quick reconnaissance proved that their rapid count of 35 full drums was just about right, all marked *Boreal Mineral Explorations*. Hansen was on the high ground above the drums with Soldier, scanning to see if there was another fuel cache further along the shore. There was nothing they could see from their elevated position, and in any case a broad expanse of drift ice was pressing in against the shore to the north.

Joanasie and Sila were willing participants in the quest for more fuel drums but they could not resist the opportunity for some physical exercise in the fresh air. They ran along the ridges and played tag to keep warm. The *aqaumasuq*—that stinky, clammy, steel tube of *qallunaat* wizardry—still filled them with wonder but it was somehow stifling their spirits. The land was healing. There was scarcely any snow on the ground, just a light dusting, but the ground was frozen now and the tundra flowers were long gone. No more sign of migratory birds either . . . Joanasie and Sila looked down at the boat and could see a few men on deck exercising. They could see their *qimmiq* outside his improved shelter chewing on a bone that Cookie had given it. So much had happened in the past few weeks of their lives, it was almost unbelievable for them. Sila looked over at Soldier, so strong and upright and handsome. She had not known this man even existed a week ago. Now she imagined a new stirring in her belly. She smiled at her own silliness.

* * *

Joanasie felt the eyes of Soldier and Commander Hansen on him. Where could the rest of the fuel cache be? There was no competing need for this type of fuel in the area. The mineral exploration with its diesel-burning equipment and generators was stalled, so what was up? Joanasie considered this and spoke through Soldier. "*Aamai*," he shrugged. Then he talked excitedly for a minute before Soldier stopped him and translated to Hansen. "There is an Eskimo camp on an island called *Qaggiujaq*, to the west of Isortoq. Tagak, the camp leader, has a big boat from the south with an engine that uses this kind of fuel. And the trading post in Igloolik has some heating stoves that can also burn this kind of fuel."

Hansen was impressed, never having heard Joanasie speak so much at once. Clearly he knew the difference between diesel fuel and aviation fuel and motor gas and kerosene. Soldier pointed out that these people are natural opportunists, and making an inventory in their heads of goods and resources that might mean their survival one day is an everyday exercise for them.

"How many Eskimos in that camp on the other island?"

"Maybe ten with the children. And they move to other places for part of the year, for fishing and caribou hunting. Now some of them will be on Baffin Island hunting caribou as the skins are best for clothing at this time of year."

Hansen nodded. "So it would seem that if we can find this Tagak and boat at his camp, or God knows where he might be hunting or fishing, we can find out where the other fuel drums are."

Soldier translated this and a moment later Joanasie nodded affirmative with a smile, happy to please.

Hansen looked over towards the small fuel cache. The drums had already been rolled down to the shoreline and he could see

Chief supervising the pumping of the fuel into the boat's tanks. As the drums were emptied, they were rolled back up to their original position and stood up with a flat rock on top so as to pass a cursory inspection from the air or the sea. Hansen looked at the steely sky and the weak afternoon sun. They would stay the night where they were and move on in the morning, backing off from the gathering ice and going up the east side of Rowley Island.

20

September 8: Rowley Island

Chief was looking over the Commander's collection of maps and sketches of Foxe Basin, noting the names given to the various islands and inlets. Soldier was beside him with a pencil writing in Joanasie's contribution of Eskimo names to the map, to minimize confusion in their route planning. Thus, *Qikiqtaarjuk* was pencilled onto Rowley Island, *Kapuivik* to Jens Munk Island, and *Qaggiujaq* to Koch Island. He noted that some of the islands had no English names at all, including the huge pancake islands they had skirted north of the mouth of Big River. And they didn't even appear as islands on some of their maps.

Chief commented, "Many Danish names here . . . Jens Munk Island, Koch Island, Steensby Inlet . . . Are we in Canada or Greenland?"

Commander Hansen chuckled. "Have either of you ever heard of Peter Freuchen, the Dane?"

Soldier nodded affirmation. "Yes. He was well known in northwest Greenland when I was there. He and his Greenlandic partner-explorer Knud Rasmussen opened a trading post in the far north and called it *Ultima Thule*, meaning the ends of the earth, or at least of the known world. Freuchen married a Greenland Eskimo woman and speaks the language fluently."

"Indeed, and Freuchen was a member of the *Fifth Thule Expedition* which explored this very region twenty-some years ago."

And now Soldier was smiling. "I remember the stories. A bear of a man, over two meters tall and absolutely fearless. One story goes that he was once caught in a blizzard and frozen into a cocoon of drifted snow behind his upturned dog sled. He cut his way out using his own feces, by shaping and freezing them into a sharp edge. And he amputated some of his own frozen toes with pliers, no anaesthesia. Later he lost the whole foot."

Chief sighed. "Let's hope that some of that spirit lingers here and rubs off on us. We may need it."

Hansen looked across at the map. "Steensby Inlet was named after a Danish anthropologist who held the theory that this region was the ancient home of the Eskimo Dorset culture."

Chief looked up. "Interesting. What did the Canadians think about these Danes running around their icebergs and handing out Danish names?"

Hansen laughed. "In those days Canada had even less presence up here than they do now. But apparently Freuchen and Rasmussen ran into some Mounties, Royal Canadian Mounted Police, on dog-sled patrols out of Repulse Bay. They got a frosty reception on the ice, and there were some nasty letters from Ottawa."

Soldier snorted. "Nasty letters? Dropping a bomb on them is much more effective!"

Chief smiled at that and said, "I wonder what the Canadians think about this new American airbase in Frobisher Bay?"

Soldier said, "When I was doing my reconnaissance at the Frobisher Bay base I saw only American flags, no Canadian ones."

Meanwhile Joanasie and Sila were considering the puzzling *qallunaat* custom of assigning human names to islands and other landforms. The Inuit custom of using descriptive terms such as "place of fish" or "place of many iglus" seemed more sensible to them. Human names could not be assigned lightly. They were personal and imbued with historical and emotional content, given their custom of naming babies after a deceased ancestor.

* * *

Krause, with his two functioning aft torpedo tubes, was the only weapons specialist left on the boat apart from young Franz. And he knew he was on to Winkler. It seemed that Winkler seized every opportunity to get Joanasie into his small workspace. The effeminate little quail delighted in showing the Eskimo his gadgets and dials. Usually it was on the headphones listening to fucking whales, or to the radio listening for any chatter while screening out news and messages from the Fatherland. Occasionally when the Commander wanted a radar sweep, sometimes just to see if it was still working, Winkler made sure Joanasie was around to marvel at his apparent prowess in the hidden realms. For one thing, it was treason for a German to demonstrate the Fatherland's technology to an enemy, to the extent Eskimos in this region could be considered Canadian. And it was shameful for an educated German to treat a savage as a being with equal learning potential. And it was a perversion for Winkler to display his lustful longings for the Eskimo, even though the native might lack the capacity to judge or even understand such behaviour. Maybe the Commander was giving Winkler the benefit of the doubt as to his sexual proclivities but Krause prided himself in having caught Winkler in the act of sodomy before his previous love, the steward, was transferred to the *Milchkuh*. Krause committed himself to keeping an eye on Winkler and the Eskimo. Sooner or later he would have something to take to the Commander to put a stop to this.

Krause was pained to think that he had found nobody on the boat to talk to about recent developments. This mission, for example, his suspicions about his crewmates sent to the *Milchkuh* . . . and larger questions such as what was happening to his Homeland and its glorious vision for a more orderly and civilized world. Krause was relatively new on this boat but still he resented the fact that the crew at large had not accepted him as one of their own. But if he had something interesting to take to the Commander maybe he could cultivate some respect . . . Then he wanted to find out if they would continue heading north to the open water, the polar sea that awaited them near the North Pole. They could finally discover, or rediscover, the mysterious genesis of the Aryan people in the purity of the boreal regions. Krause's peers in Berlin had assured him that Arctic explorers had discovered some light-skinned and blue-eyed Eskimos, Eskimos surely descended from Aryan stock in their polar base. Krause had not yet come to terms with how good Aryan stock would mix their blood willingly with Eskimos but the most likely explanation was that Aryan maidens were kidnapped and brutally raped by them. Vengeance would be sweet and just.

* * *

At 0700 hours Chief was preparing to get the boat underway and depart Rowley Island with a heading for the island that Joanasie had fingered on the map. Seaman Kuipery was on the aft deck preparing to hoist their makeshift anchor with a deck winch jury-rigged for the purpose. He felt the novelty of raising an anchor to a U-boat's deck when anchors were traditionally anathema to U-boats on patrol. In an emergency dive anchors were a delaying factor. Furthermore, wayward chains and cables could get tangled in a submerging boat's hydroplanes and propellers, and all hell could break loose in the course of being depth-charged.

Joanasie and Soldier were in the *Wintergarten* feeding the dog and making some rudimentary repairs to its shelter, which was now a sturdy weatherproof patchwork of wood and canvas, ribbed with some whale bones they had found on the beach at Rowley Island. Suddenly the dog howled and spun around toward the afterdeck. The dog lunged, only his chain halting him from a frenzied leap to the deck below. In the same instant Soldier and Joanasie heard a scream from below and turned to see Kuipery bounding toward the conning tower. A huge white beast, all dripping muscle and motivation, had clambered onto the deck and was now running full-tilt after him. The sailor was at the base of the *Wintergarten* with the polar bear closing the distance in a flash. Soldier dropped an arm down and hauled him up, his legs kicking out in panic towards the onrushing bear. Then the bear was standing up on its hind legs swatting at the howling dog and seeking purchase to haul its menacing bulk up to pursue its prey. Totally fearless, Soldier marvelled. His assault rifle was not far away but there were gawking seamen in the way. Fortunately Commander Hansen was right beside him at the moment, wearing the inherited Mauser sidearm that he had taken a fancy to. Before the Commander could react, Soldier snatched the automatic pistol from its holster. With the dog howling support in his left ear, Soldier let go with four, five, six rounds into the bear's throat, mouth and right eye. The bear dropped down on all fours onto the deck. He shook his head slowly, finally slumped down on the deck and began to die. The bear's body was still warm when Joanasie and Sila began skinning it out. The hide would be useful for clothing or trade, and they set aside the best cuts of meat for dinner. No liver, Hansen observed. He watched as Sila tossed a hunk of steaming dark meat to the dog, waiting for two seamen to help Joanasie roll the bear over so they could get the skin off in one piece.

Lutz the diesel mechanic and Winkler had stood side-by-side while watching the entire performance. Lutz squinted and said, "Somehow I think that this mangy and smelly half-wolf will be more welcome around here after this." Winkler agreed.

21

September 9: Milne Inlet

Corporal Bob Peterson heaved a box of seal meat through the doorway of the little shed behind their patrol cabin at Milne Inlet. Kidlapik, his Special Constable, roped the box to his *qamutiiq* and the two of them guided it down the slope to their dog team, which was staked out by the little creek. The dogs were howling and straining against their chains. A few of them were a little too aggressive and got a measured taste of Kidlapik's behaviour stick.

"The *qimmiqs* are looking healthy," Peterson commented. "They look eager for a good run."

The stocky Constable smiled. "Ee, mebbe more snow soon." He knew the tall Mountie was impatient to get going. Two weeks previously they had hitched a ride on a whaleboat with their dogs and gear, across the narrow saltwater inlet from Pond Inlet to Milne Inlet. This would be their starting point for the journey across Baffin Island to Igloolik. Now all they had to do was wait for a good blanket of snow on the land and the inland lakes and rivers to freeze over so they could move out.

The Corporal nodded his satisfaction at Kidlapik. Winter came much sooner to Pond Inlet in north Baffin than to south Baffin communities, what he loved to call the "banana belt". He knew that for a fact as he had previously been posted to Lake Harbour, fronting on Hudson Strait. He and his Special Constable were looking forward to doing a dog-sled patrol over to Igloolik. With no RCMP detachment there to provide administrative support and a benign touch of federal presence, with no summer sealift and the attached medical care for two years, and with a closed HBC trading post to boot, the people there could be hurting. He and Kidlapik would get in there and make a report and recommendations to Ottawa. But first they had to wait for more snow and for the water to freeze over Foxe Basin. The Corporal looked over at Kidlapik and envied him his patience. *Ajurnarmat,* he would say. There is nothing that can be done about that. Relax . . .

* * *

Tagak was up early and went out to stretch and check on things. In the first second he took in the weather situation, the sky and the wind. The next second his focus was on his Peterhead boat still linked to the barge in the little harbour below his camp, and the ice. Everything looked secure. He heard Elisapee, his older wife, call to him when the tea and bannock were ready. Things were going well, he thought. His older wife preferred to remain behind in the house he had constructed from plywood shipping crates salvaged from the trading post and church mission in Igloolik. It had a floor constructed from pallet boards and even sported three windows with real glass. It was still small enough to be easily heated while being comfortable and homey. The walls were covered with newspaper and magazine pages for insulation, and some of the pictures were interesting to look at over breakfast, or at night in the dancing light of the *qulliq* or primus stove.

Elisapee was heavy now and sometimes her bones ached in the morning. She was happy to let the younger and more adventurous, and more bed-friendly, Ragee go along with Tagak on his boat trips around Foxe Basin. Tagak's two nephews were along to help with the considerable work that came with owning such a boat, *angijuq* at 36 feet and with a coveted diesel engine. Yes, he was respected widely for owning such a boat, the only one in the whole of the Foxe Basin region north of Southampton Island. But there were some long days sometimes, hauling caribou and walrus or whale meat, sometimes moving people to fish or caribou camps in exchange for part of the harvest. There was rarely cash payment for his services, almost everything was in trade. Tagak reflected that his current work was certainly different. He had, what was that *qallunaat* word . . . a contract, from the HBC in Igloolik. He was well into his contract to use his Peterhead boat to move 400 of the 700 45-gallon fuel drums at Qikiqtaarjuk to Isortoq Fiord, towing a loaded barge that was also left behind by the exploration company. Sometime in the future, after the big *qallunaat* war was over, some more people from the south would be back to look for certain kinds of rock, using Isortoq as a base. For overseeing the fuel transport contract the HBC would keep 200 drums, having found the diesel fuel burned satisfactorily as heating oil in space heaters in the post residence. Tagak in turn would get the remaining 100 drums for his boat, and he was also promised some much-needed ammunition in Igloolik. He could only hope it was true that the trading post in Igloolik would be shortly opening its doors for a few weeks of trading.

22

September 10: Foxe Basin

William White, the rotund company clerk, was happy to be in Igloolik. Mostly because he was away from the imperious Company manager who dominated his life at the Repulse Bay post . . . The Scots, those tight-fisted and morally chaste kilt-wearing haggis-eating buggers comprised the great majority of HBC post managers, along with a few English and Irish rejects and the odd man out of Labrador. William was damn glad to be done with that weeklong journey north up the west side of Foxe Basin. Hugging the coast in the whaleboat powered by a tiny engine and steered by an enterprising Eskimo who spoke not one word of English . . . When the wind was up they had been forced to find shelter and wait it out on the land, damp and cold. William was not a rugged man, rather soft in the belly and liking his creature comforts. But now he would be a man of respect in this settlement, indeed the only white man in the whole region, and he would be holding the goods that the Eskimos craved so dearly. Thank Christ Father Bazin was away at another mission with his Catholic peers for the time being. And that there was no RCMP post here yet . . . He had brought with him some of the more essential trade goods such as ammunition, steel traps, matches, fishhooks, wire and rope, thread and twine, tobacco, tea and sugar, lard and baking powder and flour. His orders were to open up the post for three weeks of trading for white fox and wolf skins, seal skins, polar bear skins, and ivory from the walrus and narwhal. Then he would close up again and return to Repulse after freeze-up by dog sled, bundled up in caribou skins on a *qamutiiq* and chauffeured by another Eskimo.

Back in Repulse he would have to put up again with the petty social evenings with the local schoolteacher, the missionary, and of course his mentor, the so-proper Company manager and his horrible wife. At least there was no cursed Mountie posted in Repulse at present, as he had run off on a patriotic whim to join the war in Europe. But for now, William knew he was headman and he was determined that he would enjoy his time in Igloolik, the little island hugging the mainland off Melville Peninsula. Surely there would be a few agreeable young Eskimo women from the camps, whose families would come in to trade at the post and usually stay a few days in an *iglu* built for the purpose. He had a quantity of chocolate with him. And some of them, or perhaps the men in their families holding some influence, would appreciate some of the good over-proof rum in his personal stores. For once he did not mind a little grunt work. There was nobody else to do it anyway until he was able to hire a temporary post servant from the few families who stayed some distance away out at Igloolik Point. William picked up a broom and started sweeping the dusty floor of the trading post and adjoining residence. He looked out of the small window and could see the red fuel drums lined up down on the beach by the warehouse. The main objective was to keep warm, and apparently he had lots of fuel to keep the residence toasty. That was good. The trading room itself was kept cold so business would be carried out briskly and with no lingering allowed, except for someone who might be invited into the residence in the back. The layout of the trading area was just a square room with counters running along three walls, the trader and the goods behind the counter and the Eskimos out front in the open area where one could keep an eye on them. After a while William got bored and sat down in the big stuffed chair in his residence and sipped a hot rum toddy and rolled a cigarette from a tin of Players tobacco.

* * *

U-807 was submerged to periscope depth as it approached Qaggiujaq, the island where Tagak had his camp. Chief was now comfortable using the Eskimo name for the island to minimize confusion when attempting dialogue with Joanasie, Soldier translating as necessary. And that island did not even appear on some of the maps available. The boat surfaced and continued using electric propulsion as it closed the distance. Commander Hansen and Chief were on the bridge, glassing the coast. Joanasie signaled to Hansen to take the boat in toward shore, to a small bay that was out of sight from the camp. The dinghy was readied and soon Soldier and Joanasie were paddling to shore. Sila was in a fit because she was not allowed to join them. She longed to greet and feast with her friends living in the camp. Instead she was handcuffed to her bunk with a promise from Soldier that she would be unshackled when Joanasie was back on board. Krause the torpedo mechanic took all this in and smiled in partial satisfaction.

Soldier and Joanasie bounded out of the dinghy and jogged toward the camp. They circled around to ensure they were downwind of the dogs staked out along the small creek that emptied into the ocean. Soldier could see a few adults outside their huts doing chores and some children playing games. He could see a kayak, but no Peterhead boat or barge! Tagak was not here! So where was he? Until they knew that, they would not be able to fill their tanks and retreat south. They could see a few red fuel drums up from the beach but not enough to get excited about. They jogged back to the boat, having been on land less than an hour.

* * *

Hansen looked at the map with Joanasie, Chief and Soldier taking up the background. "Well, it appears that we have two choices. We can go to Isortoq Fiord to see if this Eskimo Tagak is over there with the rest of the fuel drums, or we can head over to Igloolik to see what we can find over there."

Joanasie waited until Soldier finished translating, then spoke up. "It is better to go to Isortoq now before it freezes up there along the shore. Igloolik freezes a little later as there is more ocean current there."

* * *

Before it had turned too cold, Joanasie had enjoyed the first hot bath of his life on the day before the boat departed Big River. At that time, a few of the more motivated men on deck had stripped down to shorts and hosed each other down, enjoying the heated seawater from the diesel engines. Then they wrapped a blanket around themselves and dashed below to warm up again. The seawater soap they used was sticky and left a white film on the body, but it was a lot better than nothing. For Sila it was different. Every few days Cookie would give her a bucket of heated fresh water and a bar of soap and she would wash herself in private in the aft crew quarters. Soldier was in the habit of hovering close enough to make sure none of the crew wandered back there, especially that damned Krause what with his duties in the aft torpedo room. This time was different. Soldier was caught up in a discussion with Commander Hansen and was thus delayed in following Sila aft. When he went back he surprised a young sailor sneaking a view of the bathing performance through a partially-open hatchway. What's more, he saw that the sailor had his member out of his pants and was vigorously stroking it. Intense pain around the side of his neck caused the young sailor to gasp and stumble backward. Panic marked his features as Soldier filled his vision and the grip tightened. Soldier pulled the offender's head closer to him and whispered in his ear, "If you or any other man pulls a stunt like this again, I will cut that thing off and we will find out if the dog will eat it. Now go, and pass the word before someone else exercises such poor judgment."

The man retreated past Soldier, keeping as much distance from him as possible in the cramped space, hands cupped over his crotch. Soldier peeked into the torpedo room and saw that

Sila was not even aware of this little sideshow. He stood still and took a minute to watch her bending forward and soaping her thighs. God, she was beautiful. He felt new heat in his body and wondered how much time he might have alone with her. Enough time! One thing about a U-boat, there was always a bunk close at hand. What a failed role model I am, he mused. Sila looked up when Soldier closed the hatch. Lust was written all over his face and was arcing to his groin. The beauty's teeth flashed between teasing red lips as she moved to meet him halfway. She beamed in triumph as he claimed the bar of soap to take over from where she had left off. Long and thick was her wet raven-black hair, erect were her nipples, and her natural scent was earthy and stirring. The soap, so Cookie claimed, was from Paris. But it was her raw beauty and the natural flavour of her wonderful breathing body, an angel's brew of biochemical residues, that were driving his runaway passion. He was sailing on a sudden wind to plunge his body into hers. He put his nose in her hair and breathed deeply. There was a respite from the all-pervasive diesel fumes and other odours that would advance again soon enough, but for now his nose and his lips could take delight in the scent and taste of an aroused woman. Soldier's hands were exploring Sila's nether regions, a hospitable land with little cover. "*Tipittiariktutit!*" he whispered in her ear, you smell good enough to eat. She moaned and put an arm around his waist, while the other hand went lower. "*Atii,*" she whispered back. The soap dropped to the floor. A frenzied number of minutes later, few as measured on a time-piece, Sila smiled and said, "*Quviasuktunga.*" Solder smiled back. "I am happy too."

* * *

Hansen was sitting at the table with Chief and Soldier. "Where is Joanasie?"

"In the engine room with his pal Lutz, the Obermaschinist."

Hansen smiled knowingly. Joanasie was now the diesel mechanic's shadow, always there when he needed a hand doing maintenance on the engines, the pumps, the controls. They had stopped escorting him around the boat like a prisoner. Not only did the young Eskimo show a lot of interest, he demonstrated a keen aptitude. "Happy with a wrench!" Lutz had reported.

Soldier caught the Commander's eye. "Are you still planning to drop them off on the south Baffin coast on our way back out to the Atlantic?"

"Well, either that or possibly even drop them walking distance from their family's camp west of Steensby Inlet. There are no radio sets to worry about in these parts, and we are now in that no-travel interval at freeze-up when neither the Eskimos' small boats nor their dog sleds can be used. Even if we are sighted, we would have at least a couple of weeks before word of our presence could get out. Getting home is certainly what our non-paying passengers want, and in line with what we promised them in return for their goodwill."

"Why not leave them at Isortoq if we find our fuel there? They can walk overland to their camp in less than a week from there, with their dog and little sled."

"We might need their services, their knowledge, after Isortoq if we have to go to Igloolik for fuel."

Chief pondered this. "And we can't leave them in Igloolik, where there could be a radio set."

"Exactly," said the Commander.

Hansen looked somber, eyeing Chief and Soldier in turn. "We could be down to a matter of days now before our hull freezes into the ice until next July."

"Yes," said Chief gruffly, "the men are all too aware of that. They are very anxious."

Hansen frowned. "And what are your thoughts, gentlemen? How would you like to see this patrol end? Not purely as professionals and warriors, but as men with families."

Soldier closed his eyes for a moment. "You may be surprised to hear this from me, Skipper, but the fight has ebbed out of me. Duty aside, the only time I recall ever feeling good about killing was when that damn polar bear was trying to kill me. It was survival reduced to the basics, him or me. No history, no ideology or politics. As for us, I think that Mother Nature could well do us in before any enemy warships or aircraft get us on a run for home, whatever that is now. I never thought I would ever say this, but I think now that surrender to the Canadian authorities is not so cowardly a notion." He stared at some place far away. "At Stalingrad we were ordered to fight to the last man, stand and die, and the lives of a lot of good men were wasted. Of course, one thing that kept the men fighting and not surrendering there was our knowing that the Russians would kill us anyway. With a bullet or just leaving us to starve or freeze."

"And you, Chief, what are your thoughts on our destiny?"

"I still hope to retire with my wife to the little cottage on the sea. And if we are to surrender, who better to surrender to than the Canadians?" A chuckle went around the table.

"And back to you, boss. What would you do?"

"Well, for now I am focused on getting fuel into our tanks so that in theory we can still choose from all possibilities over the next week or two, if we are lucky."

"Your thoughts on surrender?" Chief pressed.

"I think that is the most rational course of action, we have all lost enough and we have done what we could for the Fatherland. We would have nothing to be ashamed of."

Soldier, hesitated then answered, "Well, if you leave out not attacking the Frobisher Bay base, or the American planes and airmen at Nettilling Lake, and that ship the Nascopie . . . "

Chief and Hansen glanced at each other and declined to respond to Soldier's comment, even though it seemed to be spoken in less than total seriousness this time.

Hansen continued, "However, as far as I can see there are no Canadian authorities to surrender to for thousands of kilometers." Hansen smiled, adopting his thousand-meter stare.

"Oh-oh," Chief groaned. "I've seen that look before."

"Well, gentlemen, I know it is quite out of the question but my fantasy, I will call it that, would be to drive this boat through the Northwest Passage, the first such voyage by way of Fury and Hecla Strait. We would make history on the way to finding Canadian authorities in, say, Vancouver."

Chief and Soldier both broke into a laugh, and Commander Hansen joined them.

"You know," Chief spoke finally, "if this were early August and our fuel tanks were full I would say hell yes, let's try it. Raid every damn fuel cache from here to Kingdom Come, maybe even rig a sail on the tower."

"And damn it, so would I," laughed Soldier.

"We can always freeze the boat in for the winter at Igloolik like Parry did last century and just wait for a Canadian government representative to come by, probably a Mountie. Or continue into the Northwest Passage next August . . ."

"Whichever comes first," Chief chuckled.

"Remember that ship the Nascopie we saw near Cape Dorset?" asked the Commander. "Winkler's radio informs him that it is now further north of us, re-supplying an HBC trading post at Fort Ross in Bellot Strait. Only Fury and Hecla Strait and the Gulf of Boothia are separating us."

"Only . . . " grimaced Chief.

Soldier nodded. "Yes, there is probably a Mountie on that ship, but if the Yanks at Frobisher Bay catch wind of our situation here they will of course want to sink us or at least have us surrender to them, not to the Canadians."

"Right!" said Hansen. "They can scrap over us. But for now let's get that fuel into our boat. First things first."

23

September 11: Approaching Isortoq

Hansen gave the order to do a radar sweep and they picked up their target almost immediately. Within two hours Tagak's boat was in sight. The red drums on the barge were visible before the boat towing it was, and the barge looked disproportionately large compared to the 12-meter Peterhead that probably had no more than a 50-horsepower diesel engine. There were 40 of the drums on the barge, in rows five drums abreast by eight drums long.

Tagak must have been busy in the past two months hauling fuel from Rowley Island to Isortoq and God knows where else. That is what they had to find out, without the Eskimos in that boat spotting them. It was impossible to see if the boat had an antenna from this distance but it was not likely that the small vessel had a radio on board. Hansen gave the order to get the damned dog below and go to electric power and dive to periscope depth and keep the barge between U-807 and the towboat. Once the boat and barge entered the Fiord, Joanasie had assured him, he would be able to hide his boat behind a point that jutted out from the river's mouth. Then a quick reconnaissance to see how many drums of fuel were there and a determination of whether or not they would have to go to Igloolik as well . . .

* * *

Meeka was ten years old, out for a welcome stroll across the tundra to see if there might be any ptarmigans or rabbits about. She had her father's .22 single shot rifle and five bullets in her pocket, and an admonition that every shot must count. Sometimes she could get a ptarmigan or even a rabbit with a well-aimed stone, so she could try that first. She decided to walk along the coast so she could keep an eye out for seals too. That would be a nice catch, but she would take a head shot at a seal near the shore only if she were very confident she could retrieve it. There were no more mosquitos at this time of year, and she was happy about that. Soon she was out of sight and earshot of her mother, who was busy scraping caribou skins outside their tent. Meeka would try to get back to help her out again before too long, and hopefully have something for her to put in the cooking pot too. Her father was out trying to get a few more caribou. Tagak had dropped her family off here a week ago on a return trip from one of his fuel hauls to Igloolik, so they could get some caribou skins for winter clothing. *Anana* insisted on having summer caribou skins, with their typically shorter and more resilient hair, for *qulittaq* parkas and *kamiik* for their feet. The densely packed hairs are hollow, thus providing superior insulation for winter wear.

Meeka had a good view of Tagak's boat as it was once again motoring past their camp toward Isortoq, pulling that barge. She could see black smoke coming out of the pipe on the side of the boat's cabin. There was a full load of fuel drums on the barge, and she watched two squawking ravens following behind, pitching to and fro on the ocean breeze. Then something further back caught her eye. She blinked and looked again. Something there . . . It seemed that a something was rising out of the ocean, something in the shape of a chimney pipe and as high as a man standing up, and something like a little head at the top . . . It was some distance behind the barge, but she had the impression it was following behind it at the same speed. She thought she could see a small wake behind it, like the larger ones behind the boat and barge. What could it be? It was not like any animals she had ever seen. It did not even look like it was alive. Suddenly the head turned and Meeka had the chilling feeling that she was being watched. She started running back to the tent. Maybe her mother would have an idea what it was.

* * *

Tagak was feeling anxious. He had to land this load of drums and, if possible, get back to Qikiqtaarjuk again before freeze-up to move a load of his own drums to his camp. He was glad that he had already moved the HBC's allotment of fuel drums to Igloolik. That was done! Freeze-up and unpredictable weather could come at any time now and it was damn cold on his boat. The air was clear and frigid with little wind, conditions which typically prevail before the ocean glazed over. They would work into the night if necessary and then sleep on the boat so they could get away first thing in the morning. Once again he commended himself for having his brother's two sons Jaypettie and Tookilkee along as extra muscle for loading and unloading the barge and manhandling the drums from the beach up past the high water point. Tagak was also relieved to have previously found a good place to beach the barge and anchor it behind a sandbar. If the weather turned and worse came to worst he would just have to leave the barge there, first securing it well so it would stay put, what with the tidal action and break-up of the river next spring.

Tagak's wife Ragee was making some tea on their little stove. It would be good to get something warm in their bellies before starting work. It was cramped with four bodies in the Peterhead's small aft cabin, especially with his nephews' considerable bulk. He looked over the side of the boat into the black depths. No whitecaps today, just steely calm. Their best speed with the barge was only about five knots but finally they were approaching the broad opening in the Baffin coast, where the distant grey and white shoreline seemed to pull back from them. He sighed and sipped on his hot sweetened tea, knowing he was the only Inuk in this whole region who had any sugar.

* * *

Soldier and Joanasie hiked over the frozen tundra to get a look at the Isortoq fuel cache. As he walked, Joanasie thought about his sister Sila who had called out in anguish as she was handcuffed once again to her steel bunk on the boat. Joanasie recalled how guilty Soldier had looked as he checked the shackles to ensure they were secure, and how he could not meet Sila's icy glare. Meanwhile Joanasie took the lead, having walked this ground before. He visualized where the fuel cache would be, and from which direction they would have to approach. He doubted there were any dogs here but better to be mindful of wind direction as well and be safe. Joanasie prided himself in his endurance on the land. He was strong and wiry and virtually tireless. And he was travelling light today, just a small pack on his back. Soldier was carrying a pack too as well as the big rifle slung over his shoulder. Joanasie was impressed that Soldier could keep up to his pace with little obvious effort. Probably those long legs helped. There was no chat between them, just some pointing and other gesturing as necessary. Just half an hour after their delivery to shore in the dinghy they had circled around and come out over the point where Joanasie expected they would find the fuel cache. Not too far in from the river's mouth so they would have enough water depth for the barge, together with a flat beach area with a moderate slope to higher ground where it would be safe to leave the drums. There would be some tide there, as well as some spring flooding come next July with a huge volume of water and ice coming downstream. Joanasie and Soldier stopped to listen. The wind was carrying the sound of metal banging on rock as drums were rolled up the slope. Joanasie knew that would be some hard work as the drums would weigh more than twice his own weight. He smiled as he guessed who Tagak would have with him to do the grunt work. Probably his brother's husky boys who always lost to him in a foot race but who were as strong as an *aivik*, a bull walrus . . . Working together they could roll the drums up the slope and stand them up.

Ten minutes later Joanasie and Soldier were squatting and peering down at the work-scene on the beach. Tagak, with his

Mountie-style fur hat, was hoisting the last drums with a block and tackle and using a davit to swing the drums over the side of the barge and drop them onto a gravel point running off the beach. And yes, Joanasie had correctly identified the two men rolling the drums up the beach. Darkness was not far off. This meant the men would probably catch a little sleep on the boat before an early-morning departure. Soldier had finished counting the drums and pulled at Joanasie's arm, nodding for a return to the boat. Their return to the boat was much quicker with shortcuts and knowing that there were no dogs to detect their presence. Still, it was near dark by the time they stumbled down to the beach on the other side of the point. Soldier lit a small flare from the shore and soon there was an answering flare from the boat and sounds of the dinghy being paddled to shore to pick them up.

Joanasie knew he had come close to fleeing but he sensed Soldier was prepared for that. He had glimpsed a length of rope in Soldier's pack that he suspected was brought along to secure him, yet Soldier had not taken that step. And anyway Sila was still shackled in the boat. He could not leave her or endanger her in any way. Soon enough he and his sister would have their chance to escape. If the *qallunaat* could be believed, they might even be dropped off near their own camp west of Steensby Inlet.

24

September 12: Baffin Island

Corporal Bob Peterson woke up to hear Kidlapik entering the patrol cabin. The Constable was wearing a big smile as he beckoned to his boss to step outside and take a look around. More snow, lots of it! In the moonlight Peterson could see there was at least a foot of snow on the ground! And though the temperature had climbed a bit with the snow it was still a good ten degrees below freezing and there was no likelihood the snow was going to melt any time soon. He knew there was still some time before the ocean would freeze over, given the lower freezing point of salt water and the effects of wind and currents. But the smaller lakes and most rivers would be frozen over now, and with fresh snow on top. At last they could depart on their patrol and hopefully the ocean would be frozen over in Foxe Basin by the time they arrived there. By all indications this was going to be another early, cold and long winter . . . much like the last few years.

The two Mounties downed a quick breakfast of thawed and refried baked beans and canned bacon while taking another look at their map. Presently they were slinging their gear and grub boxes from the smaller storage shed down to the *qamutiiq*. They harnessed the dozen howling dogs in the fan fashion of the Eastern Arctic, kicking a few over-zealous ones. It was still early when they were ready to go. Two weeks before when they were departing Pond Inlet by boat for the Milne Inlet cabin, Kidlapik's wife had asked how long they would be away, and her husband had simply replied *"aamai"*, he didn't know. But he knew, and she knew, that this patrol to Igloolik could take as long as two months from start to finish. A storm could delay them in the rugged country between the two coasts. They could run into some open water or even some windswept terrain without enough snow for easy travel. Even with ideal conditions it would take more than a week to get across Baffin Island to the Foxe Basin coast, and things were never ideal. If they had to wait for sea ice to cross over to Igloolik, they would take advantage of that time to visit some of the Eskimo camps on this side and see how they were making out.

The two Mounties ran along holding on to the sled, to steer it and slow it down as it descended the slope to a small frozen lake, the surface of which was snow-covered with some spots of glare ice. Then they both jumped on and got comfortable as the dogs yelped with excitement and strained into their traces. The Mounties knew that soon enough they would have to hop off and help the dogs pull the sled over rough terrain.

* * *

Commander Hansen peered into the attack periscope and watched Tagak's boat with its barge in tow heading back out into

Foxe Basin, presumably to scoop up the last of the fuel drums at Rowley Island. This enterprising Eskimo would soon find out that there was no more diesel fuel there to transport. Hansen gave the order to Chief to bring the boat around the point. From Soldier's reconnaissance there were about 400 drums at the Isortoq cache, meaning they were still short 200 drums for the boat to have a running chance at getting them home to Germany without refueling. Joanasie thought the missing drums must be in Igloolik, as he could not think of anywhere else they could be of any use. Hansen rechecked his calculation, converting 600 45-gallon drums of fuel to metric tons, in turn yielding a cruising range at reduced speed, surfaced by night and submerged by day. Would it be enough to get them back to Germany? Yes, they could if they didn't have to chase fuel around Foxe Basin, burning fuel to find more fuel!

The men were lonely and miserable in the cold and damp boat, and starting to think of Christmas with their families. Home is a most powerful motivation, Hansen thought. On top of the boat's low fuel situation, food and other supplies were running dangerously low as well. They needed to stock up. They would try to get some more caribou at Isortoq, but the lean meat was not enough to keep the men healthy. They would also try to get some seals or a narwhal or beluga for its *maktaaq*, the outer skin that was rich in Vitamin C. And maybe the padlocked HBC warehouses in Igloolik would have some bounty to offer in the way of other supplies, in addition to the elusive fuel drums. The Commander could see the fuel cache from the tower now, all those beautiful red fuel drums standing out against the new-fallen snow, lined up nicely above the high water mark on the beach. Yes, Soldier's count was good. It appeared the boat could come right in by that little gravel point where Soldier said the barge had unloaded and just suck up the contents of those drums with their two transfer pumps.

* * *

Lutz had one of the fuel transfer pumps working. They were already taking in fuel from the drums as two men on shore un-bunged barrels and inserted the intake hose, which had been modified to fit the narrow openings on the drums. He cursed the other auxiliary transfer pump. It wasn't working worth a damn. He began to dismantle it with Joanasie crouching wide-eyed beside him. Lutz took apart a coupling then held up a torn gasket and a cracked spacer. "Here is the problem, right here," he announced. "No spares either, or even suitable raw materials remaining to fabricate something. Our stores are a sad memory. Maybe we can cement the spacer to hold for a while but we need a gasket."

Joanasie took the pieces from the mechanic and examined them carefully. He returned the spacer to Lutz, and slipped out with the torn gasket.

While Lutz rummaged through parts trays and boxes with mounting frustration, the Chief came in wanting an update on the problem pump. "It's going too slow. We need to be working both ends of the fuel cache at the same time and get out of here. We're too exposed."

Joanasie came back through the hatchway holding something up in his hand. "*Unaqai!*" This one maybe. Soldier translated. "Sila cut this out of a small piece of *ugjuk*, bearded-seal skin. She was carrying it in her bag to make soles for new *kamiik* for our feet before winter. It's very strong and long-lasting."

Lutz took the piece from Joanasie, exchanging glances with Chief. He examined it carefully, eyeballing it beside the old gasket. He looked up at Joanasie, a bemused yet appraising kind of look. "Yes, this might actually work."

Chief sighed in relief and winked at Joanasie as he made his exit. Joanasie smiled and gave the mechanic a hand to breathe new life into the worn pump. Ten minutes later the boat was sucking up the fuel from the drums onshore at twice the rate. Word travels fast on a U-boat and soon Sila was receiving a different kind of appraisal from the men, one different from the way she knew that men had always looked at women when their *usuit* asserted themselves over their tiny brains.

* * *

The next morning brought a little welcome early-morning sunshine to the upper side of the boat, while Hansen and Chief were below in the control room scrutinizing their crude maps and finalizing the route they would take from Isortoq to Igloolik. Soldier and the Eskimos had made a quick hunt for caribou and seals but they reported back with no kills. Soon they would get the boat underway.

Winkler was with Sila and Joanasie up in the tower. Soldier was the bemused spectator as Joanasie got busy sanding an outside surface in the tower. They were not totally confident the Commander would permit any frivolous adulteration of the mottled white camouflage paint scheme, but they would find out soon. First Winkler used a small torch to heat up the surface in the square meter of tower they had selected, and then he set to work on the image with the paints and brushes. Sila contributed syllabic lettering, using the phonetic symbols taught by the priests to speed the Eskimos' conversion to Christianity. When they were done they stood back to admire their handiwork. Behold, a black raven flying over a round white circle depicting a frozen ocean. The syllabics spelled out *Tulugaq,* Eskimo for raven. Sila and Joanasie had explained that *Tulugaq* is a renowned scavenger, tough and resilient enough to remain in the Arctic throughout the winter, when most other birds have migrated south . . . survivors and tricksters that have carved a place in the north as well as in Inuit legend.

Winkler giggled and held Sila's hand as Soldier invited the unsuspecting Commander up for inspection. Hansen frowned immediately before going quiet for a minute of contemplation. Abruptly he smiled and gave his approval with a simple nod of his head. Henceforth the boat would be known by the crew as *Tulugaq.* When the crew rotated up top to see their new logo they were pleased, and morale was stoked considerably. Chief groaned and covered his eyes with his hands, though in the end he too blessed the artwork. When Krause the torpedo mechanic had a look he asked why the writing was in pagan script instead of in German. He thought the name change was utter blasphemy.

25

September 15: Igloolik

William the clerk waddled over to the window again and looked out. Fucking snow everywhere! And where was everybody? He knew some of the people were in their camps and could not come to trade till after freeze-up. So far he had received only a dozen or so souls into his trading room, unwashed bodies bringing white fox skins and seal skins, a dozen polar bear skins, wolf skins and narwhal tusks. The Eskimos were not happy about the meager range of supplies he offered up for trade, but damn it, they would have to wait for the bloody war to be over. They had bullets and traps to go after more fur, and what was good for the Company was good for them too. The young single women who came in with the families trading at the post were a disappointment though. Some of them were very attractive but aloof . . . The ones who seemed readily available to him were not particularly attractive. Only on one occasion did he take a young woman back into his living quarters, encouraged by what he interpreted as her parent's nod of approval. He found that exercise disappointing, however. In fact, his bed had collapsed and they had to continue their coupling on the floor. Long after his visitor was gone it seemed to him that the smell of seal blubber lingered. He would have to do better than this or he would start getting homesick for Repulse.

William fixed himself a rum toddy and sat down in his easy chair with a book he had started, *Moby Dick* by Herman Melville. He reached over and turned up the wick on the lamp. Maybe tomorrow he would try to crank up the post's radio set and see if there was any traffic from the other trading posts. He knew some of the post managers in the Eastern Arctic did daily weather observations for the benefit of the Americans in Frobisher Bay and for any of their pilots unlucky enough to be flying up here this time of year. Sometimes, after they gave the weather report, the traders would stay on the air and see if they could raise anyone from the other posts to chat with, more often than not in a heavy Scottish brogue. He never thought he would be lonely enough to want to talk with another Company man in another godforsaken Arctic post but it had sadly come to that. It might at least tide him over until a young Eskimo beauty revealed herself to him. The priest in Repulse had told him that, in Eskimo folklore, an old lady lived at the bottom of the sea. If the Eskimos were good she would float up some caribou and seals and other animals to sustain the people. William grabbed his crotch. "Well, I've been good, bitch, float me up something quick to sustain this!"

* * *

Hansen gave the order to set course for Igloolik and turn the screws for 12 knots. The starboard diesel engine was still the focus of the mechanic's curses but it was time to give the engine a test-run. They would plan to arrive late afternoon with darkness falling, and would dive to periscope depth for the final 20 miles on electric power. Once near the Igloolik beach they would sit tight till midnight and do a quick reconnaissance before finalizing their plan. They had to suck up that fuel without raising the alarm in a place where there could be twenty people around, *avatiit* according to Joanasie. And maybe dogs! But Joanasie was confident that most if not all the people in the area would be camped out at Igloolik Point, out of sight and sound from the trading post. Joanasie had suggested that there could be a *qallunaaq,* a white man, in Igloolik to open the post for some short-term trading. There was no RCMP detachment there, but there could be a visit from the Mounties stationed in Pond Inlet, a community on the other side of Baffin Island. They routinely made a dog-sled patrol to Igloolik after freeze-up. The Catholic priest had a mission building not far from the HBC post, but he was thought to be at the mission in *Avvajja,* on a small island to the west of Igloolik. Or he could be at a Catholic mission in another community where saving souls was a brisker enterprise than in Igloolik at the present time.

Hansen went up to the bridge to join the Second Watch Officer and Soldier. They pointed out expanses of new ice that had formed through the evening with a cold snap and a dearth of wind. The bow was occasionally breaking through a few centimeters of new ice in large pans, but for the most part the surface of the ocean was a slushy soup of ice crystals. The sky was a steel gray and the sun a pale orb, reluctantly showing its presence above the Arctic horizon. There was some excitement when two bowhead whales were sighted, and not long after that a pod of white beluga whales. Then the whales were gone and again it was just them and the forbidding black ocean as they continued west. Watching the bow wave and the boat's wake and listening to the thrum of the boat's diesel engines gave the men up top the heady assurance that they were moving toward a tangible objective.

Now the new ice was holding larger bits of old ice that drifted south with the current from the northern strait. Fury and Hecla Strait, Hansen reflected, named after the explorer Parry's ships that had wintered in Igloolik last century. God, he would love to get up to that northern strait, the narrow opening between Baffin Island and Melville Peninsula on the mainland. He smiled in reflection that it was this same strait that had obsessed his godfather Bernhard Hantzsch as well. Joanasie insisted there was open water up there, which stayed open most of the winter thanks to the currents and the wind. He said he had friends up that way in a camp at Agu Bay. Hansen recalled that the Russians called those openings in the ice *polynyas*, while the Yanks and the Tommies called the huge opening to the northwest of Greenland simply the *North Water*.

Soldier was scanning the ocean to port. He pointed and then he passed the binoculars to Hansen. Narwhal again, five of them! Joanasie was up top too, needed for his knowledge of the area and the ice. He took a turn to watch the pod of whales. They were acting, what? Energized. Just then Winkler requested permission to come up to the bridge, passing on information that the whales were making the same sounds they made previously when approached by killer whales. He added that he was picking up clicking sounds probably emanating from killer whales, something akin to the sonar on their boat and possibly also serving to herd their prey. Joanasie nodded when this was translated and swept his binoculars behind the whales. "Ee! *Aarluk!*" Killer whales again! The narwhal were swimming through leads in the breaking ice pans and the killer whales were quickly closing the distance. Suddenly the narwhal dived and were gone. The two killer whales maintained their course for a minute then turned toward the boat. Minutes later the pod of five narwhal appeared on the starboard side of the boat swimming parallel to its course, approximately 200 meters out. Again it seemed that the pursued narwhal were staying near the boat as though it offered protection against the killer whales. Desperate action, indeed, when the narwhal themselves would have been alarmed by the sound of the boat's diesel engines and thrashing propellers. Somehow the narwhal sensed that the killer whales would be even more wary of this alien mechanical presence in their waters. Still, even Joanasie was amazed by the behaviour of the narwhal.

Everyone up top watched as the killer whales followed the narwhal and gradually closed the distance between them. Soldier did a 360-degree scan with his glasses to identify any potential human threats on the horizon. He spoke into the Commander's ear, then went over to talk to Franz, who was standing at watch as usual behind the 20 mm flak gun. Franz nodded and looked at the skipper for a confirming nod. Yes! He cracked a smile and readied the twin gun for firing through its one good barrel. He loved to shoot and he knew he excelled at it. It had been so long since he had a real target for practice, other than a piece of ice or garbage.

When the killer whales were still about 250 meters out Franz knew he had to let loose, before they were so close he would not be able to depress the gun sufficiently to target them. He quickly brought the sights and target together and fired off a ten-round burst, sweeping the rounds over the two killer whales swimming almost side-by-side. Joanasie's eyes opened wide as he saw the violent impact of the burst on the whales. They were ravaged by the exploding cannon shells and were very quickly dead in the water. Shortly the carcasses were left behind, not too soon for most of the men who had observed the shooting. The use of one of mankind's potent tools of warfare against sea mammals, even a large and feared predator such as a killer whale, was somehow discomforting. Joanasie was disturbed when the boat's departure from the scene confirmed that they would not be attempting to salvage some of the whales for food, before they sank.

Franz stared vacantly at the carnage he had wrought, his hands still gripping the gun. Soldier noticed that the only man who seemed to enjoy the show was Krause the torpedo mechanic, the brooding one, who was up top taking his turn for some fresh air. He dragged on his cigarette and suggested to Franz that he take out the smaller whales too, while he was at it. The five narwhal stayed with the boat for another few minutes then turned away to the north. Joanasie, though he shared the Inuit's deeply ingrained fear of killer whales, carried his unease below to share with his sister. Commander Hansen shook his head slowly from side to side and turned to a sober-looking Soldier. "I wish we could take that moment back. We have more in common with those predators than we care to admit."

* * *

Tagak was looking sour, so his wife and nephews were keeping quiet and trying to fade into the background. But that was not easy as they were all crammed together in the Peterhead's small wheelhouse trying to keep warm. After some feasting and an abbreviated sleep at their island camp, they had continued on to Qikiqtaarjuk with the empty barge to pick up the rest of the fuel drums. They were getting acquainted with the new ice forming up on Foxe Basin. It wasn't much yet, just skim ice and slush ice but still it made it damn difficult to tow a barge. They had slowed down from their normal slow speed of eight knots with an empty barge to just over half of that now. Good thing they did not have a load of drums on! They might have to leave the barge at the island with the drums now, secure it as best they could so the tide and ice would not take it away. It could be hard enough now just to get just his boat back to camp. He might have to get the boys up in the bow to deflect the thicker pieces of ice to ease their passage and head off damage to his wooden boat. And if some favourable winds came up soon to clear out the ice before it set in solid, he would try to return in the next week or so to make one more fuel haul with the remaining drums, these ones all his own. He would do what he could. Tagak rolled another cigarette from his tin, contemplating how the ice was early again this year, three years running! This, combined with all the old ice coming down through the northern strait, made for a short season indeed for his Peterhead boat. He noticed the nephews looking at the tobacco tin greedily so he passed the tin and papers around. He would get some more tobacco when he got to Igloolik, before the trader left and the post closed down again for the winter.

Tagak looked through his old brass telescope. He should be able to see that line of bright red drums by now. He cursed and told Jaypettie to open the cabin window so the tobacco smoke could clear. He could see the empty drums strewn about just up from the beach, the ones that he had used to fuel his boat last haul. But where were the other full drums up top? There was snow on the land but not enough to hide the drums, only to outline them even better. Tagak had an uneasy feeling as his boat tugged the barge closer to the little bay. *Aitaalunga!* Where were the drums? Then he saw them as his boat rounded a corner. The missing drums were there, but they were not in quite the same place that he left them in, and they now had rocks placed on top of them. But why the rocks? That's something you would only do with empty drums if they were empty and you wanted to weight them down so the wind would not blow them away. Or just roll them over . . . Tagak was looking even more sour now. He could only think of his old rival from Repulse Bay, the only man in the whole region besides himself who owned a Peterhead boat with a diesel engine! Yes, he is a scoundrel, but would he steal his fuel? Not likely, but if his need was great enough he might "borrow" it in the traditional fashion. Tagak scowled again. Maybe he was up this way hunting walrus. But how could he take all those drums in just a few days?

26

September 15: To Igloolik

Joanasie and Sila were alone in their sleeping space, while Soldier was out talking with the Chief. Sila looked at her brother, squeezing his hands. "I am afraid, my brother. I do not know what these men will do with us. We help them but I think they do not want to let us go."

Joanasie nodded grimly and said, "Ee. I am afraid too. They tie you up so I do not get any ideas about running away."

"It's strange because I do not think they are bad men," Sila said thoughtfully.

"But the *qallunaat* down south, the Canadians and many others over the ocean are fighting with the *qallunaat* on this boat, and their people. These people do not want the soldiers at Iqaluit to know they are here, or the *paliisi*. We have seen how they need fuel for their boat to get home. And they do not pay for the fuel!"

"Soldier is a good man, and he has said the boat boss Hansen will take us home to our camp when they have found the rest of the fuel they need."

"Yes, I know they have promised that, and I hope it is true. But I still think that if they find it necessary they would kill us, if they think keeping us alive is too risky for them."

"Strange men! They could kill us tomorrow if they needed to but still they feed our dog and try to keep it comfortable up there. And they killed those killer whales too, to save the narwhal."

"Yes, though I would have no hope for the dog if this boat has to go under water quickly again."

Sila was thoughtful for a minute, then continued. "And now we are going to Igloolik with them to look for more fuel. I have friends at Igloolik Point, and once again I will be chained to my bed."

"I thought Soldier was going to cry when he put the chains on you last time. He looked so sad."

"Yes, I know he cares for me. But I cannot see what future he sees for us, and for the one growing in here," she smiled sadly, patting her belly.

Joanasie paused, then smiled too. "And how do you know there is someone growing in you, with so little time passed?"

"Women know about such things," she said softly.

"Be careful of your feelings, sister, *qallunaat* men do not often stay with their Inuit lovers."

"Ee, I hear that is true."

Joanasie was pained to see the strong and independent Sila looking so vulnerable now, with silent tears running down her cheeks.

* * *

Soldier and Commander Hansen were smoking cigars up top.

"Cigars are frowned upon in the *Kriegsmarine*," Hansen commented. "But there are some committed cigar smokers among our ranks nevertheless."

"What is the issue with smoking cigars?"

"Well, Admiral Donitz would say it is decadent, immoral, and too Latin American. But then the Lion is also against prostitution and lust in general."

"And what he calls Negro African jungle music?" Soldier asked.

"Something like that. He is a big believer in marriage though, to a good German woman of course. Where did you get these cigars?"

"From another U-boat commander actually, one who was in Paris on leave when I was there doing the same thing. He succumbed to some jungle music there and scored some cigars from a Cuban musician who was selling them as a sideline. It was a stroke of luck running into him as it was his boat I was cruising on in the tropical waters of Cuba, the time I had to swim up that bloody river for parts. And he has owed me some cigars ever since I returned to his boat with a stash of them, along with some rum and a fresh-killed pig. All carried downriver on my Huckleberry Finn raft . . . "

"Who was this Nazi sympathizer in Cuba who helped you with the machine parts?"

"Hardly a Nazi, he left Germany before all that. He has a big plantation on a river near Matanzas. It was pretty much a brute labour operation but still he has some vehicles and machinery and they had their own machine shop and parts bin, largely self-sufficient."

"How long were you there?"

"I was supposed to head back to the boat the next night, though I had a chit to stay an additional night if forced to expand my search for the needed parts. In the end I had to stay another night."

Commander Hansen raised his eyebrows. "Business or pleasure?"

"A little of both. Turned out the German farmer was a widower who enjoyed a special relationship with his black housekeeper. Her son and I became fast friends. Hilario did his best to keep me entertained with the enthusiastic help of the locals."

"And so . . . African jungle music?"

"Ha ha, you get the picture. It was a couple of days of revelry I shall never forget. There were a hundred people, the farm workers with their families, in their own little enclave on one corner of the farm. Music you have never heard before, dance with abandon, rum and cigars, roast pig and sweet potatoes and mangos."

"Sounds like you went from heaven in Cuba to hell on the Russian front."

"Yes, indeed. And the Cuban women, Karl! Wild black and brown women who would not let you sleep!"

Hansen sighed and covered his ears. "I think you are an abject failure as a good German soldier."

"Do you think I should confess to the Lion? I feel I am dirtying this fine boat."

"Indeed you are. And now you are shifting your decadence from black women to an Eskimo woman. But who would believe such a revelation from someone on a U-boat on patrol?"

"Ah yes, that is something else to think about. On that note, my friend, I am going below to catch a nap before we reach Igloolik. I'm sure this is going to be a long night."

"Keep your hands to yourself down there or I will put Winkler between you and the Eskimo wench."

"See you in a few hours, Karl."

"Sweet dreams, Helmut."

* * *

Lutz and Joanasie were taking a break from their engine-room chores when Commander Hansen passed through with Soldier on their way to the control room.

"What is that you are holding there?" asked Hansen.

Lutz replied, "Joanasie made this part, the spacer, to go with the gasket his sister made for the problem fuel transfer pump."

"Made it? From what?"

"He carved it out of soapstone, actually from the bottom of his sister's *qulliq*, the seal oil lamp."

"You're joking!" He held it up against the light. It looked precisely like the original but minus the crack. "Will it hold up, and take high temperatures?"

"Well, perhaps not so well as steel but we will see. If the pump is operating as it should, there will be no high temperatures. In any case, the soapstone lamp has withstood very high temperatures from burning seal oil, which burns much hotter than kerosene."

"Amazing, using only a file?"

"And the drill in the machine shop."

"Brilliant." Hansen turned the piece over and over in his hands and looked up at Joanasie. "Tell me, where do you Eskimos get your wood and steel? For example, the wood and the metal pieces on your fish spear? And in your knife, and your bow?"

Soldier listened first to Joanasie then turned to the Commander. "There are many shipwrecks from the days of the American and Scottish—they call the Scottish *Siikatsi*—whalers in these waters. Joanasie and his sister were born near *Kimmirut* Lake Harbour, and only moved to the Steensby Inlet area when their parents drowned and they went north to join their grandmother who had married again into the *Iglulimiut*. As children near Kimmirut they would travel with their family to a nearby shipwreck, and spend days harvesting wood and steel. From these materials his people would make their *kakivak* fish spears, their *qamutiiq* sleds, their poles for their *tupiq*s, *ulu* knives for the women to cut meat with. Whatever was needed."

Joanasie spoke to Soldier again. "Nowadays they can get some of these things from the trading posts, in normal times. Nails, saws, and lengths of wood to make things."

"You people are born scavengers and improvisers!"

"Ee," said Joanasie with a smile after listening to the translation, accepting that as the highest compliment.

"Well, I guess we will see how this part of yours works when we get to Igloolik shortly and start taking on the fuel there."

"Ee," he agreed. "And I can see that you people are clever scavengers too."

Hansen listened to Soldier put that into German, then made a face as though grievously insulted. He laughed heartily and cuffed Joanasie on the shoulder.

27

September 15: Igloolik

Hansen, Chief, and Soldier, now sometimes called the *Triumvirate* by the crew, were on the bridge as they slowly approached Igloolik under electric propulsion, lights out and silent running. The dog, prone to howling when the mood suited him, was secured and muzzled. It was dark and there was increasing snowfall, temperature nine degrees below freezing, and negligible ice in the water. The small island of Igloolik was mostly flat with raised beaches. With just enough moonlight they could see the snow blanket on the land contrasting with the black of the ocean. Joanasie directed them in, guessing where the fuel drums would be, on the beach right below the trading post.

"You sure there won't be any Eskimos and dogs around?"

Joanasie repeated his assurance that the Inuit would be camped out at Igloolik Point, with their dogs. There could be some Inuit nearer to the post if the Company man is here now and trading has started.

Soldier shared this with Hansen, and noticed his quick glance at Joanasie. There was some risk in Joanasie flying the coop here. Soldier reassured him. "We will do the reconnaissance first, then I will bring Joanasie back to the boat and tie him up with Sila."

The dinghy was readied and pushed off from 100 meters out, where there were just a few meters of water under the U-boat's keel. Soldier, Joanasie and a seaman paddled quietly to shore and stopped to listen for a minute before pulling the dinghy up on the beach. All quiet. Joanasie took the lead. They moved to the left where they'd spotted the fuel drums and did a quick count. There were at least 250 drums, more than their estimates. Outstanding! This would make the Commander a happy man.

Soldier and Joanasie moved stealthily up the modest rise to the post. The attached residence was showing lamplight from two windows. They crept up and peered through the windows where they were not heavily frosted over. A chubby white man was sitting in a big stuffed chair reading a book. While they watched, he stopped to light a cigarette and reach for his mug. He stretched and then unexpectedly got up and came right over to the window. He looked out as Joanasie and Soldier fell to their knees right below his gaze, holding their breath. Then the chubby white man returned to his chair. Joanasie and Soldier stood up on either side of the window and walked around the white-painted and red-roofed building to meet on the other side. They saw that there were no Eskimos camped right near the post but they decided to range further out for another circuit just to make sure. Nobody! Joanasie concluded that maybe this Company man is not very friendly and therefore the people at Igloolik Point would only come here during daylight hours for trading. And the other good news was there were no signs of occupancy in the unlit Catholic mission building. Joanasie thought the boat boss Hansen would like this news. They headed back to the dinghy and lifted it into the frothy water.

Back on the boat a hasty plan was taking shape over some hot tea. With the translation and gesticulating necessary to include Joanasie in the conversation it was painfully slow going for Hansen. He was impatient to get started with the fuel transfer. But they needed a plan to deal with the presence of the trader, who might hear suspicious sounds from the beach. Plan made, Soldier took Joanasie down to their sleeping cubicle and shackled him to his bed. Sila watched wide-eyed while Soldier secured her brother then sat on a bunk to face them. "Now here is the plan, and this time you have a part to play, Sila."

As Sila listened her anger dissipated somewhat, yet she was cautious about Soldier's intentions. She stared at him a moment and then asked with restrained hope, "I am getting off the boat?"

"Yes, but your brother is staying here this time. We need to make sure you will behave and return to *Tulugaq*. We know you may have friends or relatives camping nearby to trade at the post."

* * *

Sila took deep breaths of fresh air after climbing up through the conning tower. She stood for a moment and stretched. It seemed to take her some time to get her balance back, and her outdoor orientation. She looked at the ocean, the land, the sky with the outline of a moon visible through the falling snow. It will be good to get off this stinking boat again! She climbed down the ladder to the deck and hopped into the dinghy, not waiting to be assisted by the men on the deck. It was good to be dressed in her seal-skin *atigi* parka to shield her from the bite of a wintery wind. Soon she would need to wear caribou clothing, but by then she should be at her family's camp. Her family would be so worried about her and Joanasie by now, they had been gone so long. She felt an almost overwhelming need to flee right now that she had the opportunity, but she cleared such thoughts from her mind as she stepped out of the dinghy onto shore. These men held her brother. And in their own way they held Soldier too . . .

Sila padded through the soft snow in her *kamiik* to the residence side of the trading post. What if this plan went wrong? What would happen to her and her brother? She took a breath and knocked on the door, in the manner of the *qallunaat*. She could hear some shuffling inside and then footsteps approaching the door. The bolt was drawn back inside and the door opened. In the light of the lamp that the white man was holding Sila could see his pale face. He looked uncertain, even frightened. It was no doubt unusual for someone to knock at his door this late in the day. He looked like he was about ready to go to his bed, and she could smell the heavy scent of rum on him.

William stared at the figure in the doorway and watched as the stranger brushed snow off a seal-skin parka and then dropped a fur-trimmed hood to reveal a face. William stared, dumbfounded. My God, a woman! A beautiful ravishing woman! He drank in the beauty of her face framed by a mane of raven black hair. The young woman smiled and her dazzling white teeth were set off by her perfect lips. The stricken man could only think to stagger backwards and beckon the woman to enter.

"Come in, come in," he said in her language. "Have a seat. No, no, on the couch. We can both sit here."

He just sat beside her and stared at her for what seemed forever to Sila. Finally he spoke, "What can I get you, would you like some tea? Something stronger, some rum perhaps? Perhaps some chocolate first? Are you hungry?" A nervous rush of words . . .

William busied himself in the kitchen, hardly believing his good luck. He was not sure which family this girl was from, this Nevee she called herself. But he wasn't going to let her get away. No doubt her parents would show up tomorrow with the girl in tow and expect some favourable exchanges in the trading post. Well, he would see about that. Repeat favours and repeat business was the best policy in his ledger.

He carried in a tray of tea and cookies, and slices of canned ham. She was hungry, look at her eat! Good, everything goes better on a full stomach. It was time to try a drink on her for size. He did not know if she had tasted rum before but it always did the trick. One or two down the hatch and then it was an easy sidestep to the backroom. He made up a couple of hot toddies, strong and hot but sweet. She might even think it was just another *qallunaat* drink like tea. He sat down beside her and started his drink and then got up to find his tobacco in the other room. When he returned her mug was empty already! He smiled at her in anticipation. "You liked that, didn't you? I'll get you another." He drained his own mug on his way to the kitchen.

Sila looked at the big ashtray, a sand-filled milk tin she had quickly dumped her drink into, and pushed it behind the stuffed chair. William came in with another drink and handed it to her with a flourish. He rolled a cigarette then offered it to her. She declined, saying it would only make her dizzy. It was so hot in the room, he kept his stove turned up so high. She wiped her brow. William excused himself and went back to return in a minute with a wind-up gramophone like the one she had seen three years before at the missionary's house in Kimmirut. By then she had dumped another mug's contents. He downed his too. She did not recognize the music but he told her the singer was "Bing Crosby, singing Christmas music." He told her that since it would soon be Christmas he would have to think about a present to give her. "Would you like to dance?" he asked. Sila had heard of Scottish whalers and Company men dancing jigs to the music, much to the entertainment of her people.

"Wait! I'm roasting with this *atigi* on." With one fluid motion she pulled it over her head by its hood. When William saw she was now naked down to her seal-skin pants he forgot to breathe. She said, "Can you teach me to dance?"

William decided to celebrate his good luck and pour himself another stiff one. Sila could see that his walking was very unsteady now. She asked him to show her how to make the drinks. Then she sat him down in the stuffed chair and put his feet up on a stool. She handed him another strong drink and stood in front of him swaying slowly to Bing Crosby music as he sang, "Silent Night. Holy Night, All is calm, all is bright." William was getting very sleepy. Sila looked out the window at the swirling snowfall.

* * *

Chief was satisfied that all was going well with both pumps for the fuel transfer. Stealth was the word! The work crew had managed to roll the drums down to the beach over the fresh-fallen snow and un-bung them without making much noise. The new snowfall was helping to muffle their sounds and the light wind blowing offshore helped too. Then it was just a matter of moving down the line of drums, inserting intake hoses into the drums two at a time. The fuel lines were near their maximum reach, over 100 meters from the boat, but both the transfer pumps were operating efficiently. Chief looked at his watch. They should be done in another two hours, then they would be out of here. That's good, the men were chilled now with that wind nipping at them. The steel drums and the brass hose connections were numbing to their touch when they had to remove their mitts.

* * *

Soldier was not a small man but he was trying for invisibility as he slowly walked a covert patrol from the beach and around the trading post buildings. He frequently halted and squatted down to look and listen. If he bumped into a curious Eskimo now, he didn't quite know what he would do. They could put him on the boat too but the Commander would not want that. They had enough problems with two captives. Killing a civilian and stuffing him under one of the warehouses did not appeal to him. Time to go check on Sila, he decided. He crept up to the window again, thankful for the snowfall that would cover their tracks. He peered in. The chubby white man appeared to be unconscious in his easy chair, a drink spilling from his hand. Sila was on her feet, naked to the waist and apparently dancing. Soldier could hear music faintly through the window, in spite of the gusting wind. He watched as Sila swayed with the music, breasts lifting toward the heavens, humming along with the music from the gramophone. What an incredible woman!

Movement to his right! He dropped to his knees as he waited a moment to regain his night vision. Then he made out a fur-clad figure moving between two of the small warehouses. Moving slowly, hesitantly, toward the beach. Obviously the Eskimo had heard something and was going down to investigate. Soldier got behind him, quickly and quietly closing the distance between them. He followed in the fresh snow in step with his quarry, who walked with the gait of an old man. When Soldier had closed the distance to three meters he sprang forward, catching the man unseen with an arm around his neck and choking off his windpipe. The Eskimo was a smaller man but he was surprisingly strong and wiry.

A few minutes later Soldier was dragging the unconscious man toward the door of the post residence. He knocked in code, three times fast and two slow. When Sila opened the door Soldier dragged the man in and dumped him unceremoniously on the floor beside the comatose William. Then Soldier pried the drink from the chubby man's fingers and poured it over the unconscious figure on the floor. Soldier tossed Sila's *atigi* to her and waited while she pulled it on. He then picked up a bag she had already filled with tinned food and tea and chocolate. She had left behind the foul rum, but Soldier quickly snatched it up along with another bottle he spied on the kitchen counter, dropping them into the bag along with the tin of tobacco and papers. He made a quick tour of the residence and spotted the radio set. He pulled a few wires out of their connections in the back. Soldier took Sila's hand and pulled her toward the door. "Don't worry about taking this bag of goodies. It's a very small payment for your heavenly company tonight. And besides, we helped ourselves to a few things in the warehouse too. But we didn't touch the ammunition and some other supplies your people will be needing."

Sila smiled and followed Soldier down to the beach, through the neat rows of empty fuel drums and into the dinghy.

PART FOUR

28

September 16: Northeast toward Baffin Island

The boat backed out slowly from the beach at 0400 hours with its two electric motors driving the propellers, and then it slowly turned its bow eastwards toward the narrow gap between Jens Munk Island and Baffin Island. Thirty minutes later the Commander called for both diesel engines slow ahead, a nice lazy thrum. He would have daylight before reaching the gap. After they made their way through that they should easily reach their destination west of Steensby Inlet by early afternoon, if ice did not pose a problem. And be rid of the Eskimos, his promise to them kept. The snowfall was still moderately heavy with enough moonlight to watch it disappear solemnly into the cold black ocean. Joanasie had peered at the crude map of the upper reaches of Foxe Basin and used his finger to indicate the location of his family's camp. Good, this would be finished with by the end of the day. The Eskimos would get some fresh air and exercise walking to their camp while the boat was finally getting the hell out of Foxe Basin before it turned into a skating rink.

The familiar terror of a North Atlantic gale would be most welcome about now.

Commander Hansen was in a good mood with the boat's fuel tanks more than half-full for the first time in over three months. If both engines held up they just might make it home to Germany in four or five weeks, submerging by day. If they could exit Foxe Basin before it was beset with heavy ice, and get through eastern Hudson Strait undetected and through the Labrador Sea into the Atlantic, yes, they might do all right. If they did not look for trouble . . . And if they managed to clear those hurdles, he knew he would not be ramming his boat into any enemy ships off the French coast. He would get the men ashore into Germany first, and then scuttle the boat. This would provide the basis for a credible story that U-807, incommunicado with radios down for over two months, was lost in action. By now the war was over for his men anyway. Now the challenge was for them to stay alive and eventually get home to their families and sweethearts. Yes, many German cities would now be behind enemy lines and many of the men would become prisoners of war until hostilities ceased. Some of the men might choose to seek out German units and keep fighting, or alternatively they could surrender to the British or Americans or Canadians, avoiding the Russians at all costs. The choice would be theirs individually, and the burden would be lifted from him as their commanding officer. He will then have given his men their lives back.

As for himself, he was not sure what he would do. But he could see a future for himself after this war was done. If he looked really hard, he could see a faint outline of things: a sailboat, some tropical islands, maybe a good woman. He wanted more than anything for Chief to make his dream of a cottage on the sea become a reality. As for Soldier, he hoped they would remain friends after the war. For a damned warrior he was bright and resilient. He would make out okay, even in peacetime. But he would need to be in uniform . . . a uniform suited him. Maybe Soldier would become a policeman or a fireman in his next life. He smiled at that thought.

* * *

Sila and Joanasie were ecstatic to be heading home. Well, close to home. The German *qallunaat* were determined not to be seen or reported by anybody, even by Inuit. She and her brother and their dog would be set ashore some distance from their family camp and left to walk the rest of the way home. Sila wondered who in their extended family camp would believe the direction their lives had taken over the past two months. There would be mourning for Anaanattiaq, and surprise and wonder about the new life growing in Sila's womb. She thought about Soldier. Sometimes when she was admiring his handsome face, his hard body and powerful arms, she could also glimpse pain and vulnerability. He was holding back from her now but she sensed that he was not being cruel. This man had put up a veil that she could not pass through, and she sensed it had something to do with his past. Perhaps another woman . . . She could not understand all the ways of the *qallunaat,* even this one who was different and could even speak some of their language. Joanasie and Sila readied their few possessions to leave the boat. When leaving the boat, they would retrieve the brown *tuktu* and white *nanuk* skins rolled up and stored in the forward torpedo room. The skins, when worked and dried, would be valuable for new winter clothing and for trade at the trading post. There would be too much to carry to the camp right away so the skins would have to be cached until they could get some help and return with a dog sled. She had lost her *qulliq* seal oil lamp to the fuel pump, but she still had her metal pot for making tea and boiling caribou. Everything else had been left at their summer camp at Nettilling Lake. Their grandmother and the other dogs too . . . But she still had her brother and even her lead dog, and also a little something else she had picked up along the way. Her hand moved unconsciously over her belly. And as for Soldier, maybe he would come to her after the *qallunaat* put down their guns and stopped killing each other.

* * *

Chief came in and looked at the Commander. "You are dead on your feet." Chief put his hands on the other's shoulders and pushed him gently. Hansen collapsed into the most comfortable chair on the boat, if not the whole U-boat fleet. Within seconds he fell into a deep exhausted sleep.

It seemed whole ages later that the Commander felt his body being shaken and for a foggy minute he did not know who he was or where he was, let alone what was happening. Chief was saying a word over and over, staring at him hard. Gradually the fog lifted from his mind. "Ice! Ice! Ice! Lots of it!" Chief was saying. "Everywhere! All along the shore of Jens Munk Island and plugging the gap to the north! We need you above.

The Commander sighed wearily and somehow pulled himself up the steel rungs through the tower hatch to do a quick take of the dull grey sky. He nodded to the others gathered up top as he scanned the ocean to the east, the north and south. Ice all right, what looked to be an impenetrable barrier of pack ice coming through the northern strait. Large meter-thick pans held together by new ice. *Scheisse*! Heading east through the gap was now out of the question. "Let's run south along the coast of this island and see if we can get around through the back door."

Chief lost his patience and swore. "Leave the Eskimos here on the ice! It looks solid enough for them to make it to shore. And they said there is an Eskimo camp on this island. We have to steer south, not east and north!"

Hansen scanned the shoreline of the island with his glasses. "Chief, I can see open water between this ice and the shore. Our Eskimo friends could not make it across." He paused. "Let's go southeast along this coastline and see what we can find." It seemed to the Commander that everyone up top was staring at him. Pondering, weighing, evaluating . . . He thought he saw a hint of a smile on Soldier's face but he didn't say anything. Chief was already carrying out the order, looking lost and more forlorn than ever. Three hours later they found open water near the bottom of Jens Munk Island. Hansen spoke calmly to Chief. "East and north along the inside shore."

* * *

Joanasie stood beside his sister Sila watching the shoreline pass by. They had spent some summers here, and now viewing the snow-covered hills brought back happy memories of this island known as *Kapuivik*. Inuit had lived here for more generations than people could remember. Joanasie signaled to Hansen that they were now within a day's walking distance from an Inuit camp. Not their own camp, but it would do! U-807 slowed its diesels and pointed its bow toward a small inlet. The Commander, the Chief, and the commando were breathing a shared sigh of relief. Smiles, hearty slaps on the back, sharing small jokes . . . There was a renewed hope that finally they could turn a page on this Foxe Basin craziness and make an honourable retreat.

"*Tingmisuuqtalik!*" An airplane! Sila lowered the glasses and pointed to the southwest. It was heading obliquely toward them, still far enough away to pose no immediate threat but close enough to see through binoculars that it had four engines and a war-like profile. With four engines it would not be one of the lighter aircraft being ferried to England through Iqaluit, and in any case it was too far north for the Crimson Route. It was a patrol aircraft but definitely off the beaten track, probably not looking for them but still they had to be cautious.

"*Auf Sehrohrtiefe!*" Dive to periscope depth." The Commander shook his head in silent disbelief as Sila and Joanasie speedily dragged the struggling dog to the tower hatch and somehow manhandled it through and lowered it dangling in its harness to seamen below, men who were thankful the big dog was muzzled.

Periscope depth was all they could risk here, and even for this they still wanted a minimum of 15 meters of water to keep them off the bottom. Hansen was confident they had not been spotted, but still he willed the black chop with floating ice bits to close over them protectively like a shroud.

Joanasie looked at Sila as she held the hyperventilating dog tightly by its leather harness. The brother saw the crushing disappointment in his sister's face and his heart went out to her. We were so close, he thought. Joanasie looked up to see Soldier squat down beside them to help control the dog. Then he saw Soldier's hand take Sila's hand in his own and squeeze tight. Nobody spoke. There was nothing to say for the moment.

Hansen and Chief were watching the reading on the fathometer with an almost detached interest. Their crude map indicated deeper water to the north this side of the Baffin coast but east of this island there was no clue as to depth and the presence of shoals. But they felt periscope depth was not asking for too much. The boat was proceeding at five knots when the crash came, a hard but glancing blow off a rising bottom. The keel impacted just before the bow glanced off a protrusion on the starboard side.

"*Auftauchen*! Take her up, damage reports all stations!"

Joanasie and Sila were still frozen in terror as lights flickered and crew relaxed their grips on steel holds. Some men were picking themselves up, holding bruised body parts.

Chief spoke in the Commander's ear. "No reported breaches or systems failures but there could be substantial damage to the bow plating, on top of the beating it has already taken surfacing through ice. Impacts high on the bow and now impacts low on the bow."

Hansen nodded grimly. If the strengthened hull fairing over the outer muzzle doors of the four bow torpedo tubes were stove in, and if the muzzle doors themselves were damaged, there would remain only the tube's inner doors to keep the icy waters at bay on a long journey home. This would then become the critical weak link of the boat's pressure hull, which might yet have to survive more depth charging and possibly more impacts with ice.

When they surfaced it was readily apparent that the boat had not been spotted by the aircraft. No attack! No blessing of the bombs . . .

Soldier heard sobbing and he knew where to look. He saw that Winkler was obviously stretched to his limits again. The Commander's hands were on his shoulders and his voice was soothing him. Hansen noticed Soldier's gaze and stood back as though embarrassed. Soldier caught that and sent an understanding nod back.

"Hang on, sailor, we'll make it out of this one okay, just like we always do."

Winkler felt relieved that at least the boat was back on the surface, the aircraft long gone.

"Chief is back from inspecting the bow," reported Soldier.

"Good. I'm going up top." The rungs in the conning tower were damned cold now, though his heavy mitts did their job. It was too slippery to walk on the icy deck, now elevated with maximum buoyancy, so the Commander and Chief watched as three men secured by ropes and carrying gaffs made their way back from the bow.

"From what we can see the damage to the fairing and outer torpedo doors is not beyond repair, and it's hardly the case that our torpedo tubes need to be functional. Some of the sheeting added to the casing is buckled and would reduce our speed and fuel efficiency while making us vulnerable to more ice damage. But we need a real dry-dock to do a proper assessment and any needed repairs, or . . . "

"Or . . . what?" the Commander prompted.

"Theoretically, we could run the boat up against, say, a river bank at high tide, to hold the boat on its keel. Have a better look and do some cursory welding and other repairs, and get back out on the next high tide."

"Theoretically . . . There's not as much tide on this edge of Foxe Basin. And how will we know if the following high tide will be of the same height, sufficient to float us off? And how will we keep from being frozen in if the temperature plummets or drift ice blows this way?"

"Many risks indeed, Karl."

"I suppose you already have a location in mind?"

"Well, we have an idea. Joanasie seems to grasp our predicament and has a place in mind to the east. Where Rowley River flows into Steensby Inlet. Just hours away according to our map and it appears that, at least at this moment and in that direction, there is little drift ice in our way. For our final approach we will be submerged. If there are any Eskimos camped at the river for late-season fishing we may have to abort our plan, but Joanasie thinks that is unlikely at this time and with the present trading in Igloolik."

29

September 17: Baffin Island

Corporal Bob Peterson and Special Constable Kidlapik were in high spirits. They had enough of the right kind of drifted snow, *illusaq,* in their river valley to make a fine *iglu.* They had filled themselves on fresh-killed caribou meat stewed in the pot over the primus stove and were now munching down on pilot biscuits dipped in sugar-laced tea. Kidlapik accepted the can of tobacco from the Corporal and began to roll a cigarette.

"With luck we should reach Foxe Basin in a few days. Good going now."

"Ee!"

"And with luck we can make it over the ice to Jens Munk Island and on to Igloolik without delay. If not, we visit your friends in the outpost camps on this side."

Kidlapik smiled and nodded. He was glad the Corporal was in a good mood. *Qallunaat* are not the best of company when grumpy. Grumpy from delays when some narrow stretches on rivers were not yet frozen hard enough to safely cross, and grumpy when the dogs got sore feet from pulling over difficult wind-swept terrain with not enough snow covering the ground. That was behind them now. The dogs' spirits were running high too. Soon Kidlapik would go back out of the cozy *iglu* to feed them some frozen seal meat. He would have to do that soon before he drifted off.

* * *

Joanasie stood with his sister and Soldier, looking down the slope at the boat. To an uninformed viewer it would appear that the boat had run aground, whether from inattention or lack of skill. He had seen, however, that there was an abundance of skill demonstrated here. With the tide on the rise the boat boss had to seek out a perch with the right gradient and surface composition to chance leaving the boat, at least the front half of it, high and dry to attempt repairs on the bow. The cooling water intakes for the diesel engines had to be below the surface, and the hydroplanes and propellers had to be free from contact with the bottom. It appeared that the boat was tilted about five degrees to starboard as it rested in a natural cradle between the riverbank and a sandbar. The river's current was helping to keep drift ice in the ocean from crowding around the boat. Some pans of new freshwater ice were floating down the river where it was still open due to the tidal action. To prevent the ice from stacking up against the stern were men with poles, deflecting it back into the current. From the hunters' perspective the boat looked huge, though very much out of its element, half out of the water like a beached whale.

Soldier watched the little figures working on the bow and occasionally he would see flashes as the welding proceeded. And they could hear banging as other men pounded with heavy hammers on bent steel in efforts to return it to a semblance of its original form. A few men were up in the tower scanning the sky with binoculars, while young Franz was firmly attached to the 20 mm gun. Soldier knew the Commander and Chief would be seriously nervous with the boat in that vulnerable situation. He turned back to Joanasie and Sila. They were thrilled to be on a hunt to add fresh meat to their larder. And so was he! They had shot two seals from the dinghy before the banging on the boat's hull started, and set a gillnet for any arctic char that might be still running up the river. Then they had walked inland.

The three fur-clad figures trotted over the crest and down the slope, Sila in a playful mood and hooking her arm in Soldier's. She stopped him momentarily and said, "*Kuniktaujumajuu!*" Soldier smiled and obligingly rubbed his nose against hers. His hands rose over her body. She had so much clothing on! A shame, as there were no prying eyes out here in these frozen spaces. Sila fended him off, miming the removal of his *usuq* with the snow knife she carried. Then she pointed at a small herd of caribou in a valley off to their left. The three continued to walk single-file, close enough now to begin stalking the animals that were raising their heads occasionally and sniffing at the air. Caribou are a curious animal in the absence of an identifiable threat, but they were nevertheless becoming skittish from the noise of repairs that were intermittently carried up from the boat. Soldier dropped the first five caribou, then he invited Joanasie and Sila to try their luck with his assault rifle. In short order they were putting the meat from the eight downed caribou into caribou skin bags. With *ugjuk* lines attached, the bags slid easily over the snow behind them as they headed back to the hill over the boat on the first of their two meat hauls.

* * *

Chief took off his heavy coat and shook it again before sitting down at the table with the Commander to warm up. "Well, we shaped that sheeting on the bow to render it more hydrodynamic and restored some of its shielding function. The bow has lost much of its beauty, unfortunately. The outer muzzle doors on the torpedo tubes withstood the punishment and held tight."

The Commander nodded, waiting for him to go on.

"Another hour or so and we can call it quits. Then we wait for the tide."

With this good news Cookie and helpers came in carrying pots of hot caribou stew and dumplings.

At 1500 hours, at high tide and with all the crew marched aft to give maximum floatation to the bow, the Chief gave the order to go to two-thirds power astern on both main engines. As the two powerful diesels reverberated through the hull, the two propellers struggled for purchase to pull the boat back into the river and toward the ocean. All at once the thrust conquered the resistance and the boat moved backward, dropping the bow to a horizontal plane with a modest splash. Chief breathed again when the vulnerable hydroplanes and propellers survived the exit phase of the beaching procedure. Winkler too nodded satisfaction that there was no damage to his precious hydrophone array.

With the boat back in its proper element, Chief commented on their good fortune that the boat was built before the 1944 model year, hence the design allowed the main diesels to drive the propellers in reverse. The newer versions of the Type IX boats could reverse only with the considerably reduced power of their two electric motors.

Soldier and Joanasie whooped when they saw the splash. They hurried over to the river to bag up a surprise harvest of fifteen fish from the gillnet, an efficient fishing device snagged fortuitously by one of their boat's hydroplanes off Newfoundland. When the three hunters neared the boat from their last shuttle, holding up two fat arctic char, a cheer went up from the sailors and officers up top.

With the diminishing daylight the temperature was falling rapidly. Holding proud was a full moon. That full moon would have given an extra upward pull on the tide, "*piturnivik*" Joanasie called it, to help float the boat back into its nurturing seawater, at the same time as easing the way for this late run of arctic char as they migrated upstream to over-winter in an inland lake.

* * *

Corporal Peterson and Special Constable Kidlapik studied the tracks around the leavings from a caribou hunt: blood on the snow, heads with antlers, intestines . . . There had been no new snow since yesterday so the details of the killing scene stood out starkly. Three pairs of *kamiik* footprints, one pair indicating rather large feet. Kidlapik abruptly stooped to pick up a metallic object. He held up a spent cartridge.

"What caliber?"

Kidlapik shrugged and passed it to the Corporal. *"Aamai."*

"Me neither, doesn't look like your normal hunting cartridge, eh? Big one, *angijuq*!"

"Sometimes Tagak, the Inuk at Qaggiujaq with the big boat, gets new things from the south . . . He has *kiinaujaq*, money. He will see something in a catalogue or a magazine in a HBC post or church mission and take the picture to the trader to order one for him on the next year's supply ship. Many times he has brought in things that the people had never seen before."

A little later the Mounties stood on the ridge over the river's mouth, following with their eyes the three sets of tracks sliding down the slope, dragging their catch. Two hauls up to the crest, a successful hunt . . . Down below, the tracks ended abruptly at the riverbank. Kidlapik was even more convinced now that Tagak had been here with his big boat. Even from here he could see impressions on the gravel bank where it appeared that he had beached his boat with the tide. Probably to make repairs of some kind . . .

30

September 21: Northern Foxe Basin

Sila and Joanasie scanned the ominous sea in all directions from the boat's tower. The wind was biting cold, and the caribou skins from the recent hunt in Steensby Inlet had arrived just in time. Sila had already dressed Joanasie in his new *qulittaq* and would shortly be starting on outfits for Soldier and the Commander. But those pleasant thoughts were pushed aside by more pressing ones. What would they do now? The boat had been constantly changing directions the past few days without making any real headway, pack ice coming at them from all around. The boat could hardly find enough open water to build up sufficient momentum to cut through the new ice that was forming. Old pack ice continued to push south, and some of this same ice might be circling back to them from lower in the basin. The temperature had plummeted and ice was covering the boat's deck and tower. It was perilous to move around at all but men secured by ropes were attacking the accumulating ice with hammers and axes. Sila was sure that any Inuit in this part of the inlet would hear such banging, and she smiled as she admitted to herself her hope that nobody would.

Chief and the Commander were looking very tense. Sila looked at Joanasie again, who was trying to communicate something to Soldier. In some places the ice looked sturdy enough all the way to shore. From there they could walk to their camp in a couple of days, pulling their small *qamutiiq* with the help of their dog. But she and her brother had made an important decision. They resolved that they would not leave these *qallunaat* yet, their strange kidnappers who had somehow become their friends. So skilled and with amazing tools, yet so ignorant of this unforgiving land . . . She sensed some regret on their part for their earlier promise of dropping them off near their camp, instead of leaving them at Igloolik or on the ice. That kind gesture was now endangering the lives of the crew.

Sila's thoughts were interrupted as a man passed by her. She had noticed too many times the stocky, scar-nosed, surly man called Krause staring at her and her brother with obvious ill-intent. Sometimes he even held his nose in mock disgust as he passed by them. She did not want to be alone with this man. Joanasie had tried to make light of her concerns, though he himself had given him the name *Qimmiminngaaqtuk*! Spawn of a dog! She considered talking to Soldier about this one but clearly he already had enough on his mind these past few days without her bothering him about that.

* * *

William White was looking forward to dog-sledding from Igloolik back to Repulse Bay. After a spell in this place maybe Repulse wasn't so bad after all. Things had really gone downhill after that mysterious Eskimo woman appeared at his door out of the night. Then there was the unconscious Eskimo man lying on his residence floor reeking of rum but swearing he had never touched a drop in his whole life. His radio set on the blink, and all that fuel missing from the drums on the beach, just enough left to keep him warm till he could get out of here when Koonoo was ready with his dogs . . . Trading was pretty much wrapped up here now and most Eskimos were preparing to head out to winter camps for hunting and trapping, hoping the Igloolik trading post would be open full-time again next year. His warehouses were cleaned out too, and not just from trading for the furs brought in to him. He was missing cases of powdered milk and tea along with bags of flour and sugar, but no ammunition or steel traps were missing. Strange! He had never known Eskimos to steal like this before. And with no RCMP or even a priest here he did not know what to do about it. He feared that the story of heavy drinking in his residence and the passed-out Eskimo would come back to haunt him. He thought it best to keep it quiet as possible for now and argue later that the missing fuel and warehouse stock must have disappeared after his departure.

* * *

Chief Berg-Nielsen was fit to be tied. They had hardly moved in the last week with the damn pack ice foiling every effort made to get out. Meanwhile they were burning precious diesel fuel!

The route back around Jens Munk Island was blocked, and the attempt to find open water along the Baffin coastline had been unsuccessful. They were up to the gap again between Jens Munk Island and the Baffin coast looking for an opening, hoping the winds would change so the ice could move back out into Foxe Basin. It was frigid hell, and it seemed that the ice was alive and malevolent. It was pulsing, cracking, grinding, undulating, and heaving. When ice fog rose up from freezing seawater it looked like the devil's breath.

Commander Hansen sighed and closed his eyes. When he opened them again he began to speak slowly, in a monotone. "The ice was here, the ice was there, the ice was all around. It cracked and growled, and roared and howled. Like noises in a swound."

Soldier and Chief stared at him, incredulous.

"Just a few selected words from *Rime of the Ancient Mariner* by Samuel Coleridge, my friends. It so happens that we blasted an albatross too. Not to mention a couple of killer whales, though I do not know the curse-quotient of those particular creatures."

Chief raised his eyebrows. "On that note, the Chief of the boat respectfully requests an advance administration of Grog."

* * *

Soldier was called to join Chief and the Commander in the tower. They pointed out off the bow. For the first time in a week there was a long stretch of open water, just smaller pans of new ice in it. The open water stopped abruptly in a straight line at the pack ice that ran from the land-fast ice on a long peninsula on the Baffin coast to Jens Munk Island. The boat was easing its way into a lake of open water measuring as much as a kilometer wide by perhaps five kilometers long. Soldier looked at the floating ice bits in the choppy water. "Why don't I rig my chute and hitch it to the boat and you pull me up? I can get a birds-eye view of the ice that way, and look for open water leading west."

Hansen and Chief looked at Soldier in disbelief. "You want us to launch you for a joy-ride up there and hopefully get you back in one piece, alive?"

"Yes, why not? I've done this before, admittedly in more southern seas. You know about the *Bachstelze,* the one-man observation kite some U-boats used to extend their range of vision over the horizon, when attaching a bosun's chair to a surfaced boat's extended periscope was not enough. With this wind you would only have to get this tub up to about five knots, and run from one end of this ice lake to the other. Can you do it?"

"You will die, my friend. You will freeze up and lose control, plunge into the ocean and sink before we can get you out. Or come unhooked and sail off never to be seen again."

"Well, we have to try something if we are going to get out of this mess. This is worth a try. Don't worry about me. I have nine lives and still a few left . . . "

Thirty minutes later Soldier was down rigging his chute and harness. Men were knocking new ice off the deck. Soldier was bundling up in his bulky caribou clothing with rubber overshoes on his feet to better grip the wooden decking, and goggles on his forehead. Hansen gave the order for the boat to turn back into the wind from its downwind leg, getting maximum open water for the maneuver. Eight knots into the wind was enough to launch him skyward in seconds. In just a minute he was 200 meters up, men below spooling out more line while maintaining its tension. So far so good, Chief looked at the Commander and shook his head dolefully.

Soldier looked down at the boat below, somehow looking terribly out of place even in its mottled white coat contrasted against the cold blackness of the ocean and framed by ice all around. Then he looked to the west at the ice stretched across the near horizon, and beyond. As far as he could see there was just white, white, and more white. He looked to the east, and more attentively to the south. Nothing! It was hopeless, unless the winds changed. He looked back to the west again. He wasn't sure if his eyes were playing tricks as the wind buffeted him and whipped him while he rocked to and fro on his tether. Maybe he wasn't high enough, but going higher in these conditions was out of the question. A hint, a suggestion of open water to the west came to him. A hint of open water perhaps 15 kilometers to the west, a line of hazy fog coming up where water meets ice at freeze-up. He closed his eyes and turned away for a minute before focusing again. Yes! He wasn't imagining things! It looked like open water there, for sure. But he could see no leads to get to that open water . . . Soldier felt a little slack in the line and looked down, the boat was running out of maneuvering room in the lead. He felt the tug as the men down below, themselves secured to the icy deck, commenced to reel him back in. He blew from side to side as he descended. He looked down to see the boat turning to port to match his oscillations. Minutes later, men were holding a pole up to him with a grab-ring attached. He grabbed and held on as powerful forces fought against the tether. He felt his feet hit the deck and he fell to his knees, and slid . . . He was almost over the side when the men managed to remove the rest of the slack from his tether and held on with everything they had while other men collapsed his chute. Once again, he thought, once again. Against all odds. His number was clearly not up yet. What a rush!

* * *

Krause watched Sila lavishing attention on a frozen and ice-coated Soldier after he was unharnessed and lifted up by many hands and lowered into the boat. He heard her say "*Pua*" as she pressed her nose to his own frostbitten nose and put her hands on his crusted beard and eyebrows to melt the ice. Krause recognized Soldier as a true Aryan warrior. True, he had lost his way but still he should not be sullied by this savage's cunning hands. Soldier should be saving his prized Aryan seed for a German girl. Yes, even Krause would admit that the Eskimos had earned their passage but it was past time for them to go as the U-boat completed this journey to their Aryan homeland in the Arctic. His dream had come true. He was on the very doorstep of his boreal roots bordering the open sea, where the hollow earth vented its warm air at the poles. Here, he and those who would follow him, would muster forces and carry on Germany's just struggle. A swastika rising out of the polar darkness and illuminated by the aurora borealis . . .

The details were coming to him now in waves, both in his nocturnal dreams and in his daytime visions. His duties as torpedo mechanic with only one armed torpedo tube in the stern left him plenty of idle time to plan and execute his ultimate purpose, his mission in life. Even if it cost him that life, he was just one man and it was the idea, the *gestalt*, that must reign. Krause sensed that, with his own psychic energies, he was empowering the Commander to get through this ice and proceed further north. He had heard about the open water, the ice lakes the Russians call *polynyas*, and reported by these Eskimos to lie in the north of Foxe Basin. These polynyas therefore had to be close to the boat's ultimate ice-free destination, likely stepping-stones, a garden path . . . They were almost home! He would soon show those on board who was really in charge of this mission, show the others on this boat who were casting disrespectful looks in his direction.

31

September 24: North of Jens Munk Island

Hansen stared at the barrier of ice lying off the boat's bow, closing the gap between Jens Munk Island and Baffin Island. Soldier had estimated 15 to 20 kilometers maximum to what *appeared* to be open water. He looked to the south. It was a jumble of drifting pack ice, by all bets extending right down to those huge pancake islands north of Big River. He made his decision, looking at Chief. "We will dive west under the ice and probe for open water."

"More knocking on heaven's door," breathed Chief. He knew this was coming, though. "We can only hope that the open water Soldier thinks he sees is not a mirage, and also a big fat target we can hardly miss. *Atii!*" He had picked up Joanasie's expression for "Let's go!"

* * *

Sila and Joanasie looked into each other's eyes. Joanasie could see a lot of strain in his sister's face. She had made her decision to stay on the boat and he would of course stay with her. They had again been offered the chance to take their dog and gear and get off. Take their chances on the pack ice that looked like it now made a solid platform all the way to the Baffin shore. But Sila did not want to leave Soldier with the many dangers now pressing on him. Joanasie sensed what Sila was feeling, without the need for exchanging words. They would stay with the *qallunaat* and do what they could to help them on their way south again. There would surely be another opportunity to get off the boat. But soon they were going to dive under the ice, in the way of the beluga and narwhal. The wonder and the horror of it! Soldier reminded them that the boat and crew had survived diving under the ice before, before they had joined them as passengers. Sila had noticed the mixed emotions on Soldier's face when she had made it clear she and her brother would stay on the boat with the *qallunaat* for the time being. There was no way she and her baby were walking away from him!

* * *

Krause had been waiting for the right opportunity to talk to the young seaman named Lemcke, the one who had been caught pleasuring himself while watching the Eskimo bitch take her bucket bath. Krause did not think much of the young German's morals for lusting after the wench, even if there were no good German girls close at hand to give him comfort. However, he knew that he needed an ally, that it was much more difficult to act alone. But his attempt to recruit Lemcke had failed miserably. The sailor expressed doubt that any Aryan roots were in the polar region, even if the poles had wandered and continents had shifted. The sailor said it sounded like a crock of shit to him. Krause wondered if the young seaman was just petrified by the thought of turning against someone so formidable as Soldier, though he had clearly laid out the opportunity to get even for the rude interruption to his erotic entertainment. It could be that the young seaman did not trust Krause. Possibly he even loathed him, much as the others on the boat seemed to loathe him. As he walked past the cubbyhole where the fucking dog was tied up to a pipe he saw an as-yet uncollected turd near its rear end. Since the dog was conveniently muzzled and restrained Krause saw no reason not to give it a swift kick in the ribs. And when Krause saw the male Eskimo glaring at him after the kick he just smirked, "Yes, take a good look, Eskimo. You'll get yours soon enough too."

* * *

Peterson and Kidlapik had turned away from the salt water. There was ice forming on Foxe Basin but not consistently enough to support their weight with any confidence. The Mounties steered their dog team along the land-fast ice searching for pack ice that would speed their journey. They would have to go ahead with their plan of visiting some of the outpost camps on this side, show the flag, assuming not everyone was over in Igloolik for trading. After that there would hopefully be no problems crossing over the sea ice. Corporal Peterson was trying to put a damper on his frustrations, trying to adopt the Inuit way of passive acceptance of what nature brought them. *Ayurnamat!*

* * *

Commander Hansen explained to Soldier, and through him to two distraught Eskimos, that they could not wait any longer for the ice to move out of their way. What they were going to do now was dive the boat within closely monitored parameters of depth and heading, speed and time. It was very much a dead-reckoning approach under the ice to the open water beyond. That was the idea. However, there were currents and other factors that could complicate things. And uncertainty about how far away that open water really was, and how far it stretched to the west before they would hit more ice cover again. At five knots submerged they would reach the open water in about three hours, give or take. If the surface was sufficiently free of ice pans they might be able to detect some light diffusing through the water with their attack periscope. It would still be early enough in the shortening day to wring some benefit from the retreating sun. But there were ice crystals forming at the surface, as part of the freezing process of ocean water . . . Nobody said this was going to be easy. Failing a visual approach to surface between ice fields, they would have to attempt some more bow-knocking.

In the preparations for diving there was palpable tension, but also a consensus that this was their only real option. Hansen tucked them into a warm glow of hope by telling them the soothing story of *Kapitan* Franke on U-262 the previous year while approaching Cabot Strait, between Newfoundland and Prince Edward Island. On a covert mission to pick up escaped German prisoners of war from North Point on Prince Edward Island, they had run into a solid wall of ice jamming the strait.

Franke submerged the boat for 16 hours to pass under the ice. When he surfaced the boat there was ice damage to the tower equipment and to the bow torpedo doors, but they survived the day. Unfortunately, due to some communication problems, the prisoners were not there to meet them at the designated location and U-262 had to depart without them. All in all, the audience on the *Tulugaq* found that to be a comforting tale with a most satisfactory ending.

32

September 28: Tulugaq Dives under the Ice!

Joanasie was exhausted, having spent the past several hours with Lutz maintaining the engines prior to shutting them down and switching to electric power. Everything seemed to be working to their satisfaction. "*Ikee!*" It was cold in the boat without the diesel engines to keep them warm. He had put on some of his outside clothing. Everyone else was bundled up too, many with blankets wrapped around them. Sila was busy chewing on their *kamiik* and Soldier's too to keep them soft and pliable for wear outside the boat. She murmured that doing this soothed her, kept her mind away from the numbing reality that they would soon be traveling under ice, instead of driving a dog team over it. Joanasie smiled in understanding. What they were doing now was just too large to comprehend so he also did his best to shut it out of his mind and think more soothing thoughts.

When they started up, the electric motors did not vibrate the hull in the same way that the diesels did, but there was a low pulsing hum that was enough to prod the exhausted Joanasie into the land of dreams.

Soldier had come by and nodded with approval when he saw that Joanasie had succumbed to some sleep. In a soothing tone of voice he told Sila that they were nearing what they thought was a ceiling of open water. Soldier smiled and so did Sila, but their smiles could not mask their tension.

* * *

Commander Hansen and Chief were in the control room watching instruments and talking softly. Their friendship had only become stronger in this adverse environment.

"You know, Chief, I can't help thinking what we need here is the approach used back in 1931 by the *Nautilus.*"

Chief raised his eyebrows skeptically.

"No, not the *Nautilus* fantasized by Jules Verne but the real one sent on a mission about ten years ago to operate under the polar ice. It was an American project using one of their decommissioned submarines from World War One, with Norwegian scientists on board. Their objective was to test modifications and new technologies while ultimately traveling under the ice to the North Pole. Believe it or not, they were actually to meet up with the German airship *Graf Zeppelin* at the Pole."

Chief raised his eyebrows again. "And?"

"They envisioned the underside of the ice platform as flat and uniform, so they put inverted sled runners on top of the boat, which had no tower. They would float themselves up to the ice with positive buoyancy and then just use their propellers to push themselves along on the sled runners until they ran out of ice and supposedly pop up to the surface like a cork."

"Interesting concept, indeed."

"Sometimes it is those simple notions that are revolutionary. Not that one, I'm afraid. They had some other interesting ideas as well, some of which have come down through the years to influence the design of submarines."

Chief's ears perked up at this.

"They figured if they could not surface through ice that was too thick, they would use drills to bore through the ice. One hole for bringing in fresh air for breathing and for operating the diesels when submerged to recharge the batteries, and another for venting the exhaust. The drills extended upwards from the hull using elaborate pinion gears. They never got the bugs out of the drills but you can see how this notion would have contributed to the development of our own *schnorchels*."

"Hmmm," said Chief. "Too bad they couldn't get those damned drills to work. We might be able to use a couple of them now."

* * *

Winkler was listening, always listening. The sounds of the electric motors and propeller wash reverberating off the ice cover above were different from his normal listening environment. But he put his mental filtering processes to work. Before long he could hear other sounds too. From other living creatures under the ice, big and small, sharing this underwater realm with them. The white belugas and the tusked narwhal were still around, though the effect of the ice cover made it more difficult to estimate their distance and bearing from the boat. It seemed that the magnificent creatures were sublimely comfortable diving under ice, and confident in knowing they could find open water to surface in, and draw breath. This brought Winkler at least a small measure of calm.

* * *

It was time to attempt a surfacing. The crude map on the control room table had a few soundings pencilled in and just to the north were depths a U-boat commander could take relative comfort in. But the bottom under them now was still pretty much *meta incognita*. They had had to dive a little deeper, to a depth of 30 meters under the keel, before they could begin rotating the bow upwards, the boat being almost 80 meters long . . . Hansen and Chief were tense as the depth readout was announced continuously. The Commander hung onto the periscope handles and hoped for a glimmer of light above, penetrating cold black ocean. A sign that some benevolent Arctic god was smiling upon them . . . He knew that the crew, many of them anyway, were praying in their bunks where they had huddled under blankets for the past three hours to keep warm and to slow their breathing, just in case they had to stay under for a longer time than hoped for.

Water was pumped from the bow trim cell to the stern trim cell to change the attitude of the boat in the water. The regulator tanks at mid-ship were used to control depth and the electric motors were at the ready if called upon to help slow the rate of ascent toward unknown ice coverage. This was no easy maneuver and was not covered in the training manuals. Chief gave a running commentary to the Commander as the boat eased its way to the surface, a target rise of 1.5 meters per stress-inducing minute.

* * *

A walrus hauled up on the edge of the ice floe felt a bump and a perceptible rise in the ice platform beneath him. It grunted and shifted its awkward mass forward. When nothing else transpired over the next few minutes, the walrus laid its head back on the ice to resume its snooze. Ten minutes later the huge tusked mammal was startled anew. A walrus does not have acute vision, yet it dimly registered a long sleek shape rising slowly from the deep. The shape hung briefly at its apogee, then settled into a horizontal plane while sending out a low wave, perhaps half a meter high, splashing over the ice edge. The visceral response of the tusked witness was a primeval one, matching the response to a surfacing killer whale or a polar bear in its immediate proximity. The walrus backed up and prepared for battle, if it came to that. It peered at the intrusion for some minutes, saw that the object was moving further away and not closer. Then it resumed its snooze.

* * *

Soldier was up in the tower bridge beside the Commander, both of them scanning the expanse of open water and slush ice with their binoculars. The sun was already in retreat but there was a ghostly radiance from the heavens lighting up their new harbour. Just below in the *Wintergarten* were another half-dozen men taking their turn for fresh air and a smoke. They stood in silence with their faces turned upwards. What a contrast from the hellish black icy gloom that had gripped them below. For some this glow from above was a blessing, for some a sign. Every man felt his spirits lifted, and new hope.

Soldier elbowed the Commander and pointed out a walrus resting on the ice half a kilometer away. "Still fresh meat in the locker," he said. Hansen smiled and grunted. His own spirits were lifted, though he knew enough to keep his optimism in check. He had to be coldly rational in all his decision-making. It was the way of the German warrior, and it was also the way of the Arctic survivor.

"This oasis of open sea appears to run north in a line toward Gifford Fiord on the map. We appear to be at the bottom of it and I can't see any access to open water in the west. The only direction we can move in for the time being is to the north. Hardly my preference."

Soldier regarded the Commander. "If you can get this tub up to 10 knots I can get up and take a look again with my chute. There is little wind this time and it appears we have enough maneuvering room to the north."

"Out of the question, Sergeant Wolff. This time there is too little wind to keep you airborne, and we could not get the boat up to sufficient speed to keep you airborne in this devil's brew of slush and broken ice."

"So what will we do?"

Hansen ignored the question, deep in thought as he continued to scan 360 degrees. Soldier and Joanasie readied their hunting gear and the dinghy. That walrus would provide welcome fresh meat and two nice tusks for Joanasie to trade for ammunition and supplies. It took twenty minutes to negotiate the dinghy through the broken ice and slush to the solid ice platform where they could approach the resting walrus.

* * *

Krause inhaled the smoke deep into his lungs, not sharing the excitement of the other crewmembers at witnessing the purples and greens of the aurora shimmering above, or the pale yellow orb of the moon. But he felt sublime satisfaction that the boat would be pointed north again, into the open lead. The north promised salvation, and they were inching closer to their Aryan roots in the ancestral homeland. There they would find the resources they needed to turn things around for Germany. Again they would be surrounded by blue-eyed and blond-haired countrymen, living in a temperate climate cleverly hidden in this Arctic wasteland. Fools, he thought of the Commander and his closest advisors hanging off him. Can't they see that this open water is a sign, and a pathway even the blind could see to lead them home? The worst was now behind. Ahead were only glory and discovery, and rebuilding. There would be a place there for a man of his vision!

* * *

Commander Hansen sent the last of the crew below. They were shivering now anyway as the temperature hovered at 15 degrees below freezing. The diesel engines were running to charge the batteries, and to provide heat to counter the frost build-up inside the boat's hull. Joanasie and Sila made a plea to stay up a little longer to relish the fresh air and heavenly light show, and to delay returning to the stench and gloom below. Their plea was granted. It was clear they were dressed more warmly than the other crew-members. And they would not understand anyway what he was about to discuss with Chief and Soldier . . .

"Well, gentlemen, our range of choices is as narrow as this lead in the ice, I'm afraid."

Chief nodded, having seen this coming. "Kindly break down the range of choices as you see them, in their latest incarnation."

"We can make another relatively short dive to the west from here under this ice field and do more sniffing for open water along the western shore where the current and winds are possibly doing the same thing as they are doing here. Joanasie says there is a current west of here that runs parallel to the mainland and keeps some expanses of ocean open through a good part of the winter. As far south as Hall Point, below Igloolik . . . hence good hunting for walrus."

"Any more options?"

"We continue following this lead to the north, surfaced but in a direction my whole being rejects, to see if there are any leads turning westward so we can get closer to the mainland on that side and work our way back south. If that works, we could supposedly try for that open water off Hall Point. From there we might yet find open water running south toward Hudson Strait."

There did not appear to be a lot of enthusiasm for those options, which Soldier described as a nautical form of Russian roulette.

The Commander continued. "And, perhaps more of a hallucination than an option, in strictly theoretical terms we could possibly make it through the winter in a polynya like this. If we can keep our diesels going periodically on an alternating basis—and our pumps, and our heaters—we should have enough fuel for that. And since these polynyas are an Arctic oasis attracting marine life we should get enough to eat as well. Mind you, sooner or later we would get some Eskimo visitors and word would get out."

No comment at all for several minutes.

"I really hate those options," grunted Chief finally. "My preference is to be headed south and homewards, yet in spite of that I think the option of holding our course north in this open water, surfaced and looking for leads to the west is what we must do."

"My thoughts as well," added Soldier.

The Commander eyed Chief and Soldier in turn. "There is something else we must consider too."

No comment from the two others, just anticipation on their faces, a mix of doubt and hope.

"As you know, the odds of our surviving only keep shrinking as the calendar marches on. If we can make it to Igloolik again, we can freeze the boat in there. Or run the boat up on the beach at speed and ground it proper." Silence from the other men . . .

"And?"

"We spoke lightly of this before but now I do not speak of it as a joke. We can surrender ourselves and the boat in Igloolik, after dumping our Enigma machine and code book, to any representative of the Canadian government we chance to meet there. And this would most likely be to the Royal Canadian Mounted Police when they arrive by dog-sled patrol from Pond Inlet. Hansen paused, then concluded, "Gentlemen, as things are going, this would be a matter of controlling *where* we call an end to this voyage, with our hands on the controls. This scenario seems much better than the present scenario, our future hinging on the unpredictable whims of this demon ice."

The three men remained silent as they pondered. They knew that what was decided next would probably seal their fates one way or another. Soldier looked down at Joanasie and Sila. They had contributed so much to their survival already, and it was not fair to further endanger them. At the same time, he felt the conflicting need to be near Sila and the new life in her belly. It seemed that things were on a spiral out of everyone's control.

Soldier spoke. "As a non-sailor, with fewer . . . ah . . . nautical sentiments, perhaps I can feel at liberty to offer another option."

"Please do," said the Commander.

"We can scuttle the boat right here at the floe-edge and just walk across the ice to the Inuit camp at Agu Bay. Or even to Igloolik. He pounded his fist on the side of the conning tower. "This insistence on staying with the boat and battling this onslaught of ice is what is going to doom us all."

Commander Hansen looked at Chief and Soldier. "Surrendering is one thing, but it truly goes against my nature to scuttle the boat here and now."

Soldier frowned. "Well, it seems that we are at the point now where the boat will remain in Foxe Basin one way or the other. The boat will likely come to its final rest at the bottom of Foxe Basin or perhaps it can be driven full-steam up onto a beach at Igloolik with the rising tide. Thus the boat would be a sign that German warriors have been here, much as the Inuit's *inuksuk* tells others that Inuit have been here. That notion has some merit."

Hansen smiled at Chief and then at Soldier. "Indeed. For now, I suggest we head north in this lead and see what new avenues might yet present themselves to us."

33

September 29: Gifford Fiord, Baffin Island

Soldier had seen and heard all the warning indicators. Krause was misbehaving and needed a lesson in manners. Soldier had heard from Joanasie and Sila, and even from the young sailor he had surprised taking a peek at Sila. All of them were of the opinion that Krause was a piece of shit at best, and dangerous at worst. When Soldier had taken this to the Commander, relaying Krause's babble about an open polar sea and Aryan roots at a venting portal near the North Pole, he seemed to shrug it off as bizarre but ultimately harmless. Krause was a loner, no real friends. He had some technical competence however and, besides young Franz on the 20 mm flak gun, he was the only weapons specialist left on the boat. Yes, he was an odd one and perhaps unstable, maybe even entering a cone of insanity. Typical of the enlisted men in the *U-bootwaffe*, Krause had not been groomed in Nazi ideology, and had no known sentiments of that kind prior to his technical training. It seemed to be more of a personality disintegration, perhaps together with a desperate search for a new identity.

The message from the Commander was that they would have a talk with him and hopefully reign in his personal eccentricities. Failing that he could be put in restraints. However, his stern torpedoes might be needed at some point on their long trip home. Soldier could not argue with that, but still Krause needed to know there were boundaries. All soldiers needed that. Soldier cast another glance at the polished steel wall mirror in the wardroom and presently he could see Krause coming up behind him in the passageway. Krause slowed and turned sideways to slide past Soldier. Suddenly all of the wind went out of his body and he fell to his knees. Everything was dark and swirly, and there were stars. Krause was breathing rapidly now, feeling the panic. He looked up and saw Soldier's face staring down at him. After a minute passed Soldier offered him his hand and pulled him to his feet. Then he winked and walked away while Krause swayed and moaned, struggling to stay up.

* * *

Corporal Peterson and Special Constable Kidlapik held on to the *qamutiiq* as it glided down the gradual slope from the land to the sea ice on Gifford Fiord. The dogs ran easily ahead, but alert to the whip and with the instinctive awareness that the following sled could overtake them. The Mounties managed to get the dogs stopped just before saltwater where there was some barrier ice from the tidal action in the fiord. Ice fog was rising from the cracks and leads where the tide persisted in lifting the ice and grating it against the shore.

Peterson pulled down his fur-trimmed hood and turned to Kidlapik. "We can stay here for the night and head toward the mouth of the fiord in the morning. We'll see how much ice there is further out to get across to the mainland, or else work around this side to Agu Bay on the land-fast ice. That would be quicker and easier than over the hills."

Peterson observed some good-sized snowdrifts on the land, which offered prospects of a good camping spot. Kidlapik was already jabbing his bone probe into the snow, looking for the right consistency for their *iglu*. He nodded for the Corporal to come over and get started.

Peterson retrieved the snow knife from the *qamutiiq* and outlined a circle in the snow. He began cutting snow blocks from inside the circle and placing them along the *iglu*'s circumference, trimming them so they canted inwards, and leaving an opening for the door. Then he took his snow knife and, starting at the bottom of one side of the entrance, walked around the circle cutting through the snow until he reached the top of the snow block on the other side of the opening. On this foundation, the next row of blocks was laid with the correct inward cant and with an ascending spiral from the base of the *iglu* to the top, where the last snow block would be whittled and set to complete the construction, while keeping it erect and strong. Then a small ventilation hole in the roof and a tunnel entrance to finish things up . . . A well-built *iglu* could support the weight of a man standing on it, but Peterson opted to forgo this opportunity.

Kidlapik looked up at the *iglu* from his task of staking out the dogs on the ice, out of fighting distance with each other, and feeding them. And getting some tea going on the stove behind a windbreak made of snow blocks . . . He had also been watching surreptitiously how the *iglu* was coming together, and overall it was a satisfactory job. He was pleased that this *qallunaaq* had come a long way in understanding the ways of the Inuit, the people. The Corporal before this one had not made the same effort to adapt to life in the north. That one was quite happy to sit in the RCMP detachment post and play cards and drink rum in the evening with the HBC post manager, rarely venturing out on extended patrols to learn more about the land and the Inuit. This new one, Corporal Bob, liked to get out on the land with the dogs and to hunt and fish and learn some of his language. He did not complain that there was precious little real police work up here. Kidlapik knew his job was to assist the Corporal in his job of representing the government in Ottawa, and this meant helping him communicate with the Inuit and to travel on this frozen landscape that was previously so foreign to him. And to keep him alive while he learned some land and survival skills . . .

Corporal Peterson got out his wallet and removed the crinkled picture of his girl, Colleene. He felt pride that this spunky blond pixie was in the manly business of selling Caterpillar bulldozers and heavy equipment in her home province of British Columbia. They were both looking forward to his next furlough, which would be the following year when the Nascopie arrived at Pond Inlet. Colleene would need a whole bunch of bulldozers to keep him at bay when he saw her again, if in fact she would want to keep him at bay. She was a nice respectable girl from a close-knit family of good standing in the community. On the other hand, she was a believer in proper maintenance.

* * *

It was slow going as U-807 *Tulugaq* headed north following the pathway of the lead. The water was hardly the water they knew. It was more of a gel, seawater ice in the making, and the engines seemed to be straining to give them just eight knots. The bow wave from the boat did not produce its normal white-capped turbulence. Rather, it seemed as though a membrane were stretched across the surface of the water allowing only the most rounded and gradual undulations. The broad lead through the ice field was still almost half a kilometer wide and they followed it to a point just off the mouth of Gifford Fiord. The fiord itself appeared to be mostly frozen over with some thickness of new ice, no doubt from being out of the immediate path of the current coming down through the northern strait and perhaps from lower salinity with the incoming river flow. *Tulugaq* was eased up to the edge of the sea ice in a holding position for now.

Hansen looked over at Soldier. "If the weather holds we can put you and the Eskimos with that damned dog onto the ice to do a quick reconnaissance to the west. If Joanasie is right, there should be an ice lake not all that far from here that stays open all year. If we can get there we can maybe hop-scotch over to the other side and get down to Igloolik along the shore if it's not frozen over there yet."

Soldier did not look hopeful but he launched into his crude translation to Joanasie and Sila. They were intent on breathing in the crisp Arctic air and passing a pair of binoculars back and forth between themselves, sharing their views with each other as they scanned up the fiord and to the north and west.

"Joanasie says there is some high country at the mouth of the fiord where we can get a bird's-eye view of the ice to the west. And there are usually caribou in the valleys. He suggests we may be able to bring back some meat at the same time as having a look."

"If the weather holds . . . " prompted Hansen.

"Yes, if the weather holds. But Joanasie says we can be back inside two days if we travel fast and pick up the cached meat on our return leg."

The Commander hesitated, not at all sure of how long they could hold this position if the water froze over in the lead or if the wind started to close it up. An overnight trek was risky.

"Two days then. Go now. Take flares."

Shortly Sila was unlashing the small *qamutiiq* from the wooden decking, harnessing the dog, and receiving caribou skins and winter clothing through the opened hatch. Soldier knew the dog would help pull the sled while also giving warning of bears, and hopefully alert them of any snowed-over open water in front of them. Within the hour the commando and the two Eskimos were bundled up in fur and trudging away from the boat toward land. Soldier looked at the angle of the sun in the sky and then at his watch. He tried to remember the lines of that poem " . . . and miles to go before I sleep."

Hansen watched until the figures were just dots on the white seascape. If there was any light at all in the sky, and if the weather held, that scouting party would not stop.

* * *

The three trekkers made short work of the hunting part of their expedition. Soldier quickly felled four caribou. The slope to the sea ice made it easy to slide the carcasses, antlered heads removed, down to the shore. In a few minutes they had quartered the animals and bundled the meat, hoping they could get back before the scavengers arrived. At least the sea ice here was mostly smooth, without pressure ridges, to ease the chore of pulling the sled back to the boat.

Joanasie looked up at the sky. "*Sila Piujunniisijuq.*" The weather may be turning against us. Already snow was blowing around them at ground level as they travelled along the shoreline toward some higher country. There was not enough drifted snow on the sea ice to make an *iglu*, though in a pinch they could huddle in their winter clothing under caribou skins and behind the upturned sled. Blowing snow was still a problem though. Visibility was important if they were going to locate a lead for the *Tulugaq*. The boat needed open water now, two days from now might be too late! At this time of year one could not be sure how far the open water would extend from the relatively stable location of the polynya. At its surface there was a constant interaction between air temperature, current strength, and wind. Salinity was a factor, as was snow cover with its insulating effect.

Sila had no problem keeping up with the men, so far anyway. They were taking most of the weight of the sled. The new life in her belly had started just one month ago and so far it was not much of a physical burden. Even so, the little one was never far from her mind. She wondered if a boy or a girl was growing in her, and if the baby would look something like Soldier. She tried to imagine what such a child would look like. Sila had heard of

Inuit women in camps where whalers visited, how some of these women had children from the American whalers. Or the *Siikatsi*, the Scottish whalers or Company men . . . The mixed children were not always accepted by the Inuit in the same way as one of their own. She hoped that the child would prove himself by being a good hunter. Or, if a daughter, by being a good seamstress and competent in tending the seal oil lamp to cook and keep her family warm. For now, Sila was following in Soldier's tracks but, in her wandering visions of possible futures, she was not always sure if Soldier was there with her.

34

October 1: Gifford Fiord, Baffin Island

Commander Hansen pulled up the wolf-trimmed hood on his parka and searched through the binoculars again. Too dark now to see anything, and no moon or aurora borealis tonight to light things up. There was some blowing snow on the ice but he was thankful there was no new snowfall, at least not yet. The wind was gaining strength from the west and he was concerned that their lead in the ice could narrow. If things kept up he might have to back up the boat to where the lead was wider. He did not want to do anything that would make it more difficult to retrieve Soldier and the Eskimos, but he would do what he had to do to safeguard the boat and crew. All they needed now was a blizzard to complicate things by making it difficult for the scouting party to find their way back. Just then he felt the first bite of snowflakes striking the exposed part of his face.

* * *

Petty Officer Winkler was happy to be reunited with the whales in the open water. There were pods of belugas and pods of narwhal, the sea unicorns. Mercifully there were no killer whales. He felt blessed that he could listen at leisure to the whale's amazing repertoire of grunts and squeaks and whistles and clicks. When his headphones told him the whales were very close to the boat he asked the Commander for permission to go above to watch the mammals. Request granted. The whales came near the boat again, alternately beluga and narwhal. The narwhal fascinated him the most and he was intrigued as they came straight up through the slush ice, making a hole and raising their heads with tusks pointed at the sky, for half a minute at a time while they breathed and made their subtle observations. Winkler was sure the whales were looking directly at the boat sometimes, even directly at him . . . personally. It was unnerving but strangely gratifying.

* * *

Joanasie and SIla found some drifted snow along the frozen shore that would have to do for a small *iglu*. They made short work of it. Soldier helped by slicing edges off the snow blocks with a snow knife and chinking the cracks. The dog burrowed into the snow as best it could and soon it was just another white hummock. The blizzard was picking up by the time the three humans crawled through the tight entranceway and closed the opening with a snow block. Once inside they beat the snow off their outer clothing. Sila felt at a loss not having her faithful soapstone lamp for heating and cooking. They would have no heat other than from some large candles they had brought from the boat, and from their own body heat. Their *iglu* was snug and they had a thick bed of caribou skins. Outside the *iglu* it was perhaps fifteen degrees below freezing. Inside the *iglu* it was soon warm enough to shed their outermost garments.

"How long will the blizzard go on?" queried Soldier.

"*Aamai.*" Joanasie held up fingers for first one day, then two days. A little shrug . . . Who could predict such a thing?

Sila looked at Soldier. She was going to be *iglu*-bound with this man for one or two days, and she was going to make the best of it. She would keep him warm, soapstone lamp or no soapstone lamp. She had brought some choice cuts of caribou meat along with some white back fat, frozen now from their trek. The *quaq* would be delicious when sliced thin with her *ulu*. And she would feed Soldier like a baby. Already Joanasie was making funny faces at her when Soldier was not looking, but she knew her brother would keep his back to them through the long night as the wind wailed outside.

* * *

Commander Hansen was frustrated. He gesticulated wildly to Chief. "Where the hell are they? We can't see anything in this blizzard even with the searchlights on, but we have to assume that this west wind is shrinking our lead here. We may have to move the boat back out. And if we do that we might lose them."

"We will have a little daylight in a few hours. Let's hope the blizzard lets up some by then. They have the dog's good nose, and some flares too."

"You know, Chief, most likely we won't get any good information from them. Unless they spotted signs of open water before the blizzard struck."

"And of course the question remains as to how do we get to another ice lake from here?"

No comment from the Commander, who appeared to be deep in thought.

"Karl, we have been damned lucky so far with this under-ice navigation. We have pushed our luck. Before we had a larger target almost within visible range and a solid bearing. Next time, perhaps a smaller target and a shaky bearing at best."

Hansen looked up at Chief. "Agreed, but I think it should still be a larger expanse of water this early in the winter. We will find it, then we can make our way south."

"Are you trying to get your name into the history books as a modern-day Arctic explorer? Or perhaps just beat Kapitan Franke's long under-ice dive in Cabot Strait?" Chief looked pensive. "A lot of risk for our young crew."

"Hansen rocked forward and put his head in his hands. "I think about our young crew every hour of every day. My inclination is to put this question of another dive to the men for a vote, but I think you would agree that such would only clash with our *U-bootwaffe* culture, and end up breeding new anxieties. The men need resolute leadership."

Chief nodded. "Yes, you have indeed learned that. And at this point the only other option to our present course could be Soldier's notion of leaving the boat right here and walking away from it across spotty ice. A shitty alternative for a seaman . . . "

* * *

Soldier and Joanasie raced up the hill above the point where they had cached the caribou meat. Sila stayed below to pack up the sled and feed the dog. The blizzard was spent, the air was crisp and cold, the sky was blue and the visibility was unlimited. Up and up she saw the two figures run, slipping and falling occasionally but surprisingly soon they stood on a ridge more than 200 meters above sea level. She could see them standing motionless, apparently looking west over the ice through their binoculars.

Sila's spirits were running high. She had had Soldier pinned down in close contact for two days while the blizzard raged outside their snug *iglu*. This man was normally on the move, yet he actually seemed to enjoy the forced rest. And anyway it was hardly about rest. She watched her brother and Soldier coming back down to the sea ice, cupping her mouth and shouting at them a few times when they seemed to take foolish risks in sliding and jumping and rolling down the steep descent. Soon she could hear them laughing as she hitched up the dog to the sled and prepared the other traces for themselves.

"*Atii*, Let's go," Soldier said, still breathing hard and beating snow off his caribou clothing. "We have to get back to the boat, if it is still there." Everything looked different with fresh snow on the ice, snow that was drifted into myriad shapes and contours. It was starkly beautiful. But they would have to be focused on the possibility of thin ice lurking under the snow, which is both an excellent insulator and a dangerous mask. Hopefully the dog would be alert to that.

* * *

Commander Hansen spied them first, again just small dots against a huge white canvas. The dots were moving toward them. Presumably they would be visible to the dots too, though the boat's white tower probably resembled an upright slab of pressure ice more than a German U-boat. Normally that was good. Thankfully they had not had to back up the boat too far into the wider section of the lead. The dots were getting larger fast. They must be jogging!

Soldier and the two Eskimos looked to be in excellent condition, rosy cheeks and all with just a touch of frostbite on their noses despite their time on the ice. And in good spirits too! Chief looked at the Commander and raised his eyebrows characteristically, shaking his head as if to say something like "The lord looks after fools and children . . . "

The men were happy to see the caribou meat coming down to Cookie. They were getting tired of boiled seal and walrus meat. A good many of the men had the shits, probably from the walrus meat, and the Commander was thankful that the men could relieve themselves off the aft deck onto the ice instead of lining up at the two abused toilets below. The Chief was very wary about even using the toilets at all given the maintenance issues on an over-extended mission. At least one U-boat, albeit submerged, had sunk after a toilet was flushed without following the safety protocols, and compressed air blew out the contents through an external valve in the pressure hull, which valve then failed to shut properly . . .

Hansen and Chief lost no time in shepherding Soldier and the Eskimos to the officers' table to debrief them on their scouting mission, while putting down copious amounts of tea and bannock. What had they seen besides driving snow?

Soldier conversed briefly with Joanasie then turned to the Commander. "This morning, when we climbed up the high land at the mouth of the fiord, the visibility was excellent."

"Yes, yes?"

"We could see the haze over the open water running north-south for at least 20 kilometers. '*Patuttuq*' Joanasie said. We also saw a reflection of open water from some low clouds. Judging from our straight-line trek back to this boat, we estimate the distance to the haze to be about 20 to 30 kilometers from here."

"Twice as far as last time!" Hansen and Chief got busy on the chart table. Meanwhile Soldier and Joanasie were snacking on frozen arctic char sliced with Sila's ever-sharp *ulu*. Soldier winked at Sila as she offered him another slice. He was developing quite a liking for *quaq*, the frozen fish and caribou at least. Seal and walrus, however, had to be cooked for him to keep it down. After a few minutes of silence Hansen sighed and looked up from the chart table. "A relatively long dive and a possibly narrow target. A bad combination! Four hours or more under the ice, possibly with a current to mess with our dead reckoning." He paused. "At least we should have some decent operating depths here, so slamming into a shoal would not be one of our problems."

Chief nodded. "We are reasonably confident that the current moving through the northern strait is north-south there, and probably as much as a few knots, so we can aim for the northern end of the lead." He looked at Soldier and Joanasie, rather severely. "If your estimates are accurate . . . "

"There are risks but we have to take them," concluded the Commander. "But it's a long dive and the hard part again is knowing when we are again under open water, which will probably be obscured and rendering our periscope practically useless as usual. In any case we will time our departure from here with maximum daylight at our destination.

"We don't want to miss our stop," added Chief. "I've had enough of this knocking on heaven's door for a lifetime."

35

October 2: South of Fury and Hecla Strait

Petty Officer Winkler was in a distant place as he clutched the headphones to his boyish head. He was one of the few crewmembers still not sporting a beard. With all other feelers to their external world disrupted, only Winkler's reach into the ether could help make sense of their progress through this dark and forbidding underwater environment. Besides the readings on the depth gauges, there was precious little other useful information to be processed. They were making five knots at a dive depth of 20 meters according to the manometer. The headphones were bringing him ice noises, cracking and grinding sounds, the effects of tide and current. And he could hear beluga and narwhal noises from their departure point and some even much closer, under the ice. Good, they could keep him company. Funny how he had tuned out the noise of the electric motors and propellers to the point he would have to actively switch them back on when ready, and welcome them back into his cranial spaces.

* * *

With the periscope's limited utility and without comprehensive charts and without effective sonar beamed upwards from the hull, navigation was pretty much a matter of crude calculation interspersed with raw guesswork. It was difficult to determine accurately how much clearance there was between the boat and the ice platform above. So the operative word was "enough". If there was any light filtering through open water they would have to be close enough to detect it, yet far enough to avoid smacking into ice. It was not only dangerous but nerve-racking being sandwiched between danger from above and danger from below. Chief cursed again that he was driving a blind submersible and not a true submarine designed for such operations. He was a wreck after two hours of trying to keep the boat trimmed at a consistent shallow depth and on a steady bearing allowing for a hypothetical value in the current streaming south through Fury and Hecla Strait. Hansen brought Chief more tea and watched as Chief issued commands to the men operating the hydroplanes and rudder. The Commander had taken the lead in navigation duties in the absence of the navigation officer, but Chief assisted very competently in that function as well. Once again Hansen thanked his lucky stars for having Chief, a man who was attuned to every mechanical pulse on the boat. Between this man and his well-tutored men on the steering controls, and of course the soundman Winkler, the boat was in good hands. Cool and methodical . . . professionals. But would that be enough?

The Commander and Chief conferred again over the calculations on the navigation table. "We are about to enter the region of a possible open water ceiling," Chief announced. "If our assumptions and calculations are correct . . . "

"Hmm, I note your use of that irritating 'possible' word. Slow to three knots and take her up five meters and we'll have a look through the scope. Failing that we'll try a probe." They had done this before and in spite of everything else there was definite benefit in a learning curve, and in a routine to still their beating hearts. The periscope was not picking up any light from the surface. And, with the current running for an inestimable distance under pack ice backed up in the strait, the water temperature readings would be ambiguous at best. *Scheisse*!

Plan B was next. First drop the boat 30 meters and raise the bow. Then the delicate juggling act required for a slow controlled rise to the surface. Partial blowing of ballast from mid-ships and pumping of water from the bow trim tank to stern trim tank, massaging hydroplanes, manipulating power to the electric motors, watching the *Papenberger* tube . . . Then waiting for the controlled collision and a call for damage reports . . . Or, if the gods smiled on them, a continuation of upward momentum as the front end of the boat rose above open water, until buoyancy dynamics and gravity dropped the bow back down to the surface. Yes, they had done this before and survived. Throughout the boat, tense and staring mortals hung on to pipes and ladders as the boat continued to rise vertically at this unnatural angle of 20 degrees. All hearts were stopped, lives on hold, as they waited for possible impact.

A gut-wrenching impact came as the bow met an unyielding mass of ice and was deflected downwards. "*Fluten! Fluten!* Damage reports!" It was obvious that they had not only missed the open water but also the thinner ice often bordering it.

The force of the impact was less than on that earlier surfacing encounter in Hudson Strait, but damage to the bow, though uncertain, was cumulative. Damage reports began to be relayed to the anxious Commander. No breaches, no major ruptures, no systems failures.

Shaken, the Chief focused on getting the boat back to a horizontal trim and to its previous heading and dive depth. Twenty minutes later, crew steeled themselves as the boat rose in the water column in another surfacing attempt. Again, though the rise was slowed to one meter per minute, the upward inertia of the boat's hull was spent against unyielding ice.

"*Fluten! Fluten!* Damage reports!" Again there were no breaches to the pressure hull but certainly more damage to the bow. And beyond that, shattered nerves and fallen hopes.

Commander Hansen looked spent. "Chief, we are still of this world but I fear if we do not make it up next time, things may take a bad turn for us." Hansen dropped his head into his hands. "I don't know what order to give. Do we keep going ahead, or go back on the premise we overshot the ice lake, the one Soldier says he observed? In my mind's eye all I see now is a huge white expanse of solid ice up there, holding us under." Hansen turned to a silent Chief and Soldier, crowded into the control room with him. "We have electric power for two more hours. We have to find a way out of this."

Men returned to their bunks and prayed, some cried. Joanasie and Sila faced each other on a bunk and held hands, eyes closed.

* * *

Petty Officer Winkler was petrified. But the sure way he had found to soothe himself was to listen to the whales. They were here in his headphones even now. He had learned the distinctly different sounds they made, the amazing range of their repertoire, and could even comprehend the conditions and the purposes of their sounds. Some sounds were about navigation, and some presumably about herding or guiding. Some seemed to be about basic communications including relative position of the sender, signals pertaining to danger or food availability. Other sounds smacked of being more social in nature, all about group dynamics. As he listened, eyes closed and breathing controlled, the tempo of the whale noise picked up. The sounds he heard were sounds of distress, panic, pain. Concentrated sounds, a whole orchestra of suffering, multiple whales in one location . . . He was agitated now that the sounds he was hearing were not soothing but upsetting. He tore off the headphones to stop the stimulus, his brain suddenly detached from his sensors. Then he sorted through the nuances of this unusual reception, sifted through the possibilities, let the possibilities speak to him. He put the headphones back on. Then he jumped to his feet.

"Commander!" he blurted. "I can hear whales, concentrated, all together. Making distress sounds. I have not heard this before. The closest thing was when the killer whales were chasing the narwhal."

Hansen stared harshly at Winkler, struggling to comprehend his words. "Even if you do hear the whales, and even if they are in some sort of distress, what does this mean to us? We have enough already to think about."

Winkler was surprised that the significance of his words was not clear. "Well, it means that the whales are obviously on the surface since the principal location of their sounds does not change. There is some dispersion of sounds, but there is a fixed node, which has to be at the surface. And that means that I can use the whales as a beacon. I can listen to them and give you steering directions so we can join them."

All eyes were on Petty Officer Winkler but nobody spoke. He felt a rush of self-importance knowing that the fate of the boat was once again in his hands. What he had to do here could even eclipse his guiding role in surviving that skirmish with the British submarine in the North Sea.

* * *

It was alchemy more than science, Winkler offering only minimal verbal input to the Commander. But a lot of hand signals as in port, starboard, easy, steady, slow, up . . . Hansen showed frustration but held his tongue when Winkler signaled repeatedly to orient the boat in particular attitudes to optimize the input of the hydrophone array positioned on the boat's skin. Almost an hour later Winkler raised his hand and beckoned the Commander to listen on his headphones. His face showed awe as he unconsciously looked upwards. Winkler smiled. "We have arrived!"

Hansen ordered the same bow-up surface protocol, taking all precautions to avoid another abrupt meeting of steel and ice. All hands held on and even atheists prayed as the boat slowly rose in the water column. This time, this miraculous time, the bow displaced slush and broken ice and continued skyward for perhaps five meters before coming down heavily. There was a jolt as the bow came down and broke up some harder ice at the edge of the ice lake. Then silence. Hansen routinely called for damage reports but was already bundled up and climbing upward toward the tower. Soldier and Chief were right behind, and after them Joanasie and Sila.

Nobody spoke. It took a few minutes to fathom what they were seeing. Carnage! The open water was red, as was the ice and snow ten meters back all around the circumference of this small elliptical lake in the ice. The boat was crossways in the open water and at one end their surfacing had served to make the opening a little bit larger. In the main body of the lake were numerous surfaced narwhal and beluga whales, and on the edge of the ice were numerous polar bears stalking and attacking them. The onlookers were transfixed on the scene as they watched the whales circling in the hole, steam rising in the frigid still air from their accelerated breathing after having been submerged for twenty minutes or more to avoid the danger. Or, more accurately, postpone the danger. As whales circled the lake at the edge of the ice, polar bears reached out and struck with powerful arms and razor-sharp extended claws at the breathing holes of the whales. Obviously this was weakening them as their respiratory systems began to shut down. The polar bears would then reach out and claw huge pieces of tissue from the whales' bodies, accelerating their demise. Two large polar bears cooperated in combining their awesome strength to pull an entire wounded five-meter beluga up onto the ice. Other bears moved in to share in the feasting. Some were tolerated and others were chased off to fend for themselves. There were a number of whale carcasses on the ice, and more dying whales still in the water. All the bears, eight of them ranging from two-year-olds to mature and scarred males, some measuring over three meters when they stood up to observe their prey or the boat, were covered in blood and gore. After the initial startle reaction when the boat first surfaced, the bears seemed to become oblivious to its presence in their midst. In fact, they were starving and focused on filling their bellies. They had been hungry for much of the summer as it had been difficult for them to catch seals in the open water season, and walrus are a formidable opponent. A diet of geese eggs was good but that source was long gone now too. And so these ice lake polynyas were an Arctic oasis to attract starving bears, and a potential trap for marine mammals needing to breathe air.

When Winkler came up top he was devastated. It seemed to him that the bears would kill all the whales. It was just a matter of time. More bears could be seen approaching to join in the feast from all points on the compass. Single males and females with cubs arrived, the latter holding back from the unpredictable males. The harvest looked good, however, and there was less of the usual scrapping over the kill. He watched the whales swimming, others diving and surfacing. Intentional or not, Winkler thought, their collective turbulence no doubt served to work with the current to keep the polynya open longer in a cold snap. Winkler looked up and saw the Commander and Soldier watching him.

"Shoot the bears!" Winkler said through clenched teeth.

Hansen shrugged. "Interfere with Mother Nature? The bears are feeding, trying to survive just like we are."

"The whales are dying a slow painful death, and the bears are torturing them, eating them alive. Shoot them!"

"We might have to co-exist in this pool of nature for a while. The whales are here only because they have not found other open water nearby. And the bears are here for the whales."

"All the more reason to shoot the bears. The whales saved our hides and they need us now. After the bears gorge themselves on the whales, the ones that don't sink before they can pull them up, they will come after us."

Joanasie and Sila were spellbound watching the bears and the whales. You had to be in the tower of a U-boat in a polynya to fully comprehend a scene like this. Soldier translated for them Winkler's conviction that the bears should be shot. "What do you think, should we shoot them?" queried Soldier.

Sila and Joanasie looked out at the bears, then spoke through Soldier. "Maybe some shots over their heads will scare them off." But they hardly looked convinced of that prospect.

Just then a large male polar bear, covered in blood and gore, clambered up onto the foredeck of the boat, heading single-mindedly toward the watching men. Soldier dropped the bear with two shots, then shifted his aim and fired methodically into the bears scattered around the little red lake in the ice. When he was done firing his assault rifle three more of the more aggressive alpha bears were down, and the others were in retreat. Soldier felt queasy about adding to the carnage, but he knew that their own survival came first.

Soldier turned to the Commander. "This will settle things for now, but every hungry polar bear in 500 square kilometers is headed to the smorgasbord here."

Joanasie and Sila were skinning out their fourth bear, while Soldier covered them from the tower. Three large bear skins, hair side up, surrounded the Inuit on relatively clean patches of snow. Select cuts of meat were accumulating in another two piles. Cookie had men hustling the bear meat and some salvaged whale cuts into the boat. Soldier saw Sila plunge her hands into the steaming innards of a bear to warm her freezing hands. She was clad in seal-skin *atigi* and pants, well bloodied from working too fast. No doubt she looked and smelled a lot like a seal. A newly arrived bear began stalking her, still 150 meters out. Soldier placed a bullet a meter in front of it and sprayed it with fragmented ice, enough to drive it back in the other direction. It was getting dark and it was clear that the security task would become more complicated soon. The diesels were running alternately and the men would be safe behind closed steel hatches, but still there would have to be a perimeter around the boat or it wouldn't be safe to open the hatches again. The crew coming up through the hatches would look pretty much like long skinny seals rising in their breathing holes in the ice . . . Chief supervised two men who were busy rigging more searchlights. When the two bear skinners came back onto the boat with their bounty he breathed a sigh of relief. When he asked about using the dog as part of their security set-up, to at least give warning if the bears approached, Joanasie replied that this would only attract bears looking for a dietary change. If the dog was chained it would have no chance, just as Anaanattiaq's secured dogs at their camp had had no chance when attacked by wolves.

Hansen waited till everyone had a good hot meal of bear meat. He watched Sila slicing slabs of *maktaaq*, the inch-thick layer of skin from the beluga, into edible portions for Joanasie and herself. Soldier accepted some as well. Winkler declined, though he seemed to enjoy wolfing down the bear meat. After dinner Hansen took Chief and Soldier back up top for a conference. A few other men were up as well, a number of them on bear-watch and some rotating for a smoke. The Commander cautioned Chief and Soldier to talk quietly.

Hansen started off. "Even without this welcoming committee of starving bears we would still have to eventually dive the boat again, west toward the Melville coast for more open water. Joanasie says the currents tend to keep the water open along there, between the pack ice and land-fast ice."

No comment. Hansen looked at each of the men, prompting them.

Soldier spoke. "I see there is still no option presented of our leaving the boat. Well, we have made it this far so I don't see why we can't make one more dive to the west. If we can't surface, then maybe we can make it back here."

Chief looked at Soldier. "Don't count on making it back here, Helmut. That's another long shot, I'm afraid."

Silence again.

Hansen stretched. "All right, I want you to feel out the men on their ability to withstand another dive, another blind dive under the ice. The men have been most resilient but I fear some of them may be near the breaking point."

36

October 4: Meanwhile at the Polynya

Krause was pissed! He had overheard the Commander and his cohorts planning a dive to the west. They should be heading north, where there was obviously more open water to show them the way. He would put an end to this nonsense. And he was tired of the disdainful looks being cast his way. He passed the Commander's cubicle regularly on his rounds, but this time he made a quick entry. In a minute he found what he was looking for. The big Mauser pistol, the one Hansen brought back from Big Lake and that Soldier had popped the bear with, the one that Hansen only wore when up top . . . Krause hefted it and checked it for bullets. It was unwieldy as hell, but it was fully loaded! Good. He knew all the other arms, except Soldier's sidearm, were under lock and key but he had guessed right about this one. He felt no fear, only icy resolve. He padded forward where the Commander was huddled over a mess table with Soldier and Chief, a tight little grouping as he wanted it. He nodded at them as he squeezed by, as though to continue up the passageway toward the bow. Abruptly he stepped behind the Commander, pulled the gun from under his sweater in one swift motion and pressed the muzzle against the back of his head. Soldier instinctively went for his sidearm. Krause dared him with his eyes as he tightened his finger on the trigger. Soldier raised his arms and the torpedo man held out his hand for his sidearm. Satisfied he now had the upper hand, Krause looked at the three men individually and announced, "Change of plans. We are going north! Now!"

Joanasie continued to watch all this unfold, while doing his best to keep calm. He had stiffened when he caught a glimpse of Krause through his closed curtain as the *anak* departed the aft torpedo room and moved forward. While it's true he stiffened every time he saw this vile man, this time he had sensed something different, something stronger. Perhaps it was the vacant look that his face was wearing instead of the habitual sneer. Curious, he followed Krause stealthily as he moved forward, through the engine room and control room. He kept himself out of sight as he watched Krause slip into the Commander's quarters and come out with something wrapped in a sweater. He froze when he saw Krause walk behind Hansen and press the big pistol to his head. Then he saw Soldier hand over his own gun. Joanasie rocked back on his heels, eyes closed, his body turned to stone. What to do? He could not consult with his sister as she was up in the bow torpedo room fitting a new muzzle to the dog. He had to do something! He ducked into the area where the weapons were secured, and pulled out a seal-skin wrapped bundle wedged in between two lengths of conduit. From that bundle he quickly removed his bow and quiver of arrows. He selected an arrow and notched it, taking up some of the tension on the drawstring, feeling the heft. He peered forward from his cover and waited.

Hansen was thinking fast, so was Soldier. They had to stop this quickly somehow. Soldier looked furtively over his shoulder toward the forward torpedo room, and then again, hoping to arouse suspicion. Krause saw the glances, knowing there were loyal crew, lackeys, in the bow. Possibly also some crude weapons such as knives and axes . . . The Mauser was still trained on the Commander as Krause cast a glance over his shoulder. *Thunk!* Krause looked down in genuine surprise to see the arrow shaft protruding from his belly. Then he screamed in pain, somehow keeping his gun on Hansen. Krause got a glimpse of Joanasie notching another arrow and fired at him just as the Eskimo backed out of sight again. Damn, he should have thought about those heathens. He clutched his belly and fingered the shaft of the embedded arrow. This would mess up his plans, but he would still get the boat headed north. There would soon be talented Aryan doctors doting on him, if he could just hang on that long. He heard something behind him, something like the pitter-patter of little feet when his brother and sister-in-law brought their little brat to Hamburg for a visit. He glanced up and saw the bounding Eskimo dog, big as a wolf and just becoming airborne, muzzle gone from its jaws . . . *Scheisse*! He swung the pistol's muzzle toward the new target. Only one shot off, then the impact of the dog sent him sprawling. Suddenly a grotesque fur-clad entity was pushing his head down to the floor, twisting and driving the arrow further into his stomach. He saw a gleaming crescent-shaped instrument in the right hand of the devilish figure before him. It seemed somehow that he was a detached spectator as the *ulu* sliced into his throat.

Soldier had watched this entire performance and basked in utmost satisfaction that Joanasie and Sila had so efficiently transformed the deranged torpedo mechanic into polar bear food. Life can be harsh in the Arctic, he mused.

* * *

Commander Hansen was up top with Chief and Soldier through most of the shortening daylight hours, eyes scanning the horizon. Looking for something different, something meaningful. Maybe new alternatives. The men never tired of watching the whales swimming around their little lake. There were still at least ten of them in spite of their losses to the bears. Hansen realized that most of the whales would have been underwater during the attacks, only surfacing when their need for air overwhelmed their need for safety. The whales, perhaps as many as a hundred of them in total, were in constant motion. In spite of this, their lake in the ice was shrinking and it was now less than half the size it was when the boat first surfaced. The temperature had plummeted and the wind dropped to almost nil. A few new bears had entered the scene but were holding back for the most part, though there was another carcass of a more adventurous one that was not skinned out yet. As for Krause, there was nothing left of him just ten minutes after the bears found the naked new offering on the ice. The boat's crew enjoyed watching the feast, as did Joanasie and Sila.

Hansen resolved they would have to leave soon. They couldn't stay in this hole in the ice forever . . . The feelers sent out to the men came back as a nod to do another dive to the west, holding on to the possibility of there still being a route south. Some of the men saw salvation in making it back as far as Igloolik, some even held out the hope of making it back to Hudson Strait. Hansen had no such hope, but he had no wish to scuttle his boat in this patch of open water. He would get the men to Igloolik. They would move into the trading post there and keep warm while waiting for the RCMP patrol to arrive. When he woke up this morning that is what he knew he had to do. Then he would surrender his crew and the boat and they would wait out the end of this war, which could not be far off now.

* * *

Soldier was alone with Joanasie and Sila, almost whispering. They could see he was feeling strain, not his usual confident and friendly self. "You don't have to do this. You can get off the boat and walk across the ice to the coast and make your way back to your camp in just a few days. I'm sorry you've lost your lead dog, but he died a hero. Take the small sled and some gear and food and just get off this boat. Take a rifle."

"You walk with us then," Sila pleaded with Soldier.

"That's not possible. My place is here on the boat. But soon this will all be over." Soldier looked at Sila, a faraway look in his eyes.

Faraway, but loving. Sila saw this and her heart swelled. She squeezed his hand and whispered, "Soon we will have a little one." She saw Soldier's eyes mist over, and she was not certain if it was from happiness or something else. She squeezed again. She loved this man but it was so difficult to understand him, to know him to his core.

The caribou meat and the arctic char were all gone, so Cookie made up a meal of polar bear meat and walrus meat along with some of the whale *maktaaq* snatched from the bears. The meat was necessary to maintain their strength and vigour. The *maktaaq*, high in Vitamin C, would help prevent scurvy. But there was that side effect with which the boat's two hard-pressed toilets could not cope. Shortly after the meal, a number of men hopped onto the ice alongside the boat. Facing the boat and in almost a straight line with regular spacing between them, the men unabashedly dropped their trousers to relieve themselves. The Quartermaster guarded them with a rifle.

"*Paliisikkut mittimataliingmi aggisijut!*" Joanasie exclaimed. He pointed at a dot to the northeast as he passed the binoculars to Hansen.

Soldier translated. "Ah yes, the Royal Canadian Mounted Police . . . Mounties . . . arriving from Pond Inlet. On patrol and heading to Igloolik, as expected this time of year."

Commander Hansen nodded. He had decided to stay another day while Lutz did more maintenance on the diesel engines though that hardly seemed a priority now with the need for underwater propulsion. His order to dive was orderly, almost casual, this time without the usual shouting and slamming of hatches. The approaching dog team was still a long ways off and had not stopped, which could have indicated the drivers had spotted the white tower of the boat and wanted to take a better look with binoculars. The squatting men on the ice quickly finished up their business and hopped back on the boat, fastening their pants as they went.

Commander Hansen followed Soldier through the tower hatch and secured it behind him. When the boat started to sink in their little lake in the ice, the water not so red anymore but gradually returning to black, the narwhal stopped swimming and gathered at the other end with their gaze and their tusks facing the boat. They watched the boat's conning tower drop and gradually disappear. Then it was still and quiet again. The whales continued to swim in smaller and smaller circles.

37

October 6:The Mounties stop at the
Polynya then depart for Igloolik

Corporal Peterson and Constable Kidlapik had seen the haze over
the ice lake from ten miles out. Maybe there were some Agu Bay
people hunting there. As they got closer, Kidlapik thought he
could make out something large and white standing upright in
the ice lake, like a slab of ice. But when the ice haze cleared again
and the *qamutiiq* runners had found smoother passage to enable
him to take another good look, he couldn't see anything . . . He
knew that the dazzling white of the snow and the ice haze can
play tricks on the eyes.

There were no Inuit hunting at the open water, but there
were whales in the ice lake and some bears in the near distance.
Kidlapik had heard of such things happening occasionally in this
area. The Mounties watched as whales surfaced for air, sometimes
two and even three of them raising their heads together. After
a few minutes they would dive and moments later another two
or three would arrive, apparently different animals. Amazing,
Peterson thought. Such cooperation for survival, group survival

and individual survival intertwined. He glanced at the bears that had backed off from the human presence and the howling dogs. Some bears were covered in blood and there was plenty of blood and gore around the ice lake, and the dark water appeared to have a red tinge to it. In addition to the whale carcasses on the ice, the bears had been eating the remains of some skinned bear carcasses too. Yes, Eskimo hunters have indeed been here. Kidlapik put his bare hand on the unskinned bear carcass and was surprised to find it was not wholly frozen yet. If this was animal wastage, as it certainly appeared to be, it would have to be looked into. But who would have done this? The Mounties could not even see a sign of *qamutiiq* runners in the snow, or dog tracks and feces and yellow snow. What the hell is going on here?

The snow around the ice edge on the west side of the lake was packed down by what appeared to be two sets of footprints, no doubt from the Inuit who had skinned out the bears. Corporal Peterson saw Kidlapik stoop and look at something on the ice at the other side of the open water, after noticing the dog's sudden interest and tugging on their traces. Then he made a face and backed up. "*Anak*!" Then the Mounties walked along the ice edge. They counted 10 different collections of human *anak* almost in a straight line along the ice edge and just two meters or so apart. What the hell is going on here? Who could shit so much? And why here at the ice edge? It just doesn't make sense!

Peterson pondered for a while, scanning the snow and ice for more clues. Something was really out of whack here. An airplane on skiis? No ski tracks! He thought that the only thing that could make sense of this thing was a submarine somehow surfacing here in this tiny opening in hundreds of square miles of ice and then departing again in the last few hours. But that made about as sense as little green men coming here on a fishing trip. He saw no merit in sharing such an absurdity with Kidlapik, who was acting strangely quiet. Finding no resolution, Peterson shook his head and nodded at the Constable. "Let's keep going. I'd like to go further before we stop. Besides, I suspect we wouldn't sleep very well here."

Kidlapik did his best to appear in high spirits, though he was troubled. "Ee, it's early yet and the dogs are strong." He punctuated that by throwing some hunks of bear meat to each dog while Peterson used his feet and the whip to keep the dogs from tearing into each other.

The Mounties had to detour to get around some areas of open water and so it took them an additional two days to get to Igloolik, lots of time to think about the strange things they had seen at the ice lake.

Igloolik looked damn quiet when they arrived. The trading post was closed up again, the priest was still away visiting another mission, and any Eskimos on the island were over at Igloolik Point. When they finally found an old couple passing by the post with their dogs, Kidlapik greeted them and asked them how things were. Had anything unusual happened? Have there been any visitors, perhaps from other camps like Agu Bay? No, nothing. Anybody missing? Anybody just returned from polar bear hunting? No, nobody. Very quiet . . . Petersen listened as the elderly Inuk seemed to become aroused and spoke in animated fashion to Kidlapik. It turned out he thought the trader who was here to open up the post for a few weeks was a real ass-hole. His wife calmed him down a bit and then they invited Kidlapik and

Peterson over to Igloolik Point to meet the Inuit camped there and have tea and *igunaq*, a local delicacy of fermented walrus meat. The Mounties replied that they would be happy to visit in the morning and waved them farewell.

Nothing much to report again, but that could change after tomorrow. Peterson knew he would have to note the unskinned polar bear carcass and the bear and whale meat left by the Agu Bay people. Very unusual for them to do that . . . But there were no dog tracks near the open water! The Agu Bay people would have arrived there with several teams. And the dozen piles of *anak* in a straight line! He had never heard of Eskimos doing anything like that. He didn't think there would be room for that in the report. He gradually gleaned from Kidlapik his thoughts that something supernatural had happened there, perhaps an act of shamanism. The bad kind . . . So, their theories thus far were a submarine surfaced in open water in the middle of a vast ice field, little green men on a fishing trip to planet Earth, or shamanism. Take your pick! Quite the substance for a report . . .

Corporal Peterson and Constable Kidlapik staked out their dogs and began to build an iglu, larger than their usual one. They would stay here for a week or so and see what else could be learned about the situation of these Eskimos, *Iglulimiut*, including the mystery at the open water. Then on to a couple of the other camps at Kapuivik and Agu Bay for more of the same. At the very least one could count on there being some new babies to go into the ledger, and some deaths. Disease, hunger, wildlife abundance? The government might have to provide some incentives to the HBC to keep the trading post open for longer periods until they could get another sealift in, with the aid of an icebreaker. And possibly a military-supported airlift of essential supplies in the meantime, with medical personnel onboard . . . His report would include a census and recommendations.

With the recent passing of the Family Allowance Act in Ottawa, Peterson knew these Eskimos would soon be receiving money, more likely trading credits, for every baby born and raised. Positively identifying people in these parts would be a challenge, given that the Eskimos' way of assigning names to offspring was bound to be confusing for deskbound bureaucrats. There was talk of assigning an identification number to each Eskimo to facilitate things, and indeed that southern Canadians would soon be blessed with national identification numbers as well. Things were about to change in a big way in the north, probably for both good and bad. He would flesh out a good report for Ottawa. That was his job these days, along with flying the flag, in the absence of much real crime. Heck, there wasn't even an HBC post manager here to offer him a stiff drink of over-proof rum, and a real bed in the heated residence! He considered forcing a door or window to get into the staff residence so they could get warm and comfortable, but dropped that thought as being a bad example for the local Inuit. A hot rum toddy, or two or three, would be nice to smooth things over right about now. He lowered another snow block into place in the *iglu* and trimmed its edges, jamming the trim into the cracks with his mitt to make it tight against the wind.

38

October 8: Tulugaq is on the bottom of Foxe Basin

Hansen looked up to meet Chief's eyes. Everything was quiet, and it was cold. Not surprising, since the boat lay on the bottom of Foxe Basin, almost 250 meters down. Most of the men were on their bunks breathing through *Kalipatronen* CO2 exchangers, lying still with eyes closed. The carbon dioxide in the air was at a dangerous level, and the Commander knew he had to make a decision soon. They had already expended most of their remaining battery power attempting to find a hole in the ice-crowded surface. Ampere starved and oxygen starved! This was their bleakest moment yet, and things should have gone easier. They were on their last leg to Igloolik now, and they had already made the decision to surrender. The whole crew had weighed in on the decision. Yes, they would spend time in a prisoner of war camp, but the word was that the conditions in the Canadian camps were relatively comfortable and the food was good.

Chief spoke. "The whole bow has to be stove in from our last attempts at surfacing."

Hansen nodded. The boat would hardly be hydrodynamic now with twisted and bent steel plating up front, but that didn't seem to matter much at the moment. Efficient passage on the surface, or below the surface for that matter, was a thing of the past for this boat. And its crew . . .

"We have to risk everything. Use the remainder of our compressed to blow the ballast tanks all at once. No battery power needed for that."

Commander Hansen understood the implications very well. But Chief Berg-Nielsen wanted to explain the dynamics to Soldier, who had joined them in the control room.

"What follows is a *Kriegsmarine* tutorial for the *Heer* commando on our charmed boat. Ready?"

Soldier nodded. "Let's hear it."

"Here it comes. You have no doubt come across Archimedes' Principle in your school days, and specific gravity. We have no time to discuss the fine points of physics here, but suffice it to say we are never free of their ghostly effects when we are under water. Now, in a normal controlled surfacing a precisely calculated measure of our precious compressed air is blown into the ballast tanks to eject water and lighten the boat, raising it from a given depth to the surface, working in conjunction with the hydroplanes and trim cells in bow and stern. This is a matter of calculation together with experience. When surfaced, the diesels are started and exhaust is directed into the ballast tanks to force out the residual seawater ballast, thus conserving our reserves of compressed air." Chief paused for an affirmative nod that Soldier was following before continuing.

"All that is about a normal surfacing. Now let's look at our present situation, sitting on the bottom with our oxygen and battery power for the electric motors and even the pumps sadly depleted. Keep in mind that the air pressure in our ballast tanks has to exceed the external water pressure at any given depth in order to expel the seawater. In the process of surfacing the external pressure acting on the hull decreases constantly while the air inside the ballast tanks continuously expands, increasing pressure while giving the boat a huge boost in buoyancy. The expansion potential of compressed air in our ballast tanks here on the bottom, measured in kilogram per cubic centimeter, is vastly more than at periscope depth. And it is this expansion potential that may yet save our skins. Follow?"

Again Soldier's head bobbed affirmative.

"At this point we throw our fancy calculations out the window and, as for experience in this kind of extreme no-power emergency surfacing from this depth, we have none. In this all-out procedure the devil eats the flies. Our only chance is blowing what is left of our compressed air into the ballast tanks, period. No battery power required for that . . . The overall effect will be seawater blasting out of the Kingston valves at the bottom of the boat as we initiate our ascent. The boat will accelerate upwards and, almost 250 meters later, it will smack into the underside of the ice with catastrophic force. Our hope is that the ice will give way before the boat's exoskeleton does."

Commander Hansen nodded. "And, hope that if we break through, the escape hatches won't have a meter of ice sitting on them."

Soldier looked at Hansen then back to Chief. "Sounds like quite a gamble, but it seems we have little choice." Then, forcing a smile, he spread his arms over his head a meter apart. "In any case, Joanasie says that a bowhead whale can break through this much ice."

"New ice maybe but not this damned multi-year ice that's been visiting us from the High Arctic. But still, there is a chance we will impact with enough force to break through . . . and with enough inertia that there will be no ice pans sitting on our hatches. Hansen continued. "The boat is trimmed so the tower, also strengthened to a point, should hit first. But there is no chance of adjusting the trim on our journey to the ice, though we hope to spare the bow as first point of impact."

Chief nodded again. "I will pass the word to the crew to prepare for impact and speedy evacuation, dressed for polar temperatures. If there is no serious flooding or structural damage to the boat, we can mull things over up there and decide on our next course of action. We can start up the diesels and top up our batteries and compressed air for another day."

Commander Hansen smiled sadly. "The eternal optimist . . . My only hope at this point is that the men can get off this doomed boat and walk to Igloolik and turn ourselves over to those Mounties we saw just before our last dive."

* * *

Sila was huddled together with her brother under a blanket. She did not want to die like this, at the bottom of the sea. She thought of *Nuliajuk*, the old woman at the bottom of the sea who provides for Inuit who show the proper respect for taboos and the animals they take for food. They could use a helping hand from the other world right now. Then she thought of the killer whales blown apart by the boat's big gun and their bodies left behind, and the bears, all taken in *Nuliajuk's* realm . . . Would they get any help after that? She thought of the church missions in Igloolik and Kimmirut, and the *qallunaat's* god, *Gutti*. It seemed that the *qallunaat* even had differences amongst themselves in how to approach their *Gutti*. The Catholic priests and Anglican ministers seemed to be competing for Inuit followers and sometimes wouldn't even speak to each other when they met. Sila was unsure of where she should direct her pleas and prayers, her hopes. She knew that the strength of *angakkuqs* and even *Nuliajuk* were fading where the church missions had forged a strong presence in some communities. She looked over at Joanasie, the only immediate family she had left. She would take divine intervention wherever she could find it.

Soldier lay in his bunk watching the two Inuit, the man and woman who were now so close to him, so much involved in his life. He would gladly trade his life so that these two could live. He would sign any pact with the devil to achieve this. They were not part of this madman's war, at least they should not be. They were innocents far removed from the battlefield, in body and mind. Soon he would tell them to prepare for the sudden hideous blasts of compressed air blowing water from ballast tanks, the boat's lurching off the bottom. Then the terrifying forces as the boat accelerated upwards toward the surface . . . toward the ice! He would tell them to grip their bunk frames and otherwise prepare for the inevitable impact, giving false assurances that the ice would give way so they could surface and get off the boat. Soldier had already told the Commander that he wanted the Eskimos to be first off the boat with some survival gear, should things suddenly take a turn for the worse. Soldier reached over and squeezed Sila's arm, and then inserted his hand under her *atigi* to feel her belly. He thought again about this new unborn life and what the future could hold for him, or her. Sila was convinced the baby would be a boy but she could not know for certain.

* * *

Winkler sobbed under his blanket. He found that thinking of his beloved Albert, lost with the *Milchkuh,* helped to sooth him. Soon they would be together. He was not religious, and he was sure that no God above cared about humankind after they had butchered one another for the last five years. Yet he thought that somehow he would be soon be with Albert. He was sure of it! Winkler thought too of the narwhal. He wondered if they sensed their plight, or cared. Twice these humans had saved some of them from killer whales and polar bears. But he guessed that these wonderful creatures, intelligent and sensitive as they were, would not care about them either. As he closed his eyes in exhaustion he caught a vision of his Albert being boosted to the ocean's surface in the same way he had seen a mature whale pushing up on a younger whale, mortally wounded by bear strikes, in a futile attempt to keep it from sinking. He hated the bears. They were all looking like Martin Bormann now, behind his eyelids.

39

October 10: Tulugaq Rises

Pipes rattled, valves slammed, high-pressure air hissed. In the silence of the boat, frosted by the cold, it was like the devil's beckoning shriek. Slowly, very slowly, as the hull creaked and shuddered, the boat moved. First the bow tilted up a few degrees, then the stern lifted. The slamming and creaking had stopped but the hissing continued. Lifting, rising in the water . . . Thirty-two terrified souls on the boat could feel it. Then the boat was accelerating upward, rising faster and faster . . . Those who knew would expect the uppermost part of the boat, the tower, to impact first. Then a fraction of a second later the hull would impact through its whole length. The tower could help to punch a hole while sustaining undeterminable damage in the process. Then the wooden decking would cave just before the steel plating on the deck slammed into the ice and took on new shapes. Gradually the impact would be absorbed by ice and steel as the inertial energy was expended. Then the boat might sink quickly with the death-knell of a serious breach in the pressure hull. Or, alternatively, the boat could miraculously retain its positive buoyancy as a ghost ship trapped and lifeless below the ice, until ice melt would free it the next summer so that it could drift and eventually be ground into oblivion on shallow beaches. On the other hand, the boat could shoot up through the ice, perhaps even soar a few meters skyward depending on the thickness and composition of the ice, before crashing back down to rest.

When it came, the impact was enormous and the accompanying sounds deafening. As it happened, the hull's attitude was a 5-degree bow-down angle with the tower hitting a split second before the stern. Bodies flew upwards off bunks. Water and hydraulic pipes burst and fasteners came apart. The lights went out. Some of the crew were physically injured from impacting the boat's hard surfaces, and for many there was a gap in consciousness when time itself was suspended. Shock and confusion! With a few others there was a seed of awareness that the boat had taken flight and then crashed back down, rocked sideways and gradually stilled. Eyes blinked and people stirred. People were starting to move, even more so in the control room. Just seconds after that, ready crews were running for the tower hatch and to stations under the forward and aft hatches.

Soldier hustled Sila and Joanasie into the control room. The Commander was there waiting, keen to assess damage to the conning tower. The tower was not designed to surface through ice and there was the possibility that the tower construction would funnel the ice toward the hatch in such a way that it would be impossible to open it. This was the fear that rode on Hansen as he scrambled up the ladder. Strong hands turned the wheel to open the bridge hatch. It would not open! Soldier then heaved with all his considerable strength to push the hatch open but it would not open even half way. His ability to observe the chaotic scene above was limited but it appeared there were metal debris and cable and scattered chunks of ice everywhere, some interfering with the hatch opening. He heaved again and was rewarded with a little more daylight coming in through the hatch, but still not enough! He took off his mitts and extended his hands through the opening to try to fathom what the blockages were. Joanasie climbed up beside him to peer through the opening. "I can get through there. I'm smaller." He took off his bulky caribou parka, leaving him with his seal-skin anorak. Soldier nodded and moved out of the way as the wiry Inuk moved past him and shimmied his way through the opening. Metallic sounds of bending stanchions and tugging on mired cables, together with sounds of sliding ice were magnified through the enclosed metal space of the tower.

"*Atii* . . . Push," shouted Joanasie. Soldier pushed again with all his might. He felt as though bones and tendons in his arms and wrists were about to give way, but he kept pressing. The pain was fierce. The hatch opened up a little more, enough for Sila to squeeze through dragging her caribou parka behind her. Soldier managed to compress and squeeze her seal-skin bundle and Joanasie's parka through as well, before falling back onto the ladder from exhaustion. He knew he was not going to get through that opening himself, or anyone else for that matter. He was exhausted and this was taking much too long. Just then Chief reported that the other hatches were blocked from above and could not be opened from below. Soldier called out to Sila and passed out his sidearm. "Just in case there are any big white surprises out there . . . "

Joanasie was looking around in wonder at the bridge, the shambles and the ice. There was open water all around the boat but the wind or current or both were pushing the broken ice back in around the boat even as he watched. He heard Soldier call out to him to get over to the forward hatches. Get the ice off the wooden decking so a hatch could be opened.

Chief locked eyes with the Commander as the boat shifted under them again. They were heavier in the water now than they were just minutes ago, there was definitely some uncontrolled flooding but there were no damage reports yet. Many of the crew were still disoriented or injured, including some of the few still on station attempting to assert control over pumps and valves with negligible power reserves left to draw on.

"Let's just get everyone quickly off the boat and onto the ice as soon as we get a forward hatch open."

Soldier drew in another frigid breath of fresh air through the jammed hatch and then dropped down to the control room. He kept his footing and dashed forward to ensure hands were ready to help from below to get a forward hatch opened. The Quartermaster was shouting at the sluggish crew to move faster and get their winter clothing on.

On the deck, Joanasie saw that the first escape hatch had a huge slab of ice sitting on it. He kept moving to the foremost hatch, purpose-built for loading torpedoes, and focused his efforts on removing a slab of ice to get at the wooden decking over the hatch. He found a pry bar and axe in their fasteners on the deck. He removed the bar and used it to lever and pound on the ice to get it moving and over the side, using the tilt of the deck to advantage. That achieved, he seized the axe and commenced smashing a few broken deck boards that were now an obstruction. Connecting rods between the wooden hatch cover and the steel hatch below needed to be straightened. Brother and sister together pulled and pushed at splintered wood and twisted metal. After more frenzied minutes that seemed like hours they arrived at the point that the hatch could be opened. It was not too soon as the wind was cold and the deck was slick with freezing seawater coming over the deck, which was now just inches over the ocean's surface. The two Inuit worked faster fearing that the boat might be slowly sinking. Their waterproof seal-skin *kamiik* kept their feet dry but did not grip the slippery deck well, and even with their cumbersome ice-coated mitts their hands were becoming useless in the numbing cold. "*Atii,*" Joanasie gasped through clenched teeth as they laboured to turn the locking wheel to open the steel hatch.

With a reduced ability to regulate and trim the boat, the boat was less subject to the control of human operators than to the nature of fluids and the law of gravity. The boat might yet prove to maintain positive buoyancy as a whole but the stern was rising relative to the bow. Hansen saw what was happening and assembled men to rush through the torpedo hatch when opened and clear any remaining debris. Then they could start assisting the remaining crew to get up to the deck. And quickly onto the ice . . . the ice so quickly transforming from a foe to a friend again.

The hatch came open as the two Inuit turned the locking wheel and heaved. Men with fear-haunted faces looked up desperately toward the sky. It was a cold rheumy sky but by God it was the sky. At that precise point, fluids in the multiple chambers in the boat's hull passed a tipping point and the bow dropped again relative to the stern. This time the ice on the starboard side, driven by the wind and current, pressed over the bow, thus removing any more chances for restoring trim. As the increasing weight of the ice drove the bow down suddenly and twisted the boat further to port on its longitudinal axis, the hatch moved towards the water and broken ice. Joanasie and Sila watched in horror as seawater and smaller chunks of ice began to pour into the boat through the open hatch. The water and ice combined with the shifting attitude of the boat knocked down the men who were attempting to exit. Men below cried out in terror, in anguish, in betrayal. Not at their Commander, not at the Eskimos, but at what fate had chosen at this instant to reveal to them.

Sila clung to the wooden decking as the boat tilted and she looked down at the agonized faces below while the sea poured in through the hatch at an accelerating rate. She found Soldier's face. He looked frightened too but with stoic self-control as always. He looked up and saw the frantic look on her face and seemed to smile up at her. His hand came up in a wave as in farewell, then he motioned for her to get off the boat and onto the ice. Shooing her away like a fly . . . The Commander looked somehow calm too. Sila saw in a heartbeat that this outcome was hardly a surprise to them at all, that somehow they had already come to terms with it.

Chief tried to control his panic for the sake of the men, but inside the steely calm he was racked with grief. He had foolishly indulged himself in renewed confidence that he was going to get back to his wife, to his home on the North Sea. Not now, not ever. When he moved, a drilled emergency response, to secure the interior watertight hatch to compartmentalize the flooding in the bow bulkhead, Hansen shook his head. "What would be the point, old friend? There are still a few men at duty stations back there, and even with that hatch shut and all of us behind it the boat will shortly be pulled nose-down to the bottom. Batteries dead, oxygen stores depleted. The men here in the bow still have hopes of getting off, and they know that staying right here by this flooding hatch is still their best bet for survival, with the other hatches blocked." Some of the men were stripping off their heavy outer clothing in hopes of making it up through the torpedo hatch to the surface in the few seconds after the incoming flood of seawater displaced the remaining air and lost some of its force. They would have only seconds to somehow keep afloat and pull themselves up on the ice, before their bodies shut down from the cold. And once they were on the ice, what then? But there was always a chance . . .

Joanasie slid down on wooden decking now submerged and called out to Soldier, holding out a piece of unattached cable from the debris on the deck. He threw it down and called out to Soldier again. Soldier managed to catch the length of cable in his hand but he quickly passed it to a young seaman beside him. Just then a slab of ice, held until now by some deck debris, broke free and started its downward slide. Sila shouted a warning but it was too late. The sliding ice knocked Joanasie off his feet and over the side of the boat. Sila watched him go into the narrow band of icy water bordering the hull on the port side. Like many Eskimos, Joanasie could not swim. His numb fingers tried to gain purchase on the ice face but to no avail. He went down in half a minute. There was nothing Sila could do but call out his name in desperation, over and over and over.

As the boat dropped further into the water with broken ice totally covering the forward hatch Sila noticed the freezing water was almost up to her knees. She could do nothing for the two men she loved, and nothing for the many men in the crew who had become her friends. She knew she had to think about herself and the baby. She walked up the inclining hull toward the boat's conning tower to the point where she could throw her bundles and Joanasie's parka off and hop onto the ice. She walked away from the boat a little ways, then opened up her seal-skin bundle and took out some dry caribou *kamiik* and leggings that she had made for her brother. She cried softly as she put these on. She picked up the Colt .45, looped a piece of twine through the trigger guard and hung it around her neck before putting on dry mitts. Then she unrolled two caribou skins, sitting on one and wrapping the larger one around her. She gazed upon the boat through hands pressed over her face. Mercifully she could no longer hear the men's anguished cries, but the horrific sounds of seawater flooding into the boat and of colliding ice were soul-crushing. The boat's stern rose up obscenely and slowly *Tulugaq* began its final plunge headfirst into the freezing black depths.

40

October 12: Sila Walks to Igloolik

Sila knew she was finally nearing Igloolik Point. It had been further than she imagined and she had spent two uncomfortable nights on the ice. There was little drifted snow on the sea ice for an *iglu* and anyway she did not have her snow knife with her. She had bundled herself up in her caribou skins as best she could. Soldier's big pistol hanging from her neck was reassuring but still she could not, dared not, sleep. She had no food with her and her only moisture was from munching on the top layer of multi-year ice she found along the way, its salt content having leached out over time.

Her feet felt heavier with each step. She was no longer looking over her shoulder periodically for a white shape following her tracks. She was thinking now of how good some bear meat would taste, raw bloody bear meat.

It had made little difference to her that a spent sun was dropping over Melville Peninsula or a weak sun was rising reluctantly over Baffin Island. By day her spirits lifted a little, but it was in the nights on the ice that her resilience kicked in. Under small blessings of moonlight and starlight she plodded on, one step after another toward towards Igloolik. Soon she would be able to see *iglu*s and hear dogs howling, if she could just keep going. From Igloolik she would be able to catch a ride home when the Inuit started to hunt caribou over on the Baffin coast, traveling by dog sled. Everyone would wonder what had happened to her and her brother and their grandmother. They had been gone so long, from the time the winter days were still short, and they had hitched up their dogs and left to spend the summer at Nettilling Lake. Sila recalled how everyone was happy that, thanks to her and Joanasie, grandmother's dream of spending her summer, perhaps her last summer, at Nettilling Lake was coming true. Her second husband had died and so the bonds holding her with his people had weakened. Anaanattiaq had cherished her summers at Nettilling Lake during her childhood and early adulthood. Sometimes it seemed she babbled endlessly about her good times there. Sila smiled, knowing that her memories were selective and that there were many hardships too. Hardships like losing her mother and one of her own children during childbirth there. And some of her best dogs. Near-starvation and illness had not been strangers to them either. Grandmother was tough, and some of that was in her.

Sila was so tired and so cold now, and without food or heat. She just wanted to stop and lie down to rest and dream, but Anaanattiaq whispered to her to keep going. She trudged on. She didn't know if the Inuit's *Nuliajuk* or the *qallunaat* church's *Gutti* had played a role in lifting the boat off the bottom and hurling it upward to the ice, and if the outcome was the intended one. When she dropped her bundle of caribou skins and the heavy pistol onto the ice it was hardly with conscious intent, but it served to keep her going . . .

Sila didn't know what she would tell her family about what had happened. It was all too much for someone to believe, even for her to understand herself. The *aqaumasuq* that could take them under water, even under the ice, and then come up again like a whale. These enemies of the Canadians and Americans who had somehow become her friends and her dear brother's friends . . . Tears ran down her cheeks and froze until she pulled her fur trim close around her face again. How would she explain about the baby growing in her? She would explain that her grandmother died a natural death and that her brother had drowned. There was much truth in that. As for the baby, she would remain silent about that. When they saw the baby they would gossip and speculate that she had had some romantic liaison with a Mountie or a Hudson Bay man. Such things were natural and babies were always welcome. Inuit might gossip among themselves but they were respectful and accommodating. After a while they would leave Sila alone with her secrets.

Sila knew that she would do anything for the new life growing in her. But she could not tell anyone about what happened. If she had to put into words how she helped the enemy in her own land and how this had led directly to her beloved brother's death, that would be the end of her. Too much death in her life! First her parents drowned, then her grandmother and now her dear brother, and the beloved father of her baby . . . The others on the boat too: the older kindly one they called Chief, the boat boss Hansen, the big-eared beardless youth they called Winkler . . . all gone!

She knew she would lead a solitary life. But she had to push back the madness that she felt lurking in her mind, and the will to throw her own life away, now just a seed. She had to keep herself together for the little one. Some day she would tell her grown-up child everything. She would owe that to her child. What stories she could tell her child, and they would laugh and cry together. But her child could never tell anyone what had happened, because her child would know that this would allow the seed of madness in her mother's mind to grow and flourish.

Sila could see *iglus* now, and she could hear dogs howling.

EPILOGUE

And just as fate somehow had provided Sila with the skills and the good fortune to survive with her unborn child, fate had also brought U-807, Tulugaq, to its final resting place. It settled in one of the few deep trenches in Foxe Basin, this one narrow and at a depth of almost 250 meters. The boat's long cylindrical shape stretched out so it was almost perfectly horizontal, as though a carpenter's level had been placed on the deck. Over the years it was gradually covered with silt. Occasionally a narwhal would dive down and swim along its length.

ACKNOWLEDGEMENTS

There are a number of people who have helped me immensely by reading and commenting on successive drafts of my novel: John Matthews, John Stevenson, Angus MacDonald, Perry Shearwood and Renee Wissink (all of whom have resided in Igloolik). Perry, a former teacher in Igloolik, very capably took on the editing task as well. Angus drew the maps for me, while Thomas Herbreteau provided the cover. Thanks also to Bob and Colleene Peterson, RCMP couple from Grise Fiord days, for their words of wisdom. Rob Eno, a former colleague of mine at the Nunavut Department of Environment, graciously read a draft or two of my book and was a source of information himself on such things as U-boats and the American *Crystal II* airbase in Frobisher Bay. Also thanks to Robert Trudeau, Heather Myers, Anita MacLellan (an amazing local lady who has promoted my scribblings from Portaupique to Pizzlewig and beyond), Heather Williams, Robin Burgess, and my brother Doug. Blandina Tulugarjuk helped out with the Inuktitut translation, but any errors therein are my own.

Special thanks go to my two European U-boat experts whom I met through U-Boat.net. Tore Berg-Nielsen and Maciej Florek commented on successive drafts and tried to educate me on Archimedes' Principle and such things a submariner must know. Tore was Chief on a captured German U-boat used by the Norwegian Navy well into the 1950's for training purposes, and he graciously allowed me to use his last name for the boat Chief in my book. Maciej was well-versed in the technical aspects of U-boats, the operations, and the culture of the *U-bootwaffe*. He also taught me some appropriate German cuss words. Sadly, Maciej passed away before this book was ready for print.

I would also like to acknowledge the always-generous Inuit contribution to my imperfect understanding of their land and their way of life. Inuit are a tough and persevering people. They have had to be, as much in contemporary times as in the past.

ABOUT THE AUTHOR

Larry Simpson is happily retired and lives on the Bay of Fundy in Nova Scotia. Prior to that he lived in the Northwest Territories and Nunavut for half his life, working as a Hudson's Bay Company post manager, an Inuit Cooperative manager, and lastly with the territorial governments in the economic development sector. Over the years he has lived in a dozen communities in the western, central, and eastern Arctic, including Igloolik. Three of his children were born in Iqaluit, formerly Frobisher Bay. Jean, the eldest, is still there and is proud to have Inuit status.

Larry's passions include adventure motorcycling to exotic parts of the world (usually warm spots but most recently to Tuktoyaktuk), and writing up his journeys for magazines. This is his first book.

54495490R00217

Made in the USA
Columbia, SC
02 April 2019